PRAISE FOR DREDA SAY MITCHELL:

'As good as it gets.'

—Lee Child

'A fast-paced thriller that will keep you guessing until the very last page.'

—Paula Hawkins

'A truly original voice.'

—Peter James

'Thrilling.'

—*Sunday Express* Books of the Year

'Awesome tale from a talented writer.'

—*Sun*

'Fast-paced and full of twists and turns.'

—*Crime Scene Magazine*

GONE

ALSO BY DREDA SAY MITCHELL

Girl, Missing

Believe Me

Say Her Name

Trap Door

Spare Room

One False Move (Quick Reads)

Death Trap

Snatched (Kindle Single)

Vendetta

Killer Tune

The Gangland Girls Trilogy

Geezer Girls

Gangster Girl

Hit Girls

Flesh and Blood Series

Blood Sister

Blood Mother

Blood Daughter

Blood Secrets

Big Mo Suspense Series

Dirty Tricks

Fight Dirty

Wicked Women

Play Dirty

GONE

DREDA SAY MITCHELL & RYAN CARTER

THOMAS & MERCER

Text copyright © 2025 Mitchell and Joseph Limited
All rights reserved.

Published by Thomas & Mercer, Seattle

www.apub.com

Amazon, the Amazon logo, and Thomas & Mercer are trademarks of Amazon. com, Inc., or its affiliates.

ISBN-13: 9781662515613
eISBN: 9781662515620

Cover design by The Parish
Cover image: ©Jennifer Bogle / Stocksy

Printed in the United States of America

The heart of a mother is a deep abyss at the bottom of which you will always find forgiveness.

—*Honoré de Balzac*

Prologue

'I'll kill you before I let you do this!' the woman screamed.

Voice raw and harsh, her fists pounded with manic fury against the front door of the house. She looked a mess. Her red eyes stood out like pools of blood against the sickly paleness of her skin. Dark circles beneath her eyes showed that she hadn't slept for days. Her hair was tangled, the ends matted against her shoulders. Rage made her tremble so violently it pushed her to the point of collapse.

'I know you're in there!' Her banging became brutal and hard.

Suddenly two little faces appeared at the downstairs window nearest to the door. Children. A boy and a girl. Their faces, almost pressed against the glass, were haunted, wearing twin expressions of fear and confusion. The boy's little fingers dug into the girl's arm, seeking comfort and protection, his throat muscles popping as he sucked in air. The woman's breath caught as her eyes locked with his. Her hand stopped its relentless assault against the door, falling limply by her side. Eyes clouding, she became dazed. Because, for a fleeting moment, it was another face she saw. One that had haunted her memories for such an agonisingly long time. The heaviness of that face pressed down on her chest, making it difficult to breathe.

Abruptly, a figure emerged behind the children. Another woman. A flicker of recognition danced across her features before her face became a mask of anger and accusation. Her lips tightened with contempt. With a swift motion, she snapped the curtains shut, blocking the children from seeing outside.

No! No! No! I can't see his face anymore! The woman's mind screamed a silent plea that only she heard.

The door finally opened. A man loomed in the doorway. With a long, weary sigh he looked at her. The woman outside lunged forward, her hands grasping at his shirt.

'It's not true,' she pleaded, her words choking in her throat.

As he peeled her fingers from his clothing his head reared back slightly at the stench of alcohol filling and stinging his nostrils. The fumes were pungent and fresh – a clear sign she'd been drinking before she got there.

'You've been drinking again,' he said, his voice tinged with resignation.

'I won't let you do this!' she yelled, ignoring his accusation.

'This has got to stop,' he told her firmly. There was a cold finality in his voice.

Her head rocked with denial. 'But you know it's not true! Why are you doing this?' All of a sudden, her expression and voice darkened. 'He's in the house. I saw him.'

In a rush, she skidded back and hurried towards the downstairs window. Where the children were. She knew what she had to do. She had to get inside.

Get him.

Save him.

Save him with her bare hands. Balling her hand she lifted her arm, ready to smash the window. But it never happened. Instead, a determined force gripped her fist, holding her back.

'Let go of me!'

She tried to yank her arm free. He wouldn't let go. Outraged, she swung her other hand, trying to hit him but he managed to elude her blow. They began to tussle and wrestle with each other.

As they fought, the flashing lights of an emergency vehicle lit up the street before it came to a screeching halt in front of the house. As two people emerged from it, the woman managed to break free. Darting around the man, she intended to bolt down the street. One of her shoes fell off. She stumbled and crashed to her hands and knees in the driveway. Sharp pieces of gravel dug and scraped into her palms, drawing blood.

Strong hands seized and turned her, pressing her down. Before her world went black, she managed to cry out: 'He's not dead! He's not dead!'

HE'S NOT DEAD.

Chapter 1

There's still no sign of my son. All my attempts to reach him by phone or text have gone unanswered. There has to be a limit to how many times you try to contact your child before you start to look like an anxious mother, which I don't want to. Although my boy ought to know better than anyone that his own mother has more reasons than most to be anxious. With nothing to do but wait, I'm reduced to finding reasons to walk down our front path and open and close the gate while looking up and down the road to see if he's coming. He isn't. The only other thing for me to do is reread the strange text he sent this morning in the small hours. It was short and curt.

Coming home from college tomorrow. For a few days.

That was it.

At first, I was relieved to get a message from him as he's barely managed to get in touch at all for the last few months. My attempts to get back to him though went unanswered. Any particular reason for him coming home? What time? Did he need picking up from the station? Was he in trouble of some sort? Unwell? Struggling to manage? And what prompted him to send a text like that in the small hours?

Although perhaps that shouldn't have come as a complete surprise. It's been hard enough lately to get any news at all out of him. When he does finally respond to my messages, his answers are slurred and bored. 'Yeah . . . No . . . The course is good . . . No problems . . . Gotta go now.' We all know of course that students are too busy studying and partying to keep their parents up to date with developments. Even so, I'm worried. So worried in fact, that I've been reduced to contacting my ex-husband, Mark, to see if he's talking to our boy and can explain his behaviour. The pattern is always the same.

'Yes, Alison, what is it?'

'I'm just wondering if you've been in touch with Kane lately?'

'Yes, we chatted at the weekend.'

'Did he seem OK to you?'

'Yes, of course, why wouldn't he be?'

'He didn't mention he had any problems?'

Then there will be a long sigh. 'Look, I haven't got time for this, Alison. I'm busy. If you want to know how our son is, give him a ring yourself.'

It's much too embarrassing for me to admit that his own mother can't get anything out of him.

I go back down the garden path, checking up and down the road again. There's still no sign of my boy. Why's he treating me like this? And why's he treating me like this and not his father? But I know the answer to that question – it's been ringing in my ears for years. Patiently explained by doctors, teachers, social workers and support staff.

'Your son is traumatised, Alison. He's an unusually sensitive and intelligent boy and that makes things worse. You have to handle his issues with care. You have to remember that always.'

It's true of course but it doesn't help in a situation like this. There's still a twang of anger in my belly. And what those professionals forget is that I'm traumatised too, but no one seems to be handling my issues with care. One phone call from Kane telling me where he is and when he will be home and that would calm me down. But it doesn't come.

Twilight's falling and our road is going dark. It's early spring and the trees that line it are still bare. I still live in Norfolk where I grew up; my childhood home was by the sea but now I live in a comfortable if shabby part of Norwich. It's a somewhat anonymous suburb that's generally pretty safe. But at this time of year and this time of day, those solid if dilapidated Victorian villas that make up our homes start to look slightly menacing and sinister. The empty pavements don't help. I turn to go indoors, but then I see that our road isn't empty after all. Further down, in the shadow of a tree, two youths are huddled together. They wear anonymous grey and black trainers, tracksuit bottoms and hooded jackets. They're deep in conversation with each other. They look up and down the road as if they're waiting for someone. Creeping paranoia replaces my anger. Are these shady characters dealing drugs?

I dive back indoors to alert the police. Fumbling with my phone, I check through the curtains to make sure the youths are still there. They're not. There's no sign of them. Now my paranoia turns to shame. Where did that panic come from? All kids dress like that nowadays.

A loud hammering on our brass knocker shakes the front door and me about equally. When my trembling fingers open the curtain again, I see the two youths from the street are on my doorstep, their hoods pulled down to cover their faces.

'Go away! Or I'll call the police!'

'What do you mean, call the police?' says one of them. 'It's me!' He steps closer to the window, and I see a pair of dead tired eyes staring at me. Even when he pulls his hood down to reveal his face, he's still barely recognisable. It's my son Kane, but he's lost weight. His face is pinched and haunted as if he's been living on the streets.

All I can think of to say is, 'Where's your key?'

He shrugs.

Still shaking, I open the front door. He passes me into the hall and the second youth follows. Neither of them says a word. There's no explanation as to who this other person is, never mind a hug or a kiss from my son. The pair of them make their way into our front room. After taking some deep breaths and reminding myself that I need to handle Kane's issues with care, I follow.

Kane is slumped in an armchair. His hair was long before, full and curly, but now it's matted down as if with engine grease. The plump appearance, puppy eyes and angelic hair that got him tagged as a 'pretty boy' at school are gone. The other youth is sat in another armchair. Only when he lowers his hood does it become clear that this boy is in fact a young woman. Her long hair is dyed pink and falls like curtains at the edges of her face and down over her forehead. She's wearing a nose ring and her lipstick can only be described as flamboyant. She is dressed in what look like combat fatigues with what appear to be political slogans painted on them. The most striking thing about her though are those eyes that peek out through her pink hair. Unlike Kane, whose eyes seem dead, this girl's eyes are sly and mischievous and dart around like little fish in a tank. She smiles at me.

I take a chair myself. 'You're very late, Kane, was there a problem coming home?'

'No, no problem.'

'Couldn't you have called or texted?'

He appears to be exhausted as if recovering from a long illness. 'Sorry. My phone's dead.'

I don't want to start off by asking Kane if he's OK. He's obviously not. I don't want any trouble with him. Instead I ask, 'Kane, are you going to introduce me to your friend?'

He looks at me and then at the girl as if he's just noticed her. 'Oh yeah. This is Rocky.'

I look at her. She seems to be the only one of the three of us who's comfortable. 'Nice to meet you, Rocky.'

'Likewise.' She doesn't have much conversation, only those flashing eyes.

I try again. 'Are you a student too, Rocky?'

'Yes.'

I keep trying to start a conversation but it's not working. 'What are you studying?'

'Music.'

That's something I can work with. 'I studied music too, the piano. I was hoping to make a profession out of it. That was my dream.'

Rocky will know all this. Kane must have told her. She probably knows everything about us. Or maybe not. She looks at Kane before nodding. 'I suppose it's important to have a dream.'

That appears to be the end of our conversation. I've taken a bit of a dislike to Rocky, and it looks like the feeling is mutual. I turn back to my son. 'Is the plan for Rocky to stay with us for the next few days?'

Kane appears to be completely somewhere else and is struggling to understand what I'm saying. 'Hm? Yes, that's the plan.' He thinks about what he's just said as if he hasn't heard it properly. 'If that's all right with you?'

'Of course it is.'

He turns to Rocky and gestures to her with his dead eyes which look upwards. They both rise from their chairs and make to leave the room.

I watch them go. 'Are you coming back down later for something to eat and to share your news? Let me get to know Rocky a little better?'

He looks back at me forlornly. 'Do you mind if we don't? It's been a long day. We'll see you tomorrow.'

I stand at the bottom of the stairs and watch them go up. A ping sound comes from Kane's direction. It sounds like a text on his phone. Didn't he say his phone was dead? They whisper to each other as they did on the street earlier. They're still whispering when they reach his room and close the door behind them.

Who are these two strangers? My son isn't himself at all.

Chapter 2

I sit bolt upright in bed, my heart banging against my chest. Someone is playing the piano. The notes drift up like phantoms through the house, achingly familiar and haunting. It's coming from the ground floor. That means it must be coming from . . . No! It can't be. But it is. A shiver runs right through me. There's only one room in the house that has a piano. The music room downstairs.

But who is playing it?

I've never liked this house. I grew up in a fisherman's cottage on the coast in Norfolk. It was sparse and poor but cosy and warm while the wind howled off the North Sea. There was barely enough room to swing a haddock and we all lived on top of each other, my parents, Olivia, plus all the relatives and friends who constantly visited. And Simon, of course. It's so easy to forget he was there too.

My ex-husband and I were given this house in Norwich to live in when he got a job as a caretaker at a local private school. The trust that ran the school owned property in the area and they gave him this three-storey Victorian villa to rent. When we split up, Mark persuaded the trust to let me stay in the house for a while. He got doctor's notes to prove that it wouldn't be good for our health for me and Kane to move. Now it's likely the trust has forgotten we're here. Anyway, they can afford to forget.

Since everything happened, I've slept in the attic. It's the only place in my home where the bad memories don't live. A narrow flight of stairs connects this room of sanctuary to the rest of the house. At first, I dragged a mattress up the staircase and slept on that. Over time though, a single bed was brought up, various mementos and photos, and the attic room is now a home from home. It's about the only place where I feel safe. And there's my jar, of course. The jar that sits on the bedside cabinet.

My nerves are in shreds, all kinds of dark thoughts playing through my mind. What has happened to my son to make him barely recognisable? Where is the sweet, good-natured boy who went away to uni? And who is this girl he's brought with him? Why has he virtually tuned me out of his life these past six months when he's all I've got and he knows it? I'm going to find out but for now I need to sleep, and I can't sleep with this music coming from downstairs.

The piano stops. My heart feels like it stops too. Then it begins again. It must be the girlfriend, this Rocky character, playing it. Because Kane doesn't know how to play. He wasn't the musician in the family, that was . . .

I swallow the foul taste of the memory. Why doesn't Kane tell her to stop? He of all people should know how upsetting this is for me.

My hands are shaking as I climb out of bed. The wooden floorboards are like ice under my bare feet. I open the door and peer down the darkened staircase. Shadows press in around me as I creep down the narrow stairs. Each stair creaks under my weight. I pause outside Kane's bedroom and hear him gently snoring within. The piano music echoes up from below, making my skin prickle.

I reach the ground floor, my heart pounding. The music room fills me with dread. Bile rises in my throat, my gut spasms, fighting the queasiness. The piano notes strike with the power of hammers against my skull. I've got to get her to stop playing. Now! Before it's too late.

I knock on the door of the music room. 'Rocky? Can I speak with you? Please.'

The music abruptly stops. I wait, straining to hear movement from inside, but there's nothing.

'Rocky?'

No answer. I press my ear closer. It sounds like there's no one in there.

She couldn't have slipped past me to go back upstairs, could she? I would have seen her, wouldn't I? Suddenly, the darkness is thick and heavy, almost suffocating.

I panic and rush back up the stairs, shutting the attic door tight. That's when I notice with alarm a bottle of whisky, a glass and pills scattered on the floor. I clean it up and crawl back into bed.

Despite the silence, the music is all I hear. It's eaten into my soul, stirring up something dark and gut-wrenching inside me. Because that piano hasn't been played in this house for ten years.

◆ ◆ ◆

'Can I have a word with you, please?'

It's around nine the next morning and my son is sitting at the kitchen table. Which surprises me because since he became a student he tends to sleep much later. He looks terrible. His T-shirt is soiled and his shorts have seen better days. His hair, which he's always taken great pride in, is matted and dirty. What has happened to my beautiful boy?

'What's up?' he says finally.

This time I think carefully about what I'm going to say. 'Why don't I make us a cup of coffee and we can chat?' I want to smooth my palm in a gentle mummy gesture against his T-shirt. 'I'm worried about you.'

He looks over his shoulder. Is the girl there? Rocky?

Turning back, his answer is a whispered, 'I'm all good.' He stares over his shoulder again. It's as if he is taking stage directions from this girlfriend of his. 'OK, Mum. Give me ten, fifteen minutes.'

He leaves, and for a second or two I remain frozen in the kitchen, gazing at the space Kane just vacated. I worry about him so much. He's all I have left now. Which reminds me I need to call my solicitor. My nerves kick in again.

The receptionist answers with a familiar response. 'I'm afraid Ralf's on another call at the moment. Do you want to leave a message?'

Like many people from poor backgrounds, I have an instinctive cringe when it comes to dealing with professional people. But my solicitor Ralf is rapidly de-cringing me.

'He always seems to be on a call, out on business or in a meeting. In the past week he hasn't returned my calls. So, this is the message I've got for him.' My tone toughens up. 'If he doesn't get back to me today, I am going to come down there, sit in reception and wait until he sees me.'

As I ring off, Kane reappears. He slopes over like a wounded animal and resumes his seat at the kitchen table. 'You want to talk?' he says.

I sit opposite, my troubled gaze running over his face. 'What's the matter, son? Are you ill? You're barely recognisable as my boy anymore.' I'm trying to be calm and parent-like but my worry gets the better of me. 'You don't call me. Don't text. Term time isn't over so why have you come home? Then you turn up late without ringing to let me know. You tell me your phone's dead, but I heard it ping as you went upstairs, which means it obviously isn't.' I stop myself because I now sound like a parent who's gone from caring to accusing. I take a breath. 'Please! I'm your mother. Let me help.'

His stare dances away from me. 'I'm fine.'

'Are you struggling at uni?'

His eyes drift around the kitchen and I wonder if he's on drugs. 'My tutor said I could finish my work at home. Online. Is that it?'

No, it isn't.

'I didn't know your girlfriend—'

'Her name's Rocky,' my son jumps in.

'Rocky. I didn't know that she plays the piano. Then again, I suppose I haven't had enough time to get to know her yet.'

'She doesn't.' He's looking at me directly now.

'Well, someone – I'm not saying who – but someone was playing the piano last night. Do you think you could ask Rocky if it was her – and I'm not saying it was – could you ask her, very politely, not to? You know how upsetting it is for me.'

'She wasn't playing the piano last night. She was in my room. I know, I was there.'

'Well, who was it if it wasn't her?'

'Perhaps you were dreaming.'

Was I dreaming?

Of course not. A piano playing calls to me. Just like it did last night. Dreaming? If only I had been. It's clear Kane is tired of my not-so-subtle accusations, so I switch to something else I need to speak with him about. Now this is where I have to tread very carefully. Kane doesn't react well to my mentioning the past.

'Has your father told you about his plans? To go to court?'

Kane stares down at the table. 'He said something about it a few months ago. He knew you wouldn't like it. But . . .' He draws the word out. 'He thinks it's time.'

'I'm going to stop him.'

Head flicking up, Kane sparks into life, his eyes blazing with fury. 'Why? Why would you do that? That's mad!'

I'm shocked by his reaction. I begin to explain. 'I know you think I'm crazy . . . but—'

Kane doesn't let me finish, getting abruptly to his feet, fiercely muttering, 'Not this again.'

He stomps off upstairs. I look around the empty kitchen. I'll try to talk to him again later. Then I collect the official-looking brown envelope that Mark's solicitor sent me, pick up my car keys and leave the house.

I know I've set off down a hard road of pain and heartbreak. For me and for others.

But I have to do it for my son.

Chapter 3

There's no sign of Ralf's sports car in the parking space outside his offices when I arrive but it's easy enough to find. He's parked it a street away with a fake disabled badge on the dashboard to deter traffic wardens. He does this so his receptionist can say that he's not in today. She knows me from past visits and will already be briefed with a story to fend me off. It's going to need to be a good one. I'm ready for her when I walk into reception.

'Ms Taylor. It's good to see you again.' The wary expression on her face says otherwise. She switches to bright and breezy and has her carefully prepared script ready. 'I'm afraid he's not in today, unfortunately. He's giving a lecture to students who are thinking of studying law. He knows you're trying to get in touch with him and he'll get back to you as soon as he's available.'

'He's out?'

'Yes.'

'In that case, what's his sports car doing parked in a neighbouring street? Has he lent it to you for the day?'

Ralf once told me that I'd know if he'd fled the country with the police on his tail when his sports car is discovered, unlocked in a long stay car park at one of the airports. It would break his heart to do that, apparently, but it was going to happen one day.

The receptionist moves to plan B. 'Look, I'm sorry, I have strict instructions that he's not to be disturbed.'

Not to be disturbed? Mouth tight, I move at speed around her desk and head for Ralf's office. 'You can't do that!' she says, jumping to her feet. 'Come back at once. You can't barge into his office like that. I'll call the police!'

When I do barge into his office, it's to find Ralf on one side of his desk, looking sympathetic and concerned, something he does very well. On the other side is a middle-aged woman looking wistful and forlorn. Clearly a divorce case. I know that because Ralf has put a box of tissues on the desk in front of his client. He did that for me when I divorced Mark. He doesn't appear in the least surprised to see me come through his door without warning.

He raises his palm and mouths, 'Five minutes. OK?'

Rather than face his receptionist's dirty looks, I wait outside his office, leaning against the wall in the corridor. In due course, Ralf's client appears through the door, closing it behind her. As she walks past me, she pauses, leans in and hisses, 'Divorce? Take him for everything he's got.'

I nod in agreement. But I'm not here about divorce. It's far more serious.

Beaming, Ralf greets me. 'Hey, Alison.'

After I've taken a seat I throw the brown envelope on his desk. 'Did you know about this?'

He picks it up and turns it over before putting it back down again without opening it.

'Your ex-husband's lawyer sent me notification by way of a courtesy.'

'So why didn't you get in touch with me?'

'I was planning to. I heard you made a bit of scene over this at Mark's house.'

My face burns hot at the memory of what I did, the little children's faces in the window. Ralf takes a half-smoked cigar from his desk drawer and lights it. The cigar suits him. He's a handsome man with a rather raffish appearance, more like a showbusiness agent than a lawyer. He wears smart tailored suits with the old-fashioned touch of a coloured handkerchief in his top jacket pocket and highly polished shoes. He has shoulder-length hair that hangs on the sides of his face rather like Rocky's. He's avoiding my eyes at the moment because he knows there's going to be a row.

'So, what are we going to do about it?'

He picks up a pen and begins to doodle on his desk pad. 'How do you mean?'

'It's not complicated. You've got to put a stop to it. I want you to get in touch with Mark's solicitor and tell him it's not happening.'

He avoids looking at me, focusing on his doodle. 'I'm going to be honest with you, Alison. There isn't much we can do.'

'That's strange. On your very flashy website it says, "There's always a way".'

He tears the sheet of paper from the desk pad, screws it up and lobs it into the bin.

'We could go to the high court and try and stop Mark, that's true. However, even at the reduced rates I offer you, it's going to cost a fortune to fight a case like this. Plus, you'll have to face the family again.'

I gulp.

He continues. 'All the old hatred will boil over. Accusations flying everywhere. At *you*.'

Me? The thought of it, the memory of it, leaves me trembling inside.

Ralf's voice softens. 'Things are going to be said that are better left unsaid. And then you know what will happen? We'll lose anyway and it will all be for nothing.'

Is he right? That this will all lead to more heartache? My fingers twist against each other in my lap.

His voice is soft and coaxing now. 'But you want to know the real reason why we're not going to do this? Because it's bad for you, Alison, that's why. You're better now. You've got to move on and leave all this behind. Get on with your life. I'm begging you, think about what you're doing here. Think about yourself.'

For a few moments, a kind of lightness falls over me and I catch a glimpse of what it would be like to get over it and move on. Then the darkness falls again.

'That's your advice, is it?' I ask.

He's emphatic. 'I've already drawn up a letter to Mark's people telling them we have no objection and we're happy to make a statement to that effect. All you'll have to do is sign it.'

Sign it? Turn my back on my boy? My spine stiffens as my fingers unlock. 'I can't. Mark has got to be stopped.'

Ralf considers me for a time before letting out a lengthy sigh. 'It's your choice. But if you won't think about yourself, think about how it will affect other people. Your sister, Olivia, and your brother, Simon, for example, how will they feel?'

I don't care about them.

When I don't answer, he goes on. 'What about your niece, Frances? And most of all what about Kane? How's he going to react? You think he needs this?'

'I've already told him what I'm planning. We spoke about it before I came here.'

'Considering the sensitivity of the issue, you should speak to him in person. Go see him at university—'

'He's at home at the moment,' I tersely cut in.

Ralf is surprised. 'At home? Really? Any particular reason?' He waves his hand, dismissing his question. 'Anyway, the important thing is that he's up to speed with what's going on.' He gets to his feet. 'I've got a client who will be here soon. You know, the kind of client who makes appointments first. So, if you wouldn't mind?'

I stand up too. 'If I fight Mark, you'll help me. You won't let me down?'

He looks up. 'Despite not having anything to fight with, if this is your decision of course I'll help you fight Mark's case. Have I ever let you down before?'

He's a devious and unprincipled individual. Perhaps that is what makes him a good lawyer. But it's true, he's never let me down.

Outside again, I take some deep breaths before ringing my ex-husband. It goes straight to voicemail. 'Mark! It's me. I'm going to stop you from taking this to court. Do you hear me? You're not doing it!' I inhale deeply. 'I won't allow you to have our son, MY SON, declared dead.'

Chapter 4

10 Years Ago: The Beach

The beach was deserted. That should have been a warning. An omen of the terror to come. This was the third day of the family's week-long holiday to the Norfolk coast. They were staying in a nearby hotel. Alison and her sons, Sam and Kane, were joined by her elder sister Olivia and her daughter Frances and their brother Simon. He'd come without his wife, who had taken their children to visit her parents in Ireland. That first day they'd all piled in the camper van outside Alison's house and driven less than an hour to the seaside town. When it had rolled up to the beach a sense of excitement had gripped the occupants. Well, the children at least.

In contrast, the atmosphere between the adults was strained and uncomfortable. Alison was crammed in with the children while Simon was up front behind the wheel, with Olivia beside him in the passenger seat. The moment the sisters had caught sight of each other the tension had been building. They didn't get on at the best of times, so sticking them in a van this size was asking for trouble. Simon, always the mediator, had put a brave face on it all while keeping his sisters well apart, one in the front, the other in the back.

He'd been keeping the peace for the last three days, the toll of which was becoming more visible on his face.

Alison might have felt more at ease about the family trip if her husband Mark had been by her side. Of course, he wasn't here. Bitterness clogged the back of her mouth and tongue. It had its own peculiar taste, sour and foul, a flavour that she had tasted a lot lately. The unique flavour of a marriage going wrong. Her mind went back to a few days ago when he'd told her out of the blue that he could no longer join the family outing to the Norfolk coast. Work needed him. That was always his excuse for ducking out of doing stuff with her and the boys.

An insistent tug on her arm dragged Alison away from her unhappy thoughts and back to the present. She looked down at the fingers gripping her pale blue jumper. Long and fine. Piano fingers. Sam. He was all teeth and gums, brightness glowing from his face along with a blinding smile.

'C'mon, Mum, you're in the way.'

That's when Alison realised that she was blocking their escape from the van. She got out and the children instantly spilt out of the van like escapees from prison, running towards the beach with whoops of abandon. The type of freedom only children get to enjoy.

When Alison joined her brother, he shoved his hands into his worn jeans and frowned at her. 'Are you sure about doing kiddie duty?'

For each day of the holiday an adult had been assigned to look out for the children and today it was Alison's turn.

'No problem.'

The wrinkle in his brow didn't disappear. 'You can go if you want to. I'll keep a beady eye on the next generation.'

Alison couldn't help staring longingly into the distance. Towards the place she really wanted to be. But she'd made a promise to stay with the children.

'You planning on going somewhere?' Olivia's snappy voice interrupted them as she approached, her inappropriate heels sinking into the sand. Her hardened gaze settled on her younger sister.

Alison tightened her lips because if Olivia got wind of where she really wanted to be there would be all-out war. And by the looks of her, Olivia was already spoiling for a fight. Alison had had a bellyful of this constant bickering. With a conciliatory smile, she answered, 'The only place I'm going to is the beach. With the children.'

Olivia considered her for a few seconds before announcing, 'Right then, I'm off for a walk into town.'

Half an hour later, Alison sat cross-legged on the sand. The weather had been promising in the morning but it was a fake promise. Now the occasional sun had gone and the sky was cloudy. The wind mocked the party on the beach by blowing sand in their faces. The children were doing their best. Kane and Frances were paddling in the sea, ankle deep; although the stony grey waves looked chilly, the kids didn't seem to care. Who was it who said children didn't seem to feel the cold? Sam was digging away at the sand making some type of weird sculpture. Kane and Frances were close. This always surprised Alison because Frances was nearer in age to Sam. Then again, maybe it was a small mercy, making up for their mothers not getting along.

If the adults were being adult, this holiday would be abandoned. No one wanted to be here and the weather had now come out in sympathy. More directly, Alison had somewhere else she'd rather be. Out of her sight and out of her sound, in the town itself, music was playing that she wanted to listen to in a place she wanted to go. She'd made the mistake of telling her sister about this and of course Olivia took great pleasure in reminding her that it was her turn to look after the children while she pursued some new hobby she was into. That was despite that fact that although it wasn't Simon's turn, he was on the beach too and could do the minding.

A hand touched her shoulder, startling her. It was Simon, peering at her with gentle kindness. 'I'll watch over the brats,' he told her affectionately. 'You should still be able to catch most of the performance if you run.'

Alison's heart started thumping. 'Are you sure?'

By way of an answer, he sat down next to her in the sand. Not believing her luck, grinning with heart-thumping delight, Alison jumped to her feet.

But before she set off she heard a shout. It was Sam. 'Mum, can I come too?'

Alison thought hard before she answered. What a surprise it would be for him to go with her and listen to some music. She was in a hurry and decided against it.

She yelled back, 'Next time.' Then walked away.

Alison looked up at The Whispering Waves pub. There were so many childhood memories here. Of music, people, her father. Its stone exterior was worn by the harsh sea air and time. Inside, the pub hadn't changed much, keeping its old-style vibe. Alison slipped into the back row of the horseshoe arrangement of chairs and small tables in the alcove, her eyes immediately drawn to the old piano positioned centre stage. She couldn't be sure, but she'd bet her life it was the piano that had always been there. The audience was sparse, mostly older couples and a few tourists.

As Alison settled into her seat, a small, grey-haired woman approached the piano. With a slight bow to the audience, she sat down to play.

The first notes of Chopin filled the air, and Alison closed her eyes, allowing the music to suck her in. The piece was usually a beautiful clash of contrasts, urgent yet tender, brisk but leisurely paced. However, as the performance progressed, Alison couldn't help but feel a slight disappointment.

The woman's fingers thumped away at the keys, sparring with them instead of gliding and caressing, delighting in the revelation of every note. It was clear that while technically proficient, she merely played the piece rather than truly performing it.

Despite this, Alison found herself lost in the music, the intensity of Chopin's composition making her hold her breath at times. She allowed her mind to wander, thoughts of her strained marriage and the tension with Olivia momentarily forgotten.

Suddenly, a jarring sound intruded, piercing through the music and slashing its beauty to ribbons. Alison's eyes snapped open. A wave of disquiet rippled through the audience as the noise grew louder.

Police sirens. They screeched past the building.

An awful sensation gripped Alison. Frozen fear twisted her gut.

She knew. Just knew.

Something bad had happened.

Alison jumped out of her chair and rushed outside where the gentleness of the seaside was shattered by a whirring sound from up above. A helicopter hovered over the sea in the near distance. Then a rocket shot into the air from the direction of the beach.

Now she was moving. Running. The fury of her feet against the hard street pounded in her ears. The harshness of her breathing burned deep within her lungs. Faster. Faster. She ran and ran. And with each step, Alison's heart filled with dread.

Chapter 5

As I march away from Ralf's office to my car, I accidentally bump into someone.

'Oh, I'm sorry,' says an attractive young woman in a business suit and heels carrying a tray of coffee.

'That's all right. It was my fault. I wasn't looking where I was going.'

'No problem!'

After flashing me a quick smile she walks off towards Ralf's office. I take a second look at her. I'm transfixed. I can't quite believe it's really her, so when I call her name, my voice is full of doubt. 'Frances?'

She freezes and turns around, frowning. 'Do I know you?' Before I can answer she gasps loudly. 'Oh. My. God. Aunt Alison?'

I move towards her. She's the spitting image of her mother Olivia. The dazzling smile. The cheekbones I never had. Olivia was the sister who caught the eye, while I was the plain Jane. Frances surprises me with a hug filled with warmth. It's a bit awkward because of the tray of coffee she's holding. I stand in her arms, stiff and awkward. What do you say to your niece who you haven't seen for ten years?

'How are you, Frances?' I say after she releases me.

'Good, thank you. It's been a long time.' I hear the sadness in her voice. 'How are you?'

'I'm good.'

'And Kane?'

'Good.'

Good. Good. Everything is bloody good. What liars we are.

A heavy silence falls until it's broken by Frances eyeing the coffee. 'I'd better get back to work. It was lovely *bumping* into you.' There's a twinkle in her eye at her attempt at humour.

Then it occurs to me: 'You work for Ralf?' Which surprises me because he's never got a good thing to say about her mother.

She smiles ruefully. It appears she smiles a lot. 'Sort of. I'm studying law and Ralf lets me work here as an intern in my spare time. I sent loads of letters to local firms begging for an opportunity and he was only one who replied. Anyway, look, I must get on.'

'Do you have to go? Can't we go for a drink or something? Catch up? It broke my heart that I lost touch with you after everything. That you lost touch with Kane. Both of you were only children.'

She's not smiling now. 'That's probably not going to work, Aunt Alison. If Mum finds out I'm meeting you she'll throw a fit.'

'Don't tell her. I certainly won't.'

She tries again. 'Ralf is expecting me back.'

'He'll be helping a woman to take her husband to the cleaners for the next hour. He won't even notice you're gone.'

She laughs. 'That's true. There's a place I like nearby! Meet you there in half an hour.'

◆ ◆ ◆

The pressure of the past hangs heavily between us as we sit in the coffee shop located in a quiet side street. The aroma of fancy coffees fills the air. We immediately fall into conversation, catching up on the years we have lost. It was mainly me listening and soaking up all the parts of her life I had missed. Her adventures, boyfriends, her dreams. My niece has turned into a really nice kid. I feel a sense of pride in the lovely young woman she has become.

'Mum wouldn't be too thrilled about us meeting,' Frances says, a reminder of the rift between my sister and me.

My relationship with Olivia was strained even before the tragedy that shattered our family to its core. A pang of grief and regret shoots through me, reopening wounds that had never truly healed.

'I'm glad you agreed to meet me, Frances,' I tell her, my voice trembling slightly. 'I've missed you.'

Frances reaches across the table and squeezes my hand, her touch warm and comforting. 'I've missed you too, Aunt Alison. One minute I had an aunt and the next I didn't.'

'Frances,' I begin. 'About that day . . . About Sam . . .'

Her eyes fill with a mixture of sadness and understanding, a reflection of the grief that has haunted us both.

'I think about him every day,' she says in a hushed tone. 'I loved him so much. Always will. When he played the piano the whole world came alive.'

Sam was a genius, it's true. Gifted. That's what his school called him. It's Sam's piano in the music room. That's where he would practise and play for hours. I can't go in there now because all I see is Sam, sitting at the piano, his delicate, fine fingers floating across the keys.

'I just . . . I need to know . . .' I struggle to find the words, my voice cracking with emotion. 'What happened that day? What do you remember? I've been trapped in this darkness for so long, desperate for answers. For closure.'

Gaze distant, Frances takes a deep breath. 'It all happened so fast, Aunt Alison. One minute . . . Then the next . . .' Her voice trails off, and she shakes her head, her skin pale. 'I wish I could change what happened. I wish I could turn back time.'

The years of separation between us seem to melt away, united in our love for Sam.

She tells me, 'I know what's happening between you and Uncle Mark. Because I work at Ralf's I know you're not happy about it.'

I lean back slightly, going rigid against the chair. 'Please, don't join the queue of people telling me not to fight this.'

She looks fierce. 'Aunt Alison, I would never tell you what to do. Especially concerning this. You're Sam's mother, which gives you the right to do whatever you want.'

I feel choked up. Frances is the first person to support me.

She carries on, 'Maybe I can help you.'

'How?'

'I'm a law student. Maybe I can find some court case judgements that might help. I'd do anything to help you.'

'That would be so good of you.' Suddenly, I don't feel on my own anymore.

Frances checks the large cup-shaped clock on the wall. 'Heck! I've got to go.' Quickly she grabs a napkin and writes on it. 'Here's my number. Anytime you need me, just call. I'll always be there for you, no matter what. We've lost too much time already.' She hugs me tight and whispers in my ear, 'I don't want to lose you again.'

Chapter 6

The Sisters

'Quick! Before he comes back,' Alison whispered to her big sister Olivia. At eleven years old Alison was a year younger than Olivia. Giggling, the girls rushed from their bedroom and scrambled down the stairs to the living room. The scratched, deep brown piano dominated the cramped space in their fisherman's cottage in Norfolk. The piano belonged to their father, who worked tirelessly as a fisherman by day and performed at the local pub in the evenings. Atop the piano sat a large empty jar, which he used for collecting tips after his performance.

The girls squeezed together on the piano stool, grinning mischievously at each other, then began their favourite piano duet, 'My Old Man Said Follow the Van'. If their dad caught them playing this song there would be trouble. They were strictly forbidden from learning any of the traditional working-class tunes he was famous for performing at The Whispering Waves pub, where customers gathered for an old-fashioned sing-song. Instead, he taught them classical music: Chopin, Rachmaninov, Bach. The Masters, that's what their dad called them.

But for the girls, this particular song was a classic. They adored its lively, cheerful melody, despite knowing that its lyrics told the tale of a family forced to leave their home at night because they could no longer pay the rent.

Suddenly, the front door slammed. Their fingers froze above the keys. The playful atmosphere vanished instantly. Swiftly, they transitioned into playing Chopin's 'Waltz of the Little Dog', its gentle melody flowing from their fingers as they attempted to mask their previous musical mischief. Their father's heavy work boots thumped in the passage, stopping at the open door. They felt his gaze upon them as he watched their performance. As they finished the piece and turned to face him, they noticed a sheet of paper in his hand.

'It's from the school,' he said.

Nervously, the girls stood up. Olivia, always the braver of the two, asked, 'Did we get in?'

Malcolm Wright had applied to get his daughters into the most prestigious state school in the area, not only for its excellent music curriculum and renowned piano teacher, but also in hopes that, in time, both his girls might earn scholarships through their musical talents – a potential ticket out of their working-class neighbourhood.

By rights he should have handed the letter to Olivia as the eldest, but instead he passed it to Alison. She was always so much more enthusiastic than her sister about the piano. She sucked in her breath as she read. Then leapt into the air and launched herself into her father's arms. Twisting to face her older sister, she screamed, 'We got in! We got in!'

Smiling, Olivia embraced their father too. Then she quickly drew back, her nose wrinkling at the smell of fish and his boat's engine oil. She loathed it. Then she remembered her own dreams about where the piano could take her which had nothing to do with music. She was soon squealing for joy and pointing at the piano. 'The colour of that piano isn't brown. It's gold. It's my golden ticket out of this cottage.'

Malcolm smiled with pride and satisfaction. The countless hours he had dedicated to teaching his daughters the piano after back-breaking days fishing had finally paid off. No future spent scrimping and scraping for his girls. Their lives were about to change for the better.

Chapter 7

It was bound to happen. And at the worst possible time.

I don't usually use this supermarket as it's a little grand and pricey for my pocket, but I'm in a hurry because I want to lie in wait for Mark when he leaves work for lunch. As I head for the drinks aisle my mind flashes back to last night, to the bottle and pills on the attic floor. I'm still puzzled how they got there.

And that's when I hear the humming. Someone is humming the tune 'My Old Man Said Follow the Van'. I freeze for a moment. But I know who it is already. Because the rendition is note-perfect. There's no way out of this, so I slowly turn.

It's my brother and sister.

Simon and Olivia.

My sister is merrily humming away until she sees me. She cuts the humming dead, then hurriedly looks away to examine a packet of mangetout. Simon stands slightly behind her as always. He can't resist raising his hand to give me a little wave of acknowledgement. For this, he gets a scowl from our sister. Finally, Olivia gives up the pretence of not having seen me. Lips pursed, eyes narrow, she looks me up and down. A flush of embarrassment and resentment heats my cheeks. Olivia has done well for herself. She married money, divorced money and is living life in a huge house in an affluent part of the Norfolk coast. She's the opposite of me: tall and chic, while I'm a dumpy, homely jumper kind of woman. Not only is she attractive compared to me, but she looks classy. Her clothing is designer, from her boot-cut jeans to her tanned suede jacket. And as for the handbag, God knows how much that cost.

I don't know what to say. It's been ten years since I've spoken to either of them. Ten years since the beach. So instead, I ask Olivia, 'How have you been?'

'Alison,' she acknowledges with a tight voice. 'I see you haven't changed much.'

Although I bristle at her put-me-down tone, I wish it were true. That I hadn't changed. But the years of trauma have taken their toll, left my face lined, my eyes hollow. Some days I feel like a shadow of my former self.

I answer, 'You're looking good too. How's Frances?' I pretend I haven't just come from seeing her daughter. It's for the best.

A genuine smile graces her perfectly painted lips. 'She's top of her class and making me very proud. And how's Kane?'

'He's doing fine. He was always good with his hands so he's studying engineering.'

Suddenly the tension turns to torture because we know who we aren't mentioning. Sam.

In the awkward silence that follows, Simon comes to the rescue. It turns out that he and Olivia are in the store to buy things for his daughter's fourteenth birthday party. It goes without saying there's one family member who isn't invited.

I use this opportunity to ask, 'Have either of you heard from Mark's solicitor?'

Simon shifts slightly back. Olivia does the talking for them both. 'Yes, your ex is going to court, isn't he?'

'I'm going to object.'

'Oh, Alison, for goodness' sake.'

'It's my right.'

'Is your crooked solicitor putting you up to this? He's just trying to wring more money out of you. You should have realised what a huckster he is by now, especially with women.'

Ralf was once our family solicitor, but he and Olivia fell out and she won't use him anymore. The feeling is mutual between them. I don't know what it was about but it was clearly personal. Nothing busts Ralf's good humour more than the mention of Olivia's name. *'Your sister . . . that bitch.'* I never found out what the problem was between them, although I suspect she made one too many off-colour remarks about him which Ralf got fed up with.

Simon intervenes again. 'I was just thinking that perhaps it might be nice if Alison popped over to the birthday party. You know, to say hello, catch up with the family and everything.' Even before he gets a withering look from Olivia that could roast the vegetables nearby, he's backtracking. 'You know, maybe like a drop in or something?' His voice lowers to an undertone. 'For a little while.'

Olivia is what parents call 'disappointed' in her brother. 'It's your house, Simon, you can invite whomever you like.'

Without another word to me she wheels her trolley away. No humming this time. With her back turned, Simon takes the chance to apologise. 'I tried, Alison.' Then he catches her up.

A minute or two later, while I'm examining a whisky bottle, a hand rests on my shoulder and makes me jump. The bottle falls from my grasp and smashes on the floor.

'Let's talk,' says Simon.

A shop assistant rushes to clean up the mess as Simon takes me to one side. He's strained and stressed. He looks like a worn teddy bear, with his partially bald head and plump belly. 'I'm sorry about everything. You know. *Everything.*' He seems so sad. 'I'm quite happy for you to come over to my daughter's birthday party . . . but with everything as it is . . .'

'You don't need to explain. I understand.'

There's nothing to understand. He's a weak man who was forced to choose between his sisters. He fumbles for words, but I suspect it's not me he's trying to convince, it's himself.

'There's no reason why we can't catch up from time to time . . . but if one of my children mentions that to Olivia.' He shrugs. 'We'll all be dragged back into all that again and I can't face it.' His voice starts to break. 'It's too much, Alison. Too much.' He brightens slightly, sounding hopeful. 'Perhaps if we met somewhere out of the way for lunch? We could do that?'

'If that's the only way you can manage to meet your own sister, we could do that.'

He's almost happy. 'Let's do it then. I've taken a break from teaching at the moment, so I have plenty of time.'

We swap phone numbers. Before we part, I have to ask, 'Why did you choose Olivia and not me?'

There! Out in the open. The hurt and pain for him to hear.

He doesn't answer. Instead, he kisses my cheek and is gone. I'm not surprised. Simon's not a tough guy. Hates confrontation. When we were children and my sister and I were battling, he was the one who stepped in and tried to make peace. He didn't want to fall out with either of us.

We'll certainly be having lunch though. I've got questions to ask but never had the opportunity.

He was on the beach when it happened.

Chapter 8

10 Years Ago: The Beach

Alison staggered back in horror, her mind reeling. The peaceful beach was now a scene of complete chaos. She felt like she'd walked into some living nightmare.

Police officers in dark uniforms methodically combed the sandy shore, their keen eyes scanning the undulating waves and the distant horizon for any sign of hope. The spinning red and blue lights of the police cars cast an eerie glow across the beach, their flashing amplifying the sickening dread building inside Alison. The police and other people were shouting, but she couldn't make out what they were saying.

A police helicopter hovered ominously overhead, its blades slicing through the air with a relentless, ominous thrum. The chopper's spotlight scoured the sea below. Out on the water, a Coast Guard boat cut through the waves, its crew members leaning over the sides, searching the water. Onlookers huddled together, murmuring anxiously as they watched the search unfold.

Search? Alison's mind screamed inside her skull. Who were they searching for?

Desperately, her frantic eyes scanned along the bustling beach looking for Simon and the children. Oh God, the children. Kane, Sam, Frances. Where were they? She couldn't see them amidst the sea of strange faces. Faces that blurred into a fog of confusion. Fear squeezed her throat, suffocating her until she thought she'd pass out.

Finally, she spotted them. Well, she saw her brother first. His tall body obscured the children from view at this distance. He stood strangely apart from everyone else, isolated like a hopeless castaway on some godforsaken island, who'd given up all hope.

'Simon!' she shouted, salty air rushing into her mouth.

Stumbling forward, her aching leg muscles barely cooperating, Alison drew closer. Simon's haunting features came into sharp focus, and what she saw etched upon them confirmed her worst fears – something was terribly wrong. He looked sick. His normally healthy complexion was drawn and strained, all the healthy colour had bled away, leaving only an ashen pallor. Eyes wide with distress, his gaze kept darting away from her, a habit he'd had since a kid when he'd done something he was ashamed of. That's when the children came into view.

Kane and Frances.

But no Sam.

Oh God, where is Sam?

'Sam? Where is he?' Alison cried, her voice cracking.

All at once she understood with sickening clarity what the search party's frantic shouts ringing out were for. They were desperately calling Sam's name.

Simon gasped as if he couldn't get enough air. 'Sam's missing!'

Frances stood shaking beside her uncle, her eyes full of tears, while Kane just stood there motionless, his stare vacant and unfocused. Sam's absence sent chills racing down Alison's spine. Just then her youngest boy hurled himself at her, burying his face into her middle, his wrenching, guttural sobs muffled against her body. Instinctively she hugged Kane tight, comfortingly stroking his hair.

'Aunt Alison' – Frances's high voice trembled, her breath coming in sharp, shallow gasps between body-racking sobs – 'I'm so scared. I'm sorry, I'm so sorry!' Her remaining words dissolved into unintelligible bawling as she buried her stricken face in her small hands, her shoulders shaking uncontrollably.

Swallowing hard past the lump in her throat, Alison turned back to her brother and asked again, more insistently this time, 'Where's Sam? What happened?'

Her mind rebelled against the unthinkable reality unfolding. She searched Simon's haunted eyes, silently begging for answers, for any scrap of hope to cling to, but found only a mirrored reflection of her own growing terror.

'I . . . I don't know. We were all together, and then . . .' His voice broke, trailing off, unable to find the words to articulate the unspeakable.

'What do you mean you don't know?' Her voice rose in volume.

He stammered, the horrible words catching in his tightening throat. He looked at Kane and Frances. 'I think Sam paddled out to sea—'

'Paddled out?' She looked at him as if he were speaking some unintelligible language. 'On his own? With no one with him?'

Pulling away from clutching his mother, Kane tried to explain but his haunted and haggard face with its trembling lips couldn't get any words out. It was Frances who explained. 'Sam went into the sea. I told him not to go far, Aunt Alison. But he wouldn't listen to me.' She shuddered. 'One minute he was there, the next he was gone. I told him not to do it. I told him it was dangerous.'

Alison whipped a scorching glance at her brother, eyes blazing. 'Frances told him? Why wasn't it YOU telling Sam not to go far?' she seethed, her words dripping with recrimination.

Although, when they were children, they had used all sorts of discarded material they found on the beach as makeshifts objects to float out to sea on.

Simon's haggard face crumpled in abject misery. He didn't seem to know. 'I was only gone for a minute. Don't blame me, Alison, please.'

Alison lurched at him in a blind rage. 'A minute? You were meant to be supervising them. Watching the children!'

But even as she shouted the words, she remembered who'd agreed that he could. Simon crumbled, he cried out in pure agony, 'Don't you think I know that? Don't you think I won't regret this for the rest of my life?' As if the crushing weight of his guilt was too much to bear, his head drooped. 'The rescue services think he must have been swept away by a riptide. He might still be found.'

'No!' Alison shouted, unable to process the words, shaking her head in vehement denial. 'No, no, no! That can't be true. Not my Sam. Not my little boy.'

Horrific images assaulted her mind – Sam's sweet, crestfallen face asking to join her at the recital to which she'd promised 'next time'. Now cruelly replaced by the gut-wrenching vision of him thrashing helplessly against the merciless waves, struggling to stay alive, water filling his lungs, until finally, his tiny head sinks below the foam, disappearing beneath the chilly surface.

Without consciously realising it, as if acting on autopilot, Alison suddenly broke away and started sprinting headlong towards the beckoning water. Sam was out there. She had to save him. Get him back. He wasn't dead! She refused to let herself believe that!

She was in up to her knees when powerful arms suddenly grasped her around the middle from behind and physically spun her back towards the beach.

Simon.

Gone was the broken man, replaced by the fiercely protective younger brother who would fight tooth and nail for her, do anything to shield her from harm. The children looked on wide-eyed in mute shock as she frantically grappled against his iron embrace, trying to twist free and rush back into the sea.

Back to Sam.

Back to life instead of death.

At last, utterly exhausted, Alison went limp in Simon's arms, all the mad fight leaving her body, her head sagging against his shoulder. Slowly, carefully, they sank to their knees in the sand.

'They'll find him,' Simon said to soothe her, stroking her heaving back. 'It won't be long now.'

Suddenly, a familiar voice cut through the discordant chaos like a razor blade. 'How could you let this happen?'

It was Olivia, storming across the crowded beach with a barely contained fury that rivalled the raging sea.

Looming over them, she hurled her disbelief at her sister. 'You should have been here, watching them! My daughter and your sons, where were you?'

Alison recoiled as if physically slapped across the face, the excruciating weight of Olivia's accusations crushing down upon her already fragile mental state. 'I would have—'

Olivia didn't let her finish, her savage voice brutally cutting her off mid-sentence. 'We know though, don't we, in a pub watching some guy on a piano.' Alison gaped in shocked surprise. 'What? You think I didn't know that you were going back to *that* place? That I'm an idiot? I overheard you and Simon talking before.'

Voice hoarse with barely suppressed emotion, Alison shot back, 'Ten minutes. It was only supposed to be ten minutes.'

Ten sacred minutes of precious solace for herself. Ten minutes to lose herself in the rapture of her beloved piano. Ten tiny minutes that would change her life forever.

She continued, hot tears streaming down her cheeks. 'They were supposed to be safe here with Simon.'

Olivia scoffed derisively, her words dripping with venom. 'Safe? You selfishly left them all alone, Alison! Don't you dare try to lay the blame on Simon! And for what? A bloody piano recital.' Her tone roughened. 'Why did you go there? To gloat? To remember my humiliation? You put your own indulgent wants ahead of the welfare of your own child.'

Simon pleaded with his sister. 'Olivia, please. That's enough.'

She ignored him, and what she said next would haunt Alison for the rest of her life.

'Sam's dead. And it's all your fault.'

Chapter 9

'Why are you doing this?'

I confront my ex-husband outside his workplace. It's one in the afternoon on the dot. He's as regular as clockwork in everything, you can set your watch by him. That's how I know how to find him after leaving the supermarket. Perhaps it's understandable that there was no answer to my message. He doesn't want to talk to me about having our son declared officially dead. Along with a whole new family, he's changed his profession since we were married. He's gone from school caretaker to self-employed builder to partner in a thriving construction firm.

Despite calling out to him twice, he pretended not to hear, so I had no alternative but to step in front of him. He doesn't mask how pissed off he is that I've cornered him.

'Alison, not this. Again.'

We both know what he's referring to. That day at his house, though I wish I could forget. I'd gone there to confront him about having Sam declared dead, but things spiralled out of control fast. I just snapped and started behaving like a mad woman. What made it worse was Mark's wife and kids were at the window, their faces filled with so much fear. Especially the children. His little boy watching me . . . something in my mind just snapped. I convinced myself he was Sam.

The shame of the ambulance arriving to cart me away . . .

Mark makes a big drama of checking his watch. 'Things are quite hectic at the moment, Alison.'

'Why are you doing this?'

He winces, his jaw hardening. 'We need to put Sam to rest, once and for all. By rights we should have done it after the seven-year legal period. But I gave in to you.' His lips tighten. 'I'm not giving in this time. I can't.'

'Why not?'

Huffing, he leans into me. 'Because I'm leaving. Going.'

'Going where?'

'Me and Claire and the kids are emigrating to Australia.'

I feel as if the wind has been knocked out of me. I don't know why. I mean, we divorced a year after Sam never came back and, truthfully, we fell out of love a long time before that. But it feels as if another piece of my past is vanishing for good. Another part of my life brutally gone forever.

I've no complaints about Mark's behaviour since we parted. He didn't contest the settlement, has fully involved himself in Kane's life. I can't even blame him for leaving. But we married for better or worse. On the one occasion he was cruel to me, it was his remark during an argument. 'Sure, but when the guy at the altar said that, he didn't say how much worse it was going to be.'

I plead, 'Just give me thirty minutes. That's all. Please!'

◆ ◆ ◆

'I was suffering too, you know?' Mark quietly confesses. We're sitting opposite each other at a tiny round table in a small deli not far from his office.

His words stun me. All these years I've been so locked into my own grief, so angry at the world for snatching away my beautiful boy, that I've rarely considered the depth of Mark's pain. When it all happened, he was the strong one, the one who kept it together while I fell apart. And then when he left for a new relationship I thought he'd moved on. His children a sign that he'd forgotten Sam.

'I . . . I didn't realise,' I stammer. 'You always seemed so . . . so . . . emotionless.'

He lets out a bitter laugh. 'I had to be. For you, for everyone. But inside, I was fading away. Every day I woke up hoping it was all a nightmare, that Sam would come bounding through the door, ready to delight us with the newest thing he'd learned on the piano.'

I gulp back the painful sobs trying to burst out of my throat. 'I miss him so much. Every single day. The pain . . . it's a festering wound that never gets any better.'

'It's like a part of me is missing, and I don't know how to fill that void.'

'How do you cope?'

He shrugs, a sad smile on his lips. 'I try to remember the good times.' Suddenly his eyes light up. 'Do you remember that time he played that Beyoncé tune on the piano at the school concert and all the kids just got up and started dancing? His headteacher nearly died on the spot.'

We both laugh together. Really laugh. It's been a long time since me and Mark did that. At least we still share one son.

'Have you met Kane's new girlfriend, Rocky?' I ask.

Mark's checking his watch again. 'I took them out yesterday for lunch.'

'So, you know that Kane has left university.'

Mark sighs. 'He hasn't left. He needed a break. He's spoken to his tutor who doesn't have a problem with it. Anyway, so much is online these days it won't matter if he's there or here.'

'He didn't mention he'd seen you.'

Mark shrugs. 'Why would he? They had lunch with me before going on to you.'

The distance between us is growing again.

'What's your impression of Kane?'

He doesn't understand the question. 'What do you mean, impression? He's staying with you now, so you know how he is.'

My mind flashes back to Kane this morning. 'Don't you think he doesn't . . . well, doesn't look himself?'

'If you mean does he appear like he's slept in his clothes for a week and malnourished, I think that's how all students are meant to look.'

'You don't think he's behaving a little strangely?'

He's very firm. 'He appears perfectly fine to me.'

How can his own father not notice the changes in our son?

'Don't you find Rocky a bit odd?'

'She's a nice kid. Her hair and the piercings are a bit out there but that's youngsters for you.'

'Last night, in the small hours, she was playing Sam's piano. It really upset me.'

He's baffled. 'Don't you keep the music room locked? How could she have got in there?'

'I heard what I heard. Kane thinks I imagined it, but I didn't.'

Suddenly wearing a strange expression, Mark leans across the table and takes my hand in his.

'Right! You need to listen to me. This has to stop. Now. Do you understand? Don't go down that road again or it will lead to chaos and disaster.' Again? I don't know what he means. 'The last thing you want to do is come across as a bit weird.'

'What's weird is you wanting to have Sam declared officially dead.'

He yanks his hand back, his face darkening with anger. So much anger. 'Don't you get it? We can't go on like this.'

'Sam's body was never found.'

He looks incredulous. 'You don't honestly believe he's still out there? Alive?'

'No . . .' *I don't, do I?* My voice is shaking and tiny. 'I just . . .'

His chair scrapes back as he gets furiously to his feet. 'Like I said before, me and Claire and the kids are emigrating to Australia. In six weeks.'

'What's that got to do with anything?'

He shakes his head. 'When I leave, I don't want the ghosts of the past to be haunting every step of my future.'

Chapter 10

She's playing Sam's piano downstairs again. It's two o'clock in the morning. This is torture, cruel, deliberate and sadistic. Despite my plea to Kane, THAT GIRL is doing it again. Only it's worse this time. The sound of the keys is a hammered march. Slow and deliberate. They're so loud, sounding as if they're in the attic with me. I know what she's playing. One of Sam's favourites. 'Bells of Moscow' by Rachmaninov, apparently inspired by a dream where he saw himself dead in a coffin.

How did that bloody girl know that this was Sam's favourite piece? Then Mark's words at lunch come back to me as if he's singing along with the jarring and brutal music: *She's a nice kid, a nice kid, a nice kid* . . . Repeating over and over again like a hall of mirrors.

The music plays and plays and takes me back to another time. To Sam.

I stand in the wings of the stage, my heart not stopping its pounding with anticipation and pride as I watch Sam take his place at the grand piano. Although he's had a spurt of growing recently, he still looks so small against the imposing instrument. He hates doing the suit-thing, so he's in jeans and one of his fave T-shirts, the black one with the white slogan that says, 'Shhh! I'm playing the piano.'

My Sam, my gorgeous baby boy, looks so composed, dead-on focused, that for a moment my breath catches in my throat.

His fingers touch the keys.

The music starts.

The opening notes of 'Bells of Moscow' fill the air, haunting and beautiful, taking the audience to another world. You should see the way his fingers dance across the keys. One minute feather-like caresses, the next more forceful strikes. The faces of the audience are filled with emotion. Sam's music touches you, moves you, sometimes can bring me to tears. As the piece reaches its climax, Sam's fingers fly across the keys in a dizzying display of runs, trills, and intricate patterns. His body sways with the music, his eyes closed as he loses himself in the beauty he has created. Like the audience, I am transfixed.

The music stops.

Absolute silence.

Then applause erupts. Sam stands up, a huge happy grin playing across his perfect face. He bows, the way I've taught him. And then, he rushes off the stage into my waiting arms. I embrace him tight, feeling the warmth of his body against mine. His heart racing next to mine.

I come back to the present to find I'm sitting on the edge of the bed, the cold air soaking into me. I'm clutching something to my middle and it's not Sam. It's the jar I keep by the bed. Unlike Sam, it's hard and cold in my hands. Even then, the jar is so precious to me. The piano is still playing downstairs. I have to do something. Make it stop. Her stop.

Placing the jar back in its place, I stand and head for the door. Only when the cold begins to seep through the soles of my feet do I realise that they're bare. The darkness resembles a veil, revealing parts of the house while keeping other sections shrouded like secrets. The creaking of the attic's narrow stairs adds a chilling background to the music. When I reach the landing below, the piano suddenly falls silent. Clutching the wall, I wait for it to start again. That's what happened the night before, it kept stopping and starting, as if taunting me. I stand there for what feels like an eternity but it's probably only a minute or two.

The music hasn't come back.

Feeling brave, I push through the night, down the stairs to Kane's room below. We are going to get this sorted out once and for all.

When I reach Kane's bedroom, without hesitation I knock. No, it's more than a knock, I pound my fist against it. No answer, so I do it again, louder this time. Finally, I hear movement inside although it's ages before Kane opens the door. He looks dazed, his hair all messy.

'Mum?' He rapidly blinks, trying to wake himself properly up. 'Are you OK?'

My palm sweeps tensely below my throat. 'No, I'm not. I asked you to have a word with Rocky about playing the piano at night.'

He looks confused. 'I did,' he adds in a mumble. 'Although I felt like a total idiot.'

I move closer to him, my words clipped and sharp. 'So why is she doing it? Is there a problem with her?'

Now my son looks offended. 'What kind of problem? Are you calling her nuts?'

I've pressed his button, which wasn't my intention, so I try to smooth things over. The last thing I want is to have a stand-up row with my son. 'Of course not. But I need to know why she was in the music room.'

'She's not playing the piano,' Kane informs me firmly and slowly. 'She hasn't been anywhere near the music room. I don't know what you're talking about.'

I peep over his shoulder into his room. There's no light inside so I can't tell if Rocky is in there or not. 'I'd like to speak to Rocky.'

Kane stretches his neck, the veins standing out angry beneath his skin. 'You can't.'

Rising on tiptoes, I call over his shoulder, 'Rocky? Can I speak with you? It needs to be now.'

Kane moves his body to block my view into the room. 'Mum, you can't right now. Perhaps in the morning.'

'Is she not there?' My tone is biting. 'Perhaps she's somewhere else in the house choosing some sheet music to play?'

Then Kane sweeps his hair back, his fingers fluttering through the strands. Just like Sam used to do. He's speaking to me, but it sounds like . . .

'Sam?' I ask him. 'Sam, is that you?'

The blood drains away from Sam's skin leaving him ashen. He looks horrified. Why does my son look horrified? I lean forward to take him in my arms . . .

Suddenly Sam's face switches to Kane, his features rearing up in front of me. I stumble to the side.

He almost yells at me, 'Mum, stop! You've got to stop doing this. We can't go down this road again.'

That's exactly what his dad said to me earlier. 'I don't understand.'

'Why are you always upsetting him?' The growling accusation comes from behind me.

It's Rocky. She's standing there, wearing a defiant expression and what looks like one of Kane's shirts, her silver nose ring stark against the dark.

I point an accusing finger at her. 'So, you weren't inside the room. You've been playing the piano.'

Calmly moving to stand with Kane, she tells me, 'If you weren't giving Kane the third degree you would've heard the loo flushing. That's where I've been.'

She's telling the truth because I hear the sound of the toilet's old tank still gurgling in the distance. I'm at a loss for words.

She loops her arm through Kane's, as if she's protecting him from me. His own mother. I stare long and hard at her fingers lightly stroking his arm. The fingers that have been on Sam's piano. That's what upsets me so much, thinking of someone else touching the keys where his hands have been. For years after he was gone, I paid someone to go inside the music room and clean the piano with strong disinfectant. Keep it clean, scrub the dirt away. Keep it pure. Just like Sam was.

Rocky levels a direct unnerving stare my way. 'Kane needs rest. That's why he came home.'

Kane adds, 'This business with Dad and the court has put you on edge. Like I said the other night, you're probably hearing the piano in a dream.'

Making stuff up. He doesn't have to say this, I see it written all over his face.

They shut the door in my face, leaving me standing alone in the cold. I hear them whispering inside, like two strangers plotting against me, living inside my house. Why is Rocky doing this to me?

◆ ◆ ◆

When I get back to my room, an empty bottle and scattered tablets lie on the floor. It's just like the other night. Where did they come from? How did they get there? My head starts pounding. A shaft of pain strikes between my eyes. Cringing, I reach for my jar and once again hold it against my belly. What if Kane's right and I'm making stuff up? That the music is inside my head? It's all a dream? Didn't

Rachmaninov say that a dream inspired him to compose 'Bells of Moscow'? A dream of himself dead in a coffin?

There's one thing I know for sure is true. Kane's girlfriend is playing Sam's piano. It's time I started searching for answers.

Edging the jar away from me, I look inside. There're a few things from ten years ago I keep in this jar. Not much, just a few odds and ends. Searching inside I finally find what I'm after: a crumpled business card. I straighten it out until the name is visible: Paul Simpson.

Mark, Kane, Simon, Ralf and Olivia – none of them will help me stop Sam from being declared dead. Maybe this person will.

Chapter 11

I'm back in the place of my birth.

The place of Sam's death.

On the beach the waves lap over my bare feet and my toes burrow deep into the sand under them. I welcome the feel of the water because it soothes away the pain in my feet. My arms hurt too. I must've slept wrong last night. I know this stretch of coast so well. It's moody, unpredictable and powerful. Some days the sea is gentle and inviting, lapping softly at the shore. On others, it's a terrifying beast, waves crashing with enough force to swallow a person whole. Today it's a gentle and warm day but who knows what tomorrow might bring? In front and to the sides of me is the expanse of blue ocean stretching to the horizon.

Due to its position on the coast this town is one of those where the sun both rises over the sea in the morning and sets over it at night. Only behind me is dry land. It was here, ten years ago, that my son was swept away. Well, that's what I was told. At this very spot or very nearby, it was never entirely clear where it happened. It was never entirely clear what exactly happened either, not to me at any rate.

Nothing sets my nerves on edge more than trivial incidents being described as a 'nightmare'. A traffic jam isn't a nightmare, a lost purse or bag isn't a nightmare, even an old person dying isn't a nightmare. That day though, and the days, months and years that followed were the very definition of a nightmare. Right from the moment that I first heard police sirens and helicopters in the sky, the first evil shadows that were a prelude to my son being taken away from me. Then the chaos, the disconnected and barely believable horrors that followed one after the other that day. The blizzard of images, words and whispers going on around me that couldn't be joined together. The hopeful faces and assurances, the fake hopeful faces, the soft voices and false promises.

'Don't worry, Alison, we're doing everything we can.'

Then the acrid words overheard in the background from one person to another.

'His body will be washed up in a few days.'

Kane's face was a picture of bewilderment, like a child suddenly thrust into a world he didn't understand. Poor Frances clung to my sister, her mum, her knuckles bloodless with fear. And Simon, *poor, poor Simon*, he looked even more lost than the kids, his eyes darting around as if searching for an explanation that wasn't there. The days after, interviews with the police, dumb questions, dumb answers, false reports that offered a glimmer of hope, fake news and fake blame. On and on it went, crashing over my head like being caught in the violent and murderous sea on a bad day.

It was around that time I was introduced to Paul Simpson, the local police's Family Liaison Officer. He was there to help get me through this difficult time, offer support and guidance and answer any questions I might have. I didn't want any of those things though, I only wanted my son back. He insisted I call him by his first name. They're trained to deal with devastated family of course but there was a sincerity and empathy in his eyes that was clear to me even then.

Finally, a judgement from the authorities. Sam's loss was just a tragic accident. They wanted to declare Sam dead then, but I vehemently wouldn't allow it. Until they showed me his body, I wouldn't give up hope. Sometimes it seemed like Paul was the only one who understood this. He was never judgemental like so many others and always took the time to listen.

Holding on to the rusty handrail, I go up the series of eroded stone steps that lead up the cliffs which overlook the beach and walk the path that makes its way into town. Near the centre stands the row of fisherman's cottages where I grew up. The cottages have long since been redeveloped and sold off, probably to second home-owners. I bet in the winter, virtually the entire row is dark because the residents are elsewhere.

Our old cottage home is standing proudly in its new form. There's no front garden and the little house and its door fronts the pavement. No net curtains means I can see inside from where I am. It's a vision of luxury. The walls are painted in fashionable pastel shades, expensive antique furniture is scattered around along with rugs that I imagine were tightly tied together and carried back from holidays in India and the Middle East. The floorboards are sanded, varnished and bare. They were sometimes bare in my childhood but that was because my father thought carpets were an extravagance. Something's missing in this new home though.

A piano.

So engrossed am I in my childhood that I don't even notice a woman sitting at a bureau in the corner of the room off to my right. It's a little while too before she notices me as she taps away on her laptop. She gets up from her wicker chair and comes to the window. My hesitant smile is met with a look of disdain, suspicion.

'That was once my home,' I want to call out to her, my way of putting her in her place. 'Others lived and loved here long before you set foot inside.'

Yanking her hand, she pulls the bamboo blinds down, deliberately shutting me out.

I move along until I find The Whispering Waves pub. Or what used to be it. Like the cottages, it's been renovated now, becoming a community hub, I think that's what they call it, with flats above.

Despite all these changes, when I peer through a window there are still glimpses of the pub. The outline of the bar along a wall, the alcove where the piano once stood. The space where strong-armed fishermen used to sit and drink while my father proudly looked on at his talented daughters playing music.

On a wall, the old pub sign hangs. It doesn't take much imagination to recreate the scene. It's all too easy to do if you know what you're looking for.

My heart lurches, a terrible sadness overcoming me as I remember this is where I came that day on the beach. I hadn't only come to hear the piano performance; the other reason was to soak up the nostalgia for my childhood. Sometimes the guilt is so heavy it feels as if it's dragging me under the waves with Sam.

If only I had stayed on the beach, watching over the children like a good mother should. If only I hadn't been so selfish, putting my needs before my children's. Even though I know they were in Simon's care, I still feel I abandoned them. In my mind, sometimes, I turn back time and imagine what the day on the beach would have been like if I'd stayed. I'm looking on as the children rush around and enjoy the freedom of being outside. Then Sam, it's always him, runs over to me and grabs my arm and tugs me up and towards the water. Giggling with high energy, he doesn't stop until my feet are covered over by the sea. Frances and Kane are laughing too.

No one goes into the cruel sea. No one gets hurt that day.

If only I had stayed. One stray, meaningless decision on an afternoon turned our lives upside down and now nothing will ever be the same. Guilt is such a terrible thing. You can look perfectly fine on the outside while inside guilt is ripping you to shreds.

Some days I'm so crippled by it I can hardly get out of bed. I failed my son.

Olivia's right to blame me. I'm the one who failed as a mother, as a protector. It's all my fault. I look at the building that was once our local pub and remember that this was the first place where she ever blamed me for anything. This is where the trouble between us started.

Chapter 12

The Sisters

'The Duelling Sisters.'

That was how The Whispering Waves pub was billing tonight's piano performance. Usually, the piano was played by Malcolm, but tonight, his two daughters, Alison and Olivia, would take his place. The landlord had managed to squeeze in an additional piano, making it a tight fit in the bar.

'Welcome,' the landlord announced, silencing the crowd. 'Most of you know Malcolm's girls, Ali and Oli.'

Olivia cringed at the shortened version of her name. Since she'd started hanging with the posh girls at school, she'd abandoned her childhood nickname along with her Norfolk accent. She looked up to these girls, with their money and big houses.

The landlord pointed to their dad's tip jar, balanced precariously on the line where the pianos touched. The jar accompanied their dad to all of his performances. It was precious to him, and he kept it on the piano at home.

'Be generous in your appreciation,' the landlord announced with flair. 'Now get ready for something truly spicy.'

Silence fell.

The music started. The girls started playing the first in their Spice Girls medley, 'Wannabe'. Its catchy rhythm and upbeat tempo instantly sucked in the audience, who were soon singing along to the chorus.

Alison lost herself in the music, her body swaying with each note. Though shy and reserved in public, her fingers against the keys suddenly allowed her to express all the emotions she normally found hard to show. Love. Passion. Sadness. Joy. Grief. Her mesmerising performance captivated the audience, leaving Olivia struggling to keep up.

By the final note, Alison's entire being rippled with emotion, and the pub erupted into rapturous applause and foot-stomping appreciation. The grinning landlord stepped forward, thanking the girls before sliding their father's tip jar completely onto Alison's piano, signalling that all the tips belonged to her. Olivia's cheeks burned red, her features contorted into a killer, irate expression as the jar filled up.

Later that night, Alison attempted to share the money with her sister, but, in a fit of temper, Olivia knocked the jar from her hand, sending it crashing to the ground, the soft carpet preventing it from shattering.

Olivia snapped, 'Don't think I don't know that Mrs Roberts is giving you extra piano lessons during lunchtime.'

Mrs Roberts was their music teacher at school. Alison's face filled with hot guilt because it was true. Although she defended their teacher with, 'She would do it for you too, but you don't practise much at home anymore and it shows.'

Olivia glared at Alison. 'You watch,' she said, her words laced with venom. 'One of these days, I'm going to be better than you. And I'm not talking about playing bloody music.'

Chapter 13

'Are you comfortable there? The wind's a little chilly up here on the cliffs,' Paul Simpson gently tells me.

He's the reason I dared to come back to this part of the coast.

When I first knew him, his hair was a rich chestnut, and he had a kindly face with only lines around his sharp eyes. He still looks kind but now his skin is more tanned, and his features are weathered and ruddy from constant exposure to the sea air. He's a big man, what my dad would call 'as tall as a lighthouse'. He still carries himself with the same strength and discipline I remembered from his days on the force. Time might have softened his edges, but beneath the gentle granddaddy vibe remains a firm, no-nonsense old-style cop.

After finding his card in Dad's old tip jar, I called him first thing this morning. I'd been biting my lip, worrying incessantly, fearing that the number might have been a police-issue one he'd had to surrender upon retirement, or worse, that it was no longer in service. When he answered, his deep soothing voice echoing back at me, a wave of relief washed over me, and I'd silently fist-pumped my free hand into the air.

He didn't seem in the least surprised to hear from me. He explained that it was quite common apparently for families to contact the Family Liaison Officer long after events. He was happy to talk to me about my loss. He'd been slightly floored when I'd requested to speak to him in person. He pointed out it was a long journey to make at the drop of a hat, but as he was retired now, he gave me the address of his cosy home with an elevated position overlooking the sea.

The first thing he did when we entered his garden was to take me to the bottom, where the crumbling cliff edge has eaten its way onto his property. Below is the sea which has done the crumbling.

'It's an open question which will go first, me or the house!' There's a twinkle in his eyes. 'In the meantime, come and sit down, and we can chat.'

He's an attentive host, making sure I'm comfortable and well supplied with tea and cake.

Paul's a trained listener and is ready to provide sympathy, support and advice for a woman who's lost her son, even if it was ten years ago. It takes him a while to realise that I'm not here for sympathy and support.

'The thing is, Paul, Sam's body was never found.' The fine china teacup warms the inside of my hand. 'As there was no body, the police couldn't conclude that my son was lost in a tragic accident because there's no proof.' Paul looks uncomfortable. He looks even more uncomfortable when I add, 'My husband is going to court to have Sam declared dead. Until there is proof, I'm not going to let him.'

Paul's a lot less relaxed now. 'As I'm sure the police and coastguard explained to you, when someone is lost at sea, the body isn't always recovered. In a few cases, sometimes, bodies are recovered by fishermen, trawlers, and so on, and to avoid having to engage with the authorities, the body is returned to the deep.'

I stare at him, horror-stricken at what he's telling me. 'You mean someone may have found Sam's body and thrown it back into the sea?' It leaves me feeling sick.

I quickly add, 'My father was a fisherman, and he wouldn't have done that. I'm sure none of his brethren would have either. For days afterward, the North Sea was turned over from one end of the coast to the other in an effort to recover Sam. I was told bodies are usually given up by the tide, but Sam's never was.'

Paul becomes very serious. 'I don't understand, Alison. Are you saying that you don't accept the investigation's conclusions? They were pretty definitive and backed up by all the evidence.'

'Did your colleagues consider any other possibilities?'

The corners of Paul's eyes crinkle as he glances out over the sea. 'Of course they explored every avenue. Leaving no stone unturned comes with the job. However, they were satisfied they had the facts.' He shuffles slightly. 'More or less, anyway.'

'More or less?' Carefully, I place the teacup down and stare at him questioningly. 'What does that mean?'

Paul clearly wishes he hadn't said that. He shrugs. 'What you have to understand is that in every police inquiry, there will always be things that don't quite fit together, timings that don't quite match, and statements that don't entirely agree with each other. That's normal. In a tragic case like this, when two traumatised young children have to give accounts and the adults are in shock, it's more true than usual. The most suspicious inquiries are those where everything fits together like a jigsaw puzzle.'

There's no sign of the earlier twinkle in his eyes in the expression he settles on me. 'I'm sure you wouldn't want to suggest that Kane, Frances, your brother and sister were deliberately misleading anyone?'

Of course I don't think that. But . . . ? The 'But' lingers in my mind for some reason.

'There will always be loose ends. There always are,' Paul continues. 'Sometimes more than others.'

As he picks up the teapot to fill up my cup, I press on. 'What were the loose ends?'

He settles the teapot back on the table and himself into his chair. 'I don't want to upset you, but we were disappointed we didn't find Sam's body.' Suddenly he frowns so hard that his bushy brows cover the tops of his eyelids. 'What I've learned over the years is that the sea never treats those that are swept away in the same manner.'

An expression of extreme sadness with an edge of grief shadows his features, and I wonder if he has his own personal tragedy that might be connected to the sea? When I was a girl, my father warned me: 'The sea is as breathtaking as an angel, yet as dangerous as the Devil himself.'

I ask, 'Is it possible for me to speak to the officer who was in charge of the investigation?'

Paul thinks for a minute, then dashes my hopes with a shake of his head. 'He's moved on now. Got a job with the big boys and girls in the Met in London. Plus, the investigation is closed. Unless there's any new evidence. If there is, it hasn't reached my ears.'

The thumping in my head that plagued me yesterday is back. This time in the lower part of my skull which touches the back of my neck. I know there's no more point to this. He hasn't got any information that I can use to stop Mark pursuing this. It's the end of the line. I'm not a person given to tears, but all I want to do is walk into the sea and cry.

Will anyone miss me if I never come back?

In the narrow hallway, he reaches for the door; however, he abruptly turns back to me. 'There is one thing.'

'What?'

'I was a copper for over thirty years. Call it a copper's intuition. But I've never been able to forget this case. Like I said before, sometimes there are some loose ends.'

His thick brows slash together. 'Something wasn't right. I got the feeling that pieces of the story were missing.'

Chapter 14

Daddy

We begged and begged to make you stay

But then an angel came and took you away.

By now, I know quite a number of these brass plaques and engraved stones that remember loved ones in these memorial gardens. I've been here so many times to visit Sam's. This memorial plaque in particular has always haunted me. It doesn't tell you who 'Daddy' was or who begged him to stay. There are no names on it, no dates and ages, or any indication of what happened to Daddy. I often wonder about it and feel an instinctive empathy with those children who simply called themselves 'we'.

I've come here straight from seeing Paul. I'm drop-down tired, the muscles in my legs ache like hell, so by rights I should've gone straight home. Slid into bed and pulled the duvet over my head. I haven't got long here; it will be locking up time soon. Some people might find visits to memorial gardens a miserable experience. But I never have.

This place of memories is located at the back of one of those grand cemeteries that were built in the Victorian era. With cremation becoming more of an option these days, it's become increasingly popular. The managers keep the lawn mown, the trees pruned, the flowers cleared and the plaques polished, even if the relatives have lost interest. I'm not in a hurry and even in the gathering gloom, the words can still be read. I stop by one that stands in front of a Japanese cherry tree:

Judith.

Beloved daughter, sister, wife, mother and gran.

Passed away aged 96, 23.3.2015.

Always in our thoughts.

Ninety-six? You can't complain about that. Or perhaps Judith could. Perhaps she was tired and wanted to go. I was shocked when I offered my own grandmother 'many happy returns' on a birthday, only for her to say 'not too many more I hope, dear'. Now I'm older, I get it.

Down a slope, set back slightly from the path but with no tree or bush behind it is another brass plate. On it is the outline of a piano and in that outline, there is only one word.

Sam

This is the memorial to my son, Kane's older brother by two years. There was a terrible fight over this plate. I didn't want one at all because a memorial plate meant he was dead and I wasn't willing to accept that. Stupid of course, but that's how it was. We fought and fought until eventually Mark and I compromised. We agreed on a plate with an engraving of Sam's beloved piano. But I insisted on one thing. Would not budge.

No words on it.

No 'in memoriam' or 'gone but not forgotten' or 'RIP'. When it was erected, the three of us, Mark, Kane and I came down to view it. We were the only ones. I'd fallen out with my brother and sister by then. They were invited but didn't come. We stood in the driving rain in silence. They remembered but I didn't.

Because you don't remember those who might still be living.

Kane doesn't visit his brother. When I gently asked him why he didn't he was clear: Sam isn't really there. Oddly, it was me, the person so against the plaque in the first place who became the only regular visitor. Over time this piece of brass feels like my only living connection to him. I spot a mark on it so take out a tissue which I run, slowly and lovingly, over the metal before taking a seat on a bench nearby, studying the plate.

'Your father wants you declared dead, Sam. Can you believe that? Dead. Some father he is.'

The anger is welling up in me. I don't even look round to see if someone is watching me talking out loud to an empty space. I don't feel any embarrassment. It's a common thing for the bereaved to speak to the lost. And the other way around. One writer claimed in a memoir that when he first made love to a woman after his wife died, he clearly heard his late wife call out, 'Stop that now!' He was so convinced she was in the bedroom with him that he couldn't go through with it. It's totally normal. I've seen other people doing it in these gardens, sharing news from the family. Although of course, not everyone agrees with talking to the lost.

'Can you believe it? He first tried this trick a few years ago when you'd been gone for seven years. That's how long it is before someone who's lost can officially be declared dead. He thought it was time to let you go.'

I nod to let it sink in. 'Now he's trying again. But we stopped him then and we'll stop him now.'

I share my other news with my son.

'Your brother is back from college.' I don't tell Sam about Kane's strange behaviour. He doesn't need to know about that.

'He's brought some girl called Rocky. Can you imagine any decent parent naming their daughter Rocky? She's probably made it up to make herself sound more interesting. Her real name is probably Tabitha or something. All those piercings. And the pink hair. I don't know what she thinks that's saying with the hair. It falls across her face like a criminal's mask.'

I try not to tell Sam about her playing his piano in the music room. I don't want to upset him. Unfortunately, I can't stop myself. 'She plays the piano too, so that's something you, me and her have got in common. She's touching your piano and won't stop. Two in the morning like she did last night. Perhaps she has troubles of her own and she was trying to soothe her frayed nerves or something with music.' My anxious fury bubbles up. 'Still, that doesn't give her the right.'

I stand up. 'I'm going to speak to your brother about your father's plans to have you declared dead later. If Kane is onside with me and we work something out with my solicitor, we'll put a stop to him.' As an afterthought, I add, 'I don't suppose your father has paid you a visit lately?' The empty space is silent. 'That's typical of him.'

The only time Mark did come to these gardens after the plate went up was when he followed me one afternoon without my realising. He stood at a distance and watched me speak to Sam. Then he came over, put his arm around my shoulder and led me over to this bench and sat me down. His voice was gentle but laced with worry.

'What do you think you're doing, Alison?'

I was angry at being spied on. 'I'm talking to our son. What does it look like?'

'OK, that's not wrong. But do you need to do it every day? Come down here and talk to our son? Every day? Twice a day? Is that helpful?'

I must have looked in quite a state to explain that look of something approaching terror on his face when I answered, 'You think he's gone, don't you? You've given up. Well, until there's proof, I'm never giving up on my son. Mothers don't give up on their children. Never.'

'There's not going to be any proof, you know that. Alison, I'm worried where this is going to end up. You're not well. You're being crushed by grief and guilt. You need help and I'm not sure I'm the right person to give it to you. It's not even the visiting this spot in the gardens, it's everything else that's going on.'

'Everything else? What are you talking about?'

He'd shaken his head as if at his wits' end. 'What about our other son? Our only son—'

I'd shoved him away so violently that he'd almost fallen over. 'Our only son? We have got two sons. We always will have. Sam will stay with us for the rest of our lives.'

Mark was angry too. 'What's this doing to Kane? He was there on the beach that day. What's this doing to him with his own grief and guilt? He needs you. We all need each other.'

'You think I'm going mad, don't you?' My voice had been so listless, so dead.

'I'm worried where this is going to end, that's all.'

'You don't watch crime series on TV, do you? You know what the critics say?'

He'd looked so bewildered. 'What's this got to do with anything?'

'If a character is supposed to be dead but you don't see the body, they're not dead.'

Mark hung his head in despair. 'Oh, Alison . . .'

He was right. After everything came to a head, I stopped coming to the gardens every day. Instead, my visits were confined to once a month, carefully controlled visits that I remember through a blurry haze. Back then they wouldn't let me speak to Sam.

I stand in front of Sam's plaque, my hands clasped together, head bowed as if in prayer. It's nearly dark now. I didn't want to tell him about my visit to Paul Simpson. He doesn't need to know about that at the moment until I've asked more questions. But I have to say something.

'They were all lying about what happened to you. I knew they were all along.' I reach out a hand and run my fingers over his name which I can no longer see. 'I promise you this, Sam. I'm not going to stop until I find out what really happened. That's your mother's promise.'

As I turn away and walk in the dark, my chest trembles and I shout out.

'They were all lying!'

Chapter 15

'They were all lying!'

Ralf has no problems seeing me this morning about the case but, after my dramatic announcement on the other side of his desk, he's already looking as if he'd told his receptionist every make-believe excuse in the book to keep me well away from him.

'I'm sorry, Alison, what are you talking about? Who are these liars? What are they lying about?'

'The people on the beach when Sam was lost.'

Sighing heavily, Ralf takes out one of his trademark fat cigars and lights up. After a few puffs he clarifies, 'You mean Simon? Kane and Frances? Those two little children?'

Eagerly shuffling my bum to the edge of my chair, I tell him all about my visit to Paul Simpson and how he told me something isn't right about the story of Sam's disappearance. OK, so I admit that I'm exaggerating heavily. But the thing is, if I don't raise the stakes Ralf won't help me. However, if he thinks there's something juicy for him to get his lawyer teeth into with the possibility of a win, he'll go all out. There's nothing a man like Ralf likes more than winning. Plus, the money he'll make from it, of course.

Listening impassively, Ralf makes notes while chomping on his cigar. When I fall silent, he glances up with a sceptical lift of his brow. 'Is that it? You go up the coast to talk to some out-of-commission cop, who passes on office gossip and hearsay which you're turning into the Kennedy assassination?'

Throwing his pen down, he jerks back in his chair and smashes the end of the cigar in an ashtray. 'I'm not sure what you're saying to me anymore. Are you trying to find evidence that Sam might not be dead? Or that he was kidnapped by pirates and Kane, Frances and Simon covered up for them?'

Other people will find Ralf cruel to say this to me, a grieving mother. However, I'm familiar with his sarcastic ways. As long as he gets the job done I don't care what he throws at me. Where I grew up you learned to grow a tough skin in life.

'Let me tell you something, I've been in court more than a few times for more than a few cases. The suspicious witnesses are the ones who get everything right. When you hear a cop saying that he first saw the suspect at 7.18 p.m. and at 7.21 p.m. he broke into the car and at 7.24 p.m. he drove it away, that's when you know you're hearing fairy stories.

'I dare say your new friend in Norfolk was right. We know that Sam's body was never recovered. It isn't clear why Simon lost sight of the kids and there are loose ends. But you've got to remember, poor Simon was probably in shock afterwards. The kids devastated and traumatised. Frances was eleven and Kane nine. One minute they were playing with their cousin and brother and he's gone the next.'

He's right of course. The picture he paints of the trauma my niece and living son must have experienced is stark and gut-wrenching.

When I say nothing, he goes on, 'Let's look at what we actually know about that afternoon. You're on a family holiday. You're there with Sam and Kane. Olivia is there with her daughter Frances. Simon is alone. There are no spouses or partners. You have lunch in a seaside café. It's all a bit frosty because you and your sister don't get on. Simon meanwhile doesn't have a problem with either of you.

'It's the afternoon. It's your turn to look after the children on the beach but you want to go to see a piano in a boozer where you and Olivia used to hang out as kids. Olivia says you have to stay on the beach with the children because it's your turn. She's off to do brass rubbings or something in a local church. You think she's being a bitch as per usual.' His tongue rolls gleefully around the word 'bitch'. He really doesn't like my sister. 'Simon offers to take your place on the beach, but Olivia is playing her usual witchy self and won't have it.

'But' – Ralf dramatically raises his finger in the air – 'when Olivia's gone Simon tells you to go to the pub to listen to the piano recital, he'll take on beach duty for you. Sam wants to come with you, but you say no because you want him to stay on the beach to have fun.'

I choke. Looking back, I could have taken Sam with me. If I had, he would still be with me now. I should have just taken him. It was all my fault.

Looking back is like picking at an old wound – it never heals and only leaves you hurting all over again.

'While you were at a piano performance in a pub, you become aware of a lot of activity outside. Police cars, sirens, a helicopter and what have you. A rocket goes off on the pier which means a lifeboat is being launched and the crew have to attend. You get a bad feeling and leave the pub. You get to the beach and the scene is chaos. People are everywhere. Simon is there with the children except Sam. Eventually, you hear what happened, and it's that Sam went into the sea for a swim. One minute he was splashing around, the next he was carried out by the current and then he disappeared. Simon was supposed to be keeping an eye on things but for some reason he wasn't there when Sam was swept away. That bit is a little confused. Despite an extensive sea rescue attempt for the rest of that day and into the following one, Sam's body wasn't recovered. The police interviewed Simon, Kane and his cousin Frances and concluded that this was a more or less accurate account of what happened.'

Looking up, Ralf meaningfully adds, 'Obviously, the three witnesses were in deep distress and shock so there were a few minor errors in their stories.'

This simple and brusque description of all that horror along with the total destruction of more lives than one is compressed into a flat tone in a few minutes by Ralf. It's verging on the sadistic.

He leans back in his chair. 'What your friend told you doesn't really change anything, surely you can see that?' When I don't answer, he goes on in a voice that's almost a plea. 'I mean, what do you want me to do here?'

'I want you to stop Mark declaring Sam dead and I want to know what really happened on the beach.'

He shrugs in desperation. 'How am I supposed to do that? We've got nothing here to work with.'

'Let's find something to work with.' I steal a glimpse at my phone. As soon as I returned from the memorial gardens, I texted my brother asking him to meet me this lunchtime. After all, he suggested it in the supermarket. He made excuses as to why that wasn't possible, but I persisted and, as usual, he gave in. We arranged to meet at a pub we both know, well away from Olivia's prying eyes. I didn't tell him that I want to discuss what happened on the beach that day but after the usual pleasantries that's what we'll be discussing. But I'm worried he'll find a reason to cancel on me. I turn back to Ralf. 'You're always boasting about your contacts in the police. Ask one of them to get his hands on the notes from the original inquiry and pass them on to us. Let's see what was written as opposed to the gossip and the hearsay.'

Ralf purses his lips, puts his cigar out and gives me a long stare. 'Yes, I could do that. I'll make a deal with you. If you promise to go and see someone, a doctor or a therapist, I'll get my hands on the police notes for you. You're not well, Alison, anyone can see that. Have we got a deal?'

He's right. I look terrible. All last night I lay half awake, fully clothed on my bed in the attic. I was waiting for Rocky to start playing Sam's piano again. I know she's going to. The silence when she didn't was almost as bad as when she did. Any moment, I expected it to start, and those moments were torture. But Rocky took the night off. Before coming to Ralf's this morning, I plastered my face with make-up and lippy to cover my unslept flesh and it made me look like a clown. I don't blame Ralf for thinking I'm losing it. Perhaps I am. It's even something of a relief to think that someone's worried about me.

'There's nothing wrong with my head if that's what you're suggesting.'

He raises his hands and shows me his palms to indicate he doesn't believe me. Of course he doesn't.

'Very well, I'll go and see someone.'

Satisfied, Ralf warns me with a smile, 'OK, but don't lie to me, Alison. I'll know if you lie about seeing someone, I can spot an untruth a mile off.'

'You should be able to, you've told enough of them.'

He's pleased with himself. 'Don't say that, Alison, I might put your quote up on my website as a reference.'

Ralf promises to get the police notes for me and then wishes me good luck on my 'wild goose chase'.

When I leave his office, I look for Frances. When I peer through a window, I see she's talking to a client, so I make the decision to speak to her later. She catches sight of me and breaks off from her conversation to give me a smile. I make a gesture to suggest a phone call and she gives me the thumbs up. I don't want to drag Frances or Kane into this and if Simon wants to help me, there'll be no need to.

An awful lot is riding on my brother.

Chapter 16

'Simon, open the door. Please.'

I don't shout or yell at my brother's front door. My knocking is polite and respectful. The last thing I want to do is embarrass my brother or make a scene in front of his neighbours. All I want to do is talk to him. We'd agreed to meet at the pub this lunchtime. I'd even got there early. I waited for half an hour over the agreed time before it was clear Simon was going to be a no-show. Disappointment running through me, just as I got up to leave a text pinged on my phone:

> Not going to make lunch. Terribly sorry. Got a new project going with the community centre. It's a full-on thing! Work, eh? Be in touch with you sometime next month. Apologies again. Simon x

Work, eh? That's the thing, it isn't his work. For the last twenty odd years, Simon has been a teacher in a primary school. The way I hear it, he took a sabbatical six months or so ago. Since we haven't spoken for ten years I have no idea if that's the truth or not. So, he's got plenty of time on his hands.

Simon has always been such a terrible liar. He always was when we were kids. Ralf could come up with a story that involved spies, femmes fatales and an international man of mystery and it would still be halfway believable. Simon, on the other hand, couldn't tell a tall tale if he tried. All this talk about the community centre is a load of old crap. If my brother thinks I'm going away he doesn't remember me very well.

From the pub I took a detour to the memorial gardens to update Sam and then drove up to my brother's home. There wasn't a car in the driveway, so he wasn't at home. Maybe there was a project that demanded his full attention. I made sure I parked some distance down the street because I didn't want him spotting me.

When he got home, I gave him fifteen minutes inside before making my presence felt on his doorstep.

'Simon, I'm not leaving until you speak to me.'

No answer.

I mutter to myself, 'I'll wait. There's no hurry. I've waited ten years already.'

The door flies open. It's Katie, Simon's wife. She steps out, partially closing the door behind her. Katie is much older than Simon, a good fifteen years. And she looks it with her grey bun and lined face. She's nice enough but I never understood their marriage. Maybe it's because I wanted my brother to hook up with someone his own age.

Her mouth is pinched at the corners. 'What on earth do you think you're playing at? Please go away before I call the police.'

She could call the Devil Himself, I'm not moving. 'I want to speak to Simon.'

'He's not here. He's gone away on business.'

'I know he's here because I saw him arrive in his car.' For some reason that makes her lose the colour in her face.

I don't know what Simon has told his wife about me, but it clearly isn't good. 'Look, Alison, we all know you've got your troubles and your issues but bringing them to your brother's door isn't the answer. This is harassment.'

I don't want to upset her. But . . . 'He's going to have to talk to me sooner or later. It might as well be sooner.'

She looks me up and down. 'He was never the same after that day.'

Before I can respond she goes back in the house, slamming the door behind her.

For a minute or two, I'm not sure what to do. There's no way to force my brother to talk to me. I might as well go home.

A cab pulls up outside. Suddenly the front door springs open again. Katie has reappeared, carrying a suitcase this time. She isn't alone. Either side of her are two young teenage girls. My nieces, who were four and five years old the last time I saw them. They look solemn and worried and avoid looking at me. Taking their hands, their mother guides them past me. On the road, they get into the cab, which heads off.

While I watch it drive away, icy insistent fingers grab the side of my jacket and haul me through the open doorway and into the hallway. I'm spun round and slammed up against the wall.

The air whooshes out of me as pain shudders through my body.

It's Simon. A Simon I don't recognise. His eyes are bloodshot and he appears to have been crying. His face is both sweaty and cold and it's contorted by hatred and fear. He holds me against the wall with a terrifying vibrating violence that stuns me. My brother Simon isn't violent. He's never hurt another human being in his life. His behaviour shocks me to my core.

His voice is strangled and choked. 'Why are you doing this? Why? Olivia was right about you all along. You're making trouble, you know that?' He shakes me again. I'm too shocked, winded and scared to say anything. 'We all know you're on the edge but even we didn't know you'd turn into this. And what do you think you're achieving? Do you think Sam is going to emerge fully formed from the waves and embrace his mother on the sand? Is that it?'

The image he creates leaps into my mind, leaving me gasping.

Finally, I manage to splutter, 'Simon, stop. You're frightening me. I just came to talk to you.'

It's like he can't hear me. He's lost in his own torment. There's a stricken expression burning in his eyes that fills me with dread.

'And what about the others? You don't care about Olivia or me, we all understand that. But what about Frances? What about my girls? What about your own son? If you cared for any of us, you'd let Mark have Sam declared dead. Let us all get on with the rest of our lives in peace.'

His words tumble, half-shaped and spoken as if he has preprepared a speech to deliver but now he can't remember how it goes.

He shakes me again. 'Why don't you just go back to that lunatic asylum you were in, take to the booze and pills again and leave us all alone? What about that idea?'

What lunatic asylum? What's he talking about?

Now and again, for a second, he seems to remember he's really my brother Simon and his voice breaks, his grip loosens and he struggles with this fiend who appears to have taken possession of him. His face is briefly overcome with horror at what he's doing. But he loses the struggle, his voice sharpens again, his grip tightens and he slams me against the wall again. 'This is the end, do you understand?' Spit froths at the corner of his mouth. 'I want you out of this house. Don't get in touch with me again. Ever!'

Like I'm nothing but a rag doll Simon throws me out. I tumble forward and end up in a heap on the stony driveway. For a few moments, I'm on my knees winded and dazed. And stupefied. What just happened?

This is my brother Simon. My baby brother. The little boy who always stepped in to break up arguments between Olivia and me when we were children. The man with a horror of confrontation who always took the easy way out of a dispute, if it would spare him an argument.

Struggling to my feet, wiping the grit from my palms, I stumble to my car and finally collapse into the driver's seat.

The guilt kicks in at once. In all that flood of abuse, my brother made one fair point. What about Kane, Frances and his two daughters?

Perhaps I shouldn't have promised Sam in the memorial gardens that I wouldn't stop until I found out what really happened.

When I get home, I spend a long time in the car, physically unable to get out. When my phone alerts me there's a text, it's ignored. Only when I finally manage to get out, do I check who's contacted me.

Simon.

I'm tempted to delete it. I don't need round two of more abuse. But curiosity gets the better of me.

Forgive me, it says. I don't know what got into me. I've been under a lot of stress lately. That's why I asked Katie and the girls to go visit her sister for a few days. I'm going to write you a letter tonight that will set your mind at rest about things. It might be quite a hard read but it's for the best. It might at least stop you blaming yourself for everything. Your loving brother xxx

I reply at once:

Let's meet. Now. Talk to me instead of a letter. I won't get angry, Promise.

No response.

If he's writing me a letter I won't have long to wait. A day or two?

I know he won't text back but I send him another message anyway:

I've loved you since Dad placed you as a baby in my arms when I was four. Nothing you could do would make me stop loving you.

Chapter 17

I'm still shattered by the incident with Simon when I finally reach home. My back aches from where he banged me into the wall. My heart hurts too. I'll just have to bide my time and wait for his mysterious letter.

My mood gets worse when I find Rocky in *my* kitchen putting something in the microwave. Even supposing I want to be sociable it's not with her. She doesn't think I can see her watching me from under the tips of her pink hair.

After sending her a sharp nod, I step inside and begin ferreting around in the cupboards, looking for something to drink. There's nothing left except a bottle of cooking sherry, so it will have to be that. I can't face going out again.

'Are you all right there?' Rocky's voice behind me makes me tense. 'You seem a little stressed.' Is she really concerned about me or is that amusement I hear in her tone? Laughing at her boyfriend's mother? Where did Kane find this mocking girl?

I consider not answering, but quickly decide against it because I have got manners.

Twisting around, I say, 'I'm fine, thank you. Where's Kane?'

The microwave pings. Then she tells me, 'He's gone out. He got an urgent phone call. It stressed him out.'

I freeze, worry eating away at me. 'Really? Where's he gone?'

She takes her ready meal out. 'I dunno. I'm not his keeper.'

Suddenly, I'm spoiling for a fight and she's a good candidate for one. 'You're his girlfriend, aren't you? Aren't you interested in where he goes? Why he's upset?'

She doesn't answer, merely smiles. If it's possible for a smile to be snide, this one is it. Rocky leaves the kitchen, the wafting steam from her meal rising up and masking her face, without another word.

I take my sherry up the two flights of stairs to the attic. Open up the skylight and suck in much-needed air. Fill my lungs up until I feel more balanced. I almost collapse into the Peacock chair under the skylight and sip the sherry. I should really have used a glass but what's the point of that, it will only mean washing up. Tipping back the bottle will do. It's after my fourth sip, as my head comes down, that I notice something is missing from the room.

The tip jar.

It isn't in its usual place on the bedside cabinet. Panic starts setting in.

The tip jar is so cherished to me. It may look like a simple jar but it is the most treasured object I have left of my dad. He'd keep it on the piano at home and take it with him wherever he played. With awe, when I was a young girl, I'd watch it fill up with coins, customers showing their appreciation. I remember one night someone put a twenty-pound note in it. Dad had every right to spend that tip on himself, but he didn't. He used that twenty to take me and Olivia and Simon to the cinema, or The Pictures was what we called it. I don't recall what we saw; however, I remember us all singing on the way back home. It was the one time Dad permitted us to sing 'My Old Man Said Follow the Van'.

There was something so special about how our pockets would jangle with change when our father took us home, walking the dimly lit streets in the twilight, each of us carrying a bottle of pop with a straw in it.

The tip jar is a reminder of the hard, selfless passion and dedication he'd committed himself to trying to give his kids a better life. Although, for me, looking back there was nothing wrong with our lives. I loved living in our cosy cottage and hearing the slapping of the sea at night. I was proud of who we were. In the wake of Sam's passing, the tip jar became a lifeline, a source of comfort during my hellish grief. When the guilt threatened to overwhelm me, pull me under, I would cradle Dad's jar close and let the rush of memories of Dad take me back to those cherished evenings spent listening to him playing piano. The same hands that gutted fish were a wizard across the keys.

Now my jar is missing.

I begin searching and start by dropping to my knees beside the bed. A knot of tension tightens in my belly. The tip jar has to be here somewhere. It must have fallen off the bedside cabinet and rolled under the bed. That's the only explanation that makes sense. I peer into the darkness beneath the bed. But it's empty, save for a lone sock and dust that makes me cough. Pushing myself up, I clench my jaw. *Where else? Where could it be?*

'Come on,' I mutter, my voice steady despite the increasingly out of control alarm building inside me. 'Where are you?'

I move through the attic, opening drawers, checking the wardrobe and inside the bedside cabinet. In the living room, I scan the bookshelf, removing books and checking behind picture frames. My movements are quick but controlled. I'm vaguely aware of a frame nosediving to the ground, but I can't spare it a thought. The jar is all that matters right now.

After I've turned over the kitchen, huffing badly, I stand in the middle of the room, surveying the mess I've created. Glasses, plates, cups, cutlery all out and shoved to the side. The doors to the cupboard under the sink are wide open, yawning like the silent scream I'm barely holding back.

I notice the microwave isn't fully closed and that reminds me of who else is now living in my house.

My fist pounds against Kane's door with such fury the bones of my hand hurt. Rocky opens up. She's changed into a fashionably jagged hemmed T-shirt with a political slogan: 'Uncover the truth. Reveal the lies.' It feels like a pointed jab at me. Or am I just being paranoid?

'Where is it?' I rasp. I don't like the way I sound slightly unhinged.

Rocky searches my tightening features. 'Where is what?'

'You know,' I spit back.

Calm down. Be calm. But I can't. That jar is my link to Dad and Sam.

'My tip jar.'

She looks incredulous. 'Your tip jar? Do you do circus tricks on the high street? Balancing things on your nose, that kind of thing?'

How dare she mock me! 'Just give it back to me.'

Suddenly she looks grave. 'You're being serious, aren't you. This isn't a joke.'

'A joke?' I can barely contain my anger.

'I don't know. It wasn't me. Maybe Kane took it.'

'He would never do that. My son knows how important it is to me.' My frustration builds.

'Why is this jar so important to you?'

It's not just her question which throws me but her sincerity too. Defiantly I reply, 'It belonged to Kane's grandfather. It . . .' I want to explain to her about Dad receiving tips for his wonderful talent; however, I suspect she won't understand. So instead, I say, 'It is very precious to me. I don't suppose you'd understand what that means.'

'This,' Rocky answers. She raises one of her fingers to show me one of the many silver rings she wears. It's striking, actually three rings interlocked together. 'It belonged to my sister,' she continues. 'We went down to London and had a day shopping in Camden. We both liked silver much more than gold. As soon as she saw that ring she had to have it.'

As I listen to her, I realise this is the first personal thing that I've found out about Kane's girlfriend.

'Why are you wearing it instead of your sister?'

For a moment, Rocky rubs her finger and thumb around the ring. 'She was killed by a drunk driver.' I gasp. 'Two years ago. I wanted to bury her with her ring, but she left instructions saying she wanted me to have it.'

I'm stunned and saddened by her loss. And also by my assumption that Rocky wouldn't understand how a simple object can be a link to someone who is lost, that it's so much more than a mere physical thing, it's a link to valued memories. How could I have been so dismissive? So quick to judge? Rocky knows the pain of loss.

Which one of us hasn't known grief?

Nevertheless, I remind myself that my tip jar is missing. Kane would never have taken it. Which leaves only one other person. I take two steps back from Rocky, clearly signalling that our moment of intimacy is over.

'I suppose it wasn't you playing my son's piano either? Who told you "Bells of Moscow" means as much to me as my tip jar does?' I chuck the old accusation at her.

I turn my back on her. Behind me she calls out, 'Are you sure you left it where you think you did?'

◆ ◆ ◆

'Are you sure you left it where you think you did?'

Rocky's question echoes uncomfortably in my mind as I sit on the Peacock chair, my legs folded under me. It's God knows what time in the morning. Still dark, I couldn't sleep, what Rocky said preying on my mind. What if she's right and I took the jar and left it somewhere else? My memory has played tricks on me before. How many times have I convinced myself of something, only to be proven wrong? The jar could be anywhere.

Maybe I'm losing my grip, the stress of the upcoming court case leaving me second-guessing myself.

Suddenly my phone rings. Who could be calling me at this crazy time? I get out of the chair and walk across the room to pick up my phone. It's Frances.

'Aunt Alison—'

'What's happened?' Only bad phone calls come at this hour.

'Mum got a call from Aunt Katie. Uncle Simon went out for a drive and never came back home.'

My heart plunges when she tells me: 'He was last seen at the beach.'

Chapter 18

10 YEARS AGO: RIPPLE EFFECTS – THE GATHERING

'I'm not coming out. Leave. Me. Alone,' Alison listlessly uttered.

Nearly two months had passed since Sam was lost and an anguished heaviness hung over her house in Norwich. Her once vibrant home, filled with the melodies of Sam's piano and the laughter of a happy family, was now a place of a strange silence, a mere shell of its former self.

Although today was different. Mark had organised a get-together in memory of Sam, hoping to bring some solace to their grieving hearts. The main room and garden brimmed with family and friends, their hushed tones and sombre expressions a testament to the shared sorrow that had brought them together.

But Alison refused to join them. She remained locked in their bedroom, a self-imposed exile from the world that dared to move on without her beloved son. How could they gather here, in the very house where Sam's presence lingered in every corner, and pretend that life could go on?

She sat on the edge of the bed, her once alert eyes now dull and ringed with dark circles. Her hair hung in limp, unwashed strands while her rumpled and stained clothes clung to her body.

Mark knocked again at the door. His muffled voice pleaded, 'People are here for you, for us. They want to support us. Everyone is asking after you.'

Alison shook her head vehemently, her fingers clawing and digging into the mattress. Her lips twisted with contempt. 'How dare they come here, acting like Sam is really gone?'

Mark swallowed the words that he wanted to tell his wife – that their son was never coming back. He didn't because it seemed so cruel. However, he didn't know how much more of this he could take.

Silence stretched between them, heavy and suffocating. Then, the door creaked open and a small figure slipped inside. Kane, their nine-year-old son, approached his mother, his young face riddled with sorrow and fear.

For a second he hesitated before moving to her. It frightened him to see his mother like this. 'Mum,' he whispered, his small hand slipping into hers. 'All the people are asking to see you.'

Something in his innocent plea, in the way his fingers tightened around hers, broke through the walls of Alison's grief.

With a shuddering breath, she nodded. 'For you, I'd do anything.'

With robotic movements she got up and went to the bathroom to clean up and to make herself as presentable as possible. She avoided her reflection in the mirror, unable to face the naked grief she would see.

As she descended the stairs, the murmur of voices grew louder. Her gaze landed on Mark, deep in conversation with her sister Olivia. She could hear what they were saying but it all sounded disjointed and muddled up. She fixed her stare on her sister with a flicker of annoyance. Of course, Olivia would be here, ready to pass judgement, no doubt still blaming her.

Olivia's eyes met hers and Alison flinched at the pity that lurked beneath the surface. It was a look she had grown to despise along with the whispered, 'Poor Alison.'

When she reached them, Olivia's chilled lips touched her on the cheek, her expensive perfume swirling around her. Mumbling a greeting to her sister, she quickly headed down the stairs. And wished she hadn't because the weight of the sympathetic gazes of those gathered pressing down on her. Condolences and well-meaning platitudes washed over her, but she barely registered the words. They were empty, meaningless in the face of her loss.

Abruptly, Alison froze, not believing what she was seeing. People were in Sam's music room. White-hot anger surged through her.

'Get out!' she screamed, her voice raw and shrill. 'All of you, get out of his room! You have no right to be there!'

Stunned faces turned toward her, eyes wide with shock and confusion. Kane stood frozen, his small form trembling as he watched his mother unravel before his eyes.

Alison pushed past the gathering, her breath coming in ragged gasps. She went to go inside the music room but couldn't. It was like a wall was blocking her.

Chest heaving, face strained she demanded in a deadly calm voice, 'Leave! Now! I want everyone out of my house. Out!'

Leaving Olivia, Mark flew down the stairs two at a time. 'Alison, calm down. They're just trying to—'

'I don't care!' She blew up in his face. 'They act like they understand, but they don't. No one does!' Her voice crumbled. 'Not even you, Mark. You don't understand either.'

Olivia stepped forward, her expression a mix of concern and exasperation. 'You need help. You can't go on like this.'

Alison rounded on her sister, a bitter laugh escaping her lips. 'Help? Where was your help when I gave up everything to take care of our father? When I sacrificed my dreams so you could chase yours?'

Tears streamed down her face, but she made no move to wipe them away. 'And now, you come here, judging me, acting like you have all the answers. Well, you don't. None of you do.'

Alison stumbled until her back pressed against the wall. Her stare was distant, her gaze unseeing. Kane rushed to her side, his small arms encircling her shaking form. The house was silent, the air thick with tension. Mark's shoulders slumped, the burden of his own grief and the realisation of his wife's deteriorating state pressing down on him.

Olivia's terse voice cut through the stillness, firm and resolute. 'Mark, it's time you faced the fact that she needs specialist help. Call the doctor.'

Chapter 19

'He's dead,' I choke out, my voice cracking with despair.

I'm standing on the windswept seafront, my hand trembling as I clutch the phone to my ear. The sea is wild today. Dangerous. The waves tumble over each other, some vaulting high into the air and crashing violently against the rocks. There's a fury out there.

Please don't let Simon be caught up in it. Please.

I've rung Ralf because there's no one else to ring.

'Who's dead?' Ralf sounds frustratingly calm.

'My brother. Simon. He took off in his car last night and hasn't been seen since.'

Ralf isn't convinced. 'You need a bit more than that to go on before you conclude he's dead. He's probably run off with another woman and if you've met his wife, who could blame him?'

'How can you say a thing like that?' This is one time his crappy remarks are not appreciated.

He continues, not taking any notice of me. 'Maybe he's on the verge of being arrested for embezzling his employer or something and he's skipped the country. It's always the quiet ones you have to watch.'

'He's taken some time off teaching. He's worked straight for twenty odd years in that job and simply needed a break.'

'There you are.' There's the snap of his desk drawer in the background. In my mind I see him lighting up one of those smelly cigars. 'He's had a breakdown. The newspapers are filled with reports of teachers cracking up in the classroom these days. People disappear all the time, it doesn't mean they're dead.'

My stare turns to further down the road, where a car is parked at an angle on a double yellow line.

'They found his car this afternoon.'

Simon's car is cordoned off by police tape with a lone cop standing guard. It was found with the driver's door half-opened.

'It was found a few hundred yards from where . . .' For a moment I choke up. Then manage, 'From where Sam was lost. Some witnesses saw Simon on the beach, staring at the sea and the police think he went in. I drove up here as soon I heard.'

'Alison, I'm so sorry.' For once he's dead serious.

'It's my fault,' I choke out. 'I went to see him yesterday evening. I should've left him alone. But I only wanted to talk to him about what happened to Sam ten years ago. I must have upset him badly because he turned violent, which isn't like him. He threw me out. I sent him over the edge. It's my fault.'

Exasperated, Ralf tries to put me straight. 'Don't tell me you're going to take this on as well? Is there anything you won't take the blame for? Stop playing the martyr.'

He takes a breath. 'If he didn't even know why you were there, what possible reason could he have for flying off at you and then driving off to God knows where? If the earth was hit by an asteroid, you'd be going around telling people this asteroid is on me. If it's anybody's fault, it's that ex-husband of yours. He kickstarted all this off again. Let's face it, without wishing to be disrespectful, it's not surprising Simon felt guilty about Sam. He was meant to be keeping an eye on the children that day and he fell down on the job. Maybe now it's all being brought up again, he couldn't cope.'

Ralf pauses for a moment before adding, 'Or maybe there was something else about Sam's loss he felt guilty about.'

I'm nettled by what Ralf seems to be suggesting. 'What's that supposed to mean?'

'Nothing.' I can almost hear his mind going around. 'But your cop friend thinks that the full story didn't come out. Maybe Simon knew what that full story was.'

'Don't be so bloody ridiculous.'

I cut the call. The last thing I need is for Ralf to be planting bad seeds in my head because the problem with those types of seeds is their roots take hold and they grow, strangling everything else until only darkness is left.

'Alison?'

It's Paul Simpson, his weathered face etched with sympathy. 'I heard about your brother.'

Word travels fast in a place like the town I grew up in.

It suddenly occurs to me. 'I should've called you. Asked if you knew anything.'

Nodding with a gentle smile he tries to reassure me. 'I know the lead officer in charge of the search. She's the best. If anyone's going to find Simon, it's her. Don't give up hope, he might still be found.' His tone changes. 'Let's find somewhere to sit. We need to talk.'

The café we end up in is filled with young professionals with laptops – a clear sign that the area is being gentrified. The scents of bitter coffee and salt air mingle in the atmosphere.

As our teas are settled on the table, Paul, with a wistful expression, tells me, 'I remember this street back in the day. One of the houses was owned by a woman who would open up her kitchen and serve all manner of treats and delights. And, I still can't believe this, a man would be playing a piano at the end of the road almost off the cliff.'

'That was my dad.' I give him my first genuine smile in . . . I don't know how long. 'Malcolm Wright. He played mainly in The Whispering Waves, but every now and again he'd play up here. He said the sea smelt different here. Sweet and free.'

Paul looks at me with wistful eyes. 'I had no idea that Malcolm was your father. Now I remember, he had two daughters who played the piano. I suppose you were one of them.'

Smiling I nod back. 'Sam played too. He was more gifted than either me or Olivia. He was going places.' I expect him to say, 'I'm sorry' like anyone else, but he doesn't. Then I remind myself that he was a Family Liaison Officer so knows the ways of grief.

Abruptly, I look down at my tea and suddenly want something else. What I really want is a stiff drink.

The sound of Paul's voice distracts me, thank goodness.

'Alison,' he begins, his voice low and hesitant. 'I've found out something that . . . Well, I'm not sure how to tell you this.'

The air squeezes inside my chest. 'Just tell me.'

He sighs, wrapping his palm around the warmth of his cup. But he doesn't lift it. 'I've been speaking with one of the officers who was on the original case. We play golf together sometimes.' He pauses, considering what he has to tell me. 'It's about your sister, Olivia.'

I freeze, my teacup halfway to my lips. 'Olivia? What about her?'

My mind starts racing a mile a minute because I can't think what he'd have to tell me about Olivia.

Paul takes out a small notebook and flicks the pages until he finds what he needs. 'We know she wasn't on the beach when . . .

when it happened.' He glances up at me and frowns. 'But do you remember where she said she went?'

The day on the beach flashes through my mind. There are so many things I don't recall, but Olivia isn't one of them. She stands out so vividly. Her sour superior expression and leopard-print sky-high heels as she grills me about leaving the beach.

Nodding, I answer, 'She went to the nearby church. She wanted to do some brass rubbings, I think, for her interior design work. I don't understand what this could have to do with anything?'

Paul's expression tightens. 'The thing is, the investigation found no sign of her at the church. None at all.'

I set my cup down, my hand shaking slightly. 'What do you mean? She must have been there. Where else would she have gone?'

He takes a deep breath. 'Security cameras picked her up getting into a taxi. She ended up further down the coast.'

The words hit me like a physical blow. I struggle to process what he's saying. 'That . . . that can't be right. Olivia wouldn't lie about something like that. Not with Sam . . .' I can't finish the sentence.

'I'm sorry, Alison. But the evidence is clear. When the investigation questioned her about it, she said she got muddled up about which church she was going to.'

I shake my head, disbelief warring with a growing sense of unease. 'But why would she go further down the coast? It doesn't make any sense.'

Paul leans back, his eyes filled with sympathy. 'The CCTV footage showed her heading in a direction where there's no church. It's . . . puzzling, to say the least.'

'But she wasn't on the beach, right? She couldn't have had anything to do with . . . with what happened to Sam.'

'She definitely wasn't on the beach. That's a clear fact,' Paul confirms. He sips from his breakfast tea. 'Maybe it's nothing.

People make mistakes, get confused about details. Especially in traumatic situations.'

But I can't shake the feeling that there's more to this. 'Then why didn't she tell the truth? Why lie about where she went?'

'Lie might be too strong a word. She genuinely may have got mixed up.' Paul shrugs. 'As I said, it might be nothing, but . . .'

'But it might be something,' I finish for him.

We sit in silence for a moment, the cheerful atmosphere of the café at odds with the turmoil inside me. I stare out the window at the sea, as it shifts and changes shape.

Paul tries to reassure me although his expression is grave. 'What your sister told the investigation could all be explained by the chaos of the moment.'

'Surely Olivia must have remembered later where she was. Why didn't she contact the lead officer with the correct details?'

Paul doesn't answer. He knocks back the remainder of his tea and gets to his feet. 'I've got to go.' He smiles, adding by way of an explanation, 'My annual appointment with the doctor to check my old ticker is still running well.' He becomes serious again. 'I'll keep digging and asking about the investigation. Hope they find your brother.'

As he turns, I ask, 'Does this mean that you'll help me find out what happened to my son?'

Twisting back he meets my penetrating stare. 'I'm already helping you. Together, we'll find out what happened that day on the beach.'

When I'm alone, one question is stamped in my mind:

Why did my sister lie about where she was?

Chapter 20

As I step into the hotel lobby, a violent shiver rushes down my spine. Something about this place makes me uncomfortable. The air is thick and heavy, weighed down by an unsettling sense of unease. There are funny looks from the receptionist as if she knows me. Perhaps it's something about the rundown grandeur of the place with its curling wallpaper and its chipped coving that jars. It's only after I've collected the key to my room that I realise what it is that's not right. The room number is attached to the keyring on a piece of plastic and shows a seagull with a bucket and spade. It's this naff detail that finally shatters the fog of my trance-like state. The realisation hits me like a tidal wave, threatening to pull me under.

This is the hotel we all stayed in ten years ago while the police searched for Sam. I must have come here in a trance, retracing my fateful steps. Panic rises in my throat, urging me to run, to escape this place that holds so many haunting memories. But it's too late because when I turn I realise it's about to get much worse. Waltzing into the reception like she owns the place is my sister. Olivia.

But it's not all bad news because beside her is her daughter Frances.

My sister and I stare at each other across reception like two gunfighters. Olivia then steps forward until we're face to face. Frances follows behind. She shakes her head slightly at me which

I take to be a warning not to mention to her mother we've been in contact. We're not supposed to have seen each other since we stayed at this hotel ten years ago.

Looking me over with disdain, Olivia rubs her lips together in that nasty way she does sometimes. 'You've got a nerve coming here after what you've done.'

'What have I done, Olivia?'

What have YOU done? That's what I should throw in her face. *Where were you really that day on the beach?* I want to ask her but . . . Now, with Sam's loss hanging between us like a ghost, I find myself hesitating. The words stick in my throat. Because confronting Olivia about her lie means confronting everything else too. The resentment, the choices we've made, the vastly different paths we've taken. The blame she chucks at my feet about that day. Tired of her resentment towards me. Yes, resentment. It comes off her like waves of poison each time she's near me. I don't get it. I mean, come on, Olivia got everything she ever wanted – the wealth, the status, the picture-perfect life far removed from our working-class roots. She married into money, scrubbed away any scent of the diesel fuel Dad used to power his fishing boat. She reinvented herself as Lady Toffee Nose as she always dreamed of being.

The exhaustion of it all makes my bones ache.

And the facts are she wasn't on the beach, so her being somewhere else probably has nothing to do with anything.

Instead, I allow my sister to tell me what she thinks I've done wrong now.

'Simon's wife told me you were harassing him the night before he left. Asking him all manner of questions about Sam. Making a scene and refusing to leave. Now he's disappeared. You think that's a coincidence?'

The ferocity of her assault staggers me. 'Katie had no idea why I came to the house, nor did Simon. I'd arranged to meet him for lunch but when he was a no-show I got worried.' I ignore the contemptuous scoffing sound she makes. 'I went to his house to see him. We spoke . . .' I nearly tell her about Simon's behaviour towards me. 'We just talked. I didn't hassle him.'

'Like you didn't hassle Mark and his wife and kids,' she sneers. How did she know about that incident outside Mark's house? Olivia's outrage grows. 'There's no way *my* brother would have agreed to see you for lunch or anything else. Not yesterday! Not any day! You're a liar!'

The receptionist pretends to attend to some paperwork while some guests crane their necks to see what's going on.

An embarrassed Frances takes her mother by the arm. 'Mum, come on.'

Olivia snatches out of her grip, the colour on her face high with fury. 'I suppose you followed us to this hotel, did you? What's the plan? To harass me and my daughter as well?'

Is she right? Is that why I'm here? To stir up trouble? Olivia leaves me confused.

My sister doesn't wait for an answer and instead marches off towards the lifts. Before she follows, Frances flashes a quick apologetic smile and mouths, 'Later.'

There's no way that I can leave this hotel now that Frances has offered to talk, even though the manky carpet in my room sticks to the bottom of my shoes like it's holding on to me for dear life. The only saving grace is that I'm in a different room from ten years ago.

I open the window and inhale sharp salty air. I feel the rush of it go into my lungs. Memories of the tragedy on the beach I look at come rushing back to me.

After the interview with the police, I don't remember how I got back here. There was constant pressure on my arm, which I think was Mark. I can't be sure. There was definitely a police officer present because I remember him saying, 'It might be better for you to go home.'

The reason I've never forgotten this is that the texture of his voice was so grating and got right inside my head to the bone of my skull to the point of wanting to slam my hands over my head and scream for him to go away.

'We'll assign you a Family Liaison Officer who will make sure you know about any new developments.'

Go home? While Sam was *out there*? In the cold? Wet? Suffocating dark? Never. I refused to go. Mark tried to persuade me to come home. But what kind of home would it be without Sam? If it had been up to me, I'd still be here ten years on, waiting until he was found. It was a week later that things finally came to a head and Mark dragged me out of here. Well, that's what I've been told. I don't remember.

I step back from the window. The room smells as if it's been flushed out with stagnant sea water and blasted with grains of sand. Nothing is right in here, from the wonky light shade to the door which doesn't quite extend to the floor. While I wait for Frances to contact me I sit on the bed and as soon as I'm still, Olivia's words creep into my head like a plague of insects. Maybe she's right to blame me for what happened here ten years ago. Despite Ralf trying to convince me that Simon's situation is not down to me, deep down I know it is. If my brother's filled with guilt about taking his eye off the kids on the beach that all comes back to me. However, sometimes I have moments of intense anger where I'm tempted to blame Simon. He made a simple mistake that day and it meant my son was taken away from me. A simple mistake, like a minor error of judgement while driving that leads to a fatal crash.

But Olivia will never let me forget who she really blames. She knows how to really hurt me. She learned it so well when we were girls. The pain is bad because it's been a such long time since she had the opportunity to be cruel in person and I'd forgotten what she can be like.

The contortions on her face. Her voice gasping as she struggles to get as many bitter words into a sentence as she can. Her rummaging through her rusty toolbox of malice to find a new way to torment me. Her real contempt for me started the day Daddy nearly died.

Chapter 21

The Sisters

Alison sat by her father's bedside in the hospital while Olivia stood on the opposite side. Alison was seventeen. Olivia eighteen. Malcolm Wright lay heavily sedated, his breathing harsh and laboured. It was Alison who had discovered him collapsed and hunched over the piano at home, and she had wasted no time in calling an ambulance and her sister.

After waiting for hours, the doctor finally opened the door and invited them to join him outside.

'It's his body,' he began, but Olivia didn't give him a chance to finish.

'We know it's his body,' she snapped, her voice laced with impatience and frustration.

Inwardly, Alison winced at her sister's outburst. Olivia always seemed to be on the verge of losing her cool these days, at least at home. At school, however, she had crafted a completely different persona. The queen bee of a group of rich kids who were seen as the ultimate 'in' crowd. Her graceful gestures, flawless make-up, and cleverly accessorised bargain clothes were all carefully chosen to give an air of indulgent culture.

Recovering from her show of bad temper, Olivia hastily added in her refined, measured voice that had suffocated her Norfolk accent, 'Sorry, doctor. It's just been such a shock.'

The doctor nodded in understanding and continued, 'What I mean is that his work as a fisherman has taken a toll on his body. Heavy lifting and awkward positions have all placed a strain on him. Also, he has a poor respiratory system.' He stared at them gravely. 'His days as a fisherman are over. He's going to need constant support at home to get around.'

The sisters were left in an awkward silence, their minds reeling from the news. It didn't help that the closeness they had once enjoyed was long gone.

Gaze filling with sadness, Alison broke the silence. 'What's poor Dad going to do now? Fishing is in his blood.'

Olivia, her lips tightening as she thought, responded, 'The question we need to consider is who is going to look after him. There's that council-run care home a few miles down the road.'

Alison was outraged at the suggestion. 'We can't do that.'

'What other alternative is there?' Olivia shot back.

'We look after him,' Alison stated firmly.

Olivia responded in disbelief, 'We? You've got a scholarship, Ali. A bloody scholarship to one of the best music academies in the country. The Guildhall School of Music and Drama. In London, for heaven's sake.'

Alison's school had been ecstatic when their application to the academy had been accepted, recognising her as one of their most gifted musicians. Although overjoyed, Alison remained shy of the limelight.

Olivia's ranting continued. 'They turned down my application. I would've killed to get in there. The opportunity to study in London.' Her mouth dripped with disdain and bitterness. 'And what do you want to do? Fucking throw it all away.'

Alison's anger flared. 'The only reason you wanted that scholarship was to go to London. You never cared about the piano. All you care about is living the high life like your friends in groovy London.'

'And what's wrong with that?'

Alison shook her head in despair. 'How can you even think like this? Dad gave up so much of his free time to teach us the piano. That's why he collapsed. Not from all the years of fishing but from all the times he should have been resting after work and instead was teaching us. I saw the pain on his face many times as he was hunched over the piano.'

'Well, I'm not looking after him,' Olivia retorted.

'Are you ashamed of him? Is that why on our first day at school you told me not to tell anyone Dad was a fisherman?'

Olivia didn't answer. Instead, she stepped back and lengthened her neck. 'My future is not going to be spent in a fisherman's cottage.' Then she turned on her high street heels – she couldn't afford designer yet – and was gone.

Alison searched inside her bag and found her father's tip jar. She placed it beside his bed for good luck. Then she made the phone call.

'It's Alison Wright,' she choked. 'I need to talk to someone about my scholarship. I won't be coming anymore.'

Chapter 22

The four walls of the hotel room are closing in on me. This whole hotel stinks of poisonous memories. I grab my purse and hurry down to the bar where I knock back a couple of whiskies in quick succession before taking a third out onto the hotel's blustery terrace where I'm mercifully alone.

Out here though there's the sea staring back at me. It's black with just a few dancing white and yellow lights from the pier. In the distance is the sound of revellers on boats, others playing fruit machines, pretending to throw each other into the sea while disco tunes wail from the amusement arcades. For a week after Sam was lost, I'd come down here, wade knee-deep into the waves and call his name. Eventually, my minders or passers-by would come and fetch me and take me back to the hotel.

It's strange, but I don't remember Paul being one of them. He must have been around offering support I didn't want or need.

It's almost a relief to see Olivia and Frances coming back to the hotel. Frances is slightly ahead of her mother, who's talking in urgent, clipped tones on her phone. It's difficult to catch her words as she's still some distance away but some of them drift across the damp air.

'No, don't worry about that . . . Everything's taken care of . . . Alison's here of course, to . . .'

When Olivia catches sight of me sitting on my own on the gloomy terrace, she quickly rings off, sends me a long, stony stare before eventually averting her gaze. Behind her mother's back, Frances flashes her hand four times at me indicating she'll be around twenty minutes. Which is fine with me because I can down another whisky.

Frances finally emerges, and because she's dressed in a black trackie bottom and top, her figure hugs the wall of the hotel and terrace like a shadow avoiding the lights.

Perching next to me, she says, 'I'm so sorry about Mummy earlier.'

I stop her. 'There's no need to apologise. She's understandably upset about Simon.' Which prompts me to check my phone for any emails or texts from the police. Nothing. Poor Simon.

Come home, brother! Please!

'I take it your mother doesn't know you've slipped away?' I ask Frances.

Snorting with laughter, she tells me, 'Don't worry about her. She's already asleep. Like a dead man as they say in Germany. She always does, sleeping the sleep of the unjust.'

'What do you think's happened to Uncle Simon?' Frances's voice floats in the inky night, her face bathed in shadows.

On the opposite side of the road to the hotel we've made our way down a flight of weather-beaten wooden steps onto the sandy beach below where we found a dry spot on a breakwater that serves as a bench, hidden away from prying eyes. We huddle together.

It's my guilt that answers her question. 'With the right support he could have moved on. If we hadn't fallen out, I could have helped with that. I never blamed him.'

'Come on, Aunt Alison, he was no kind of man, was he? It was embarrassing the way he cringed and fawned around my mother. I sometimes wondered if she had something on him.'

I'm uncomfortable with my brother being talked about like this and want to change the subject. 'You don't like your mother very much, do you?'

Frances is furious. 'Like her? I hate her. She's a truly awful person.' She stops for a moment and decides that the word awful doesn't do my sister justice. 'She's actually evil.'

I've never had reason to believe that Olivia has ever treated other people the way she treats me. Rather the reverse in her daughter's case. 'Why don't you like her?'

Frances doesn't answer at once, merely raises her hands. They're caught in a shaft of light from the pier, and I can see her wiggle her delicate fingers. 'You don't know the half of it: she's selfish, greedy, arrogant, deluded and she doesn't care about anyone except herself. She's no kind of mother. She's got narcissistic personality disorder. Look it up, Aunt Alison. She ticks all the boxes and another bunch of boxes that aren't even there.'

The venom is heartfelt and quite frightening.

But she isn't finished. 'She's little better than a whore. Do you know the number of strange men I met around the breakfast table on Saturday and Sunday mornings? A constant parade of them, she didn't even have the decency to throw them out before I got up.'

Frances's gaze goes distant, lost in her world of bad memories. 'My father told me on one of his visits when I was older, he thought she had sex with his best man at the wedding. I believe it, it's the sort of thing she would do, just for a laugh. Of course, she slung my father out as soon as she could. She was only after his money, then she's swanning around like Lady Muck while my poor father was stuck in rented accommodation.'

She looks directly at me. 'I often thought you were lucky being ditched by my mother after Sam went. Sometimes I wished I could live with you and Kane. I was always close to him. And Sam.'

She falls quiet, sounding exhausted after unleashing this bitter tirade. I'm no friend of my sister but it all sounds a little over the top. 'I floated the idea that you could carry on seeing us,' I said, 'and that Kane could carry on seeing you and your mother, but it was ruled out.'

Frances is triumphant like a barrister who's trapped a murderer in the witness box. 'See? See? That's exactly what she's like.'

I'm embarrassed to bring up the subject of the day Sam was lost because I don't want to hurt her. It must be a deep and lasting wound for my niece, and I don't know how she's coped over the years. But I can't keep quiet any longer.

'Frances,' I tentatively start. 'What happened that day?'

I need to ask her again because new memories may have come back to her.

Shifting, she looks across at the sea. 'All I remember is Kane running down the beach, screaming. He was hysterical. He was screaming over and over that Sam was swept away but he wasn't making a lot of sense.'

Sniffing, she lifts her chin as if she welcomes the wind battering her face. 'Considering Uncle Simon was a teacher, you'd have expected him to be calm. He wasn't. He flew into a panic.'

Her head whips around to me and she looks terrible. Colourless and worn down, all traces of the modern hip young woman gone.

Her words come out in a jumble. 'I rushed into the sea yelling Sam's name and Uncle Simon had to drag me back. Kane couldn't stop screaming and crying. Uncle Simon made a few phone calls—'

I go rigid. 'More than one?'

'I don't know. Maybe.' Her palm runs over her mouth in doubt. 'I know for definite he called the police.'

There're tears in her eyes, and I feel bad for asking. But what other choice do I have?

There's a flash of light as she pulls her phone from her pocket. 'I'd better get back, Aunt Alison, in case Mother wakes and wonders where I am. But do you mind if I ask you one last question?'

After my curious nod she continues. 'Are you thinking there's something you haven't been told about the loss of Sam? That there was something else going on? Although I was there and I didn't notice anything else. I would have told you and the police if there was.'

'Do you think your mother was seeing one of her men that day?'

After thinking for a while, she shrugs. 'I don't know. To be honest, I tried not to think about my mother too much back then.'

Suddenly Frances is on her feet. 'I really must go back.'

Before she goes, Frances hugs me and whispers, 'If I find out anything, I'll let you know.'

Chapter 23

'Where's my son?' I brusquely demand of Rocky.

With no news about Simon, I've come back home, hoping that Simon's letter might be waiting for me. But there's no sign of it. I'm dead on my feet, feeling a bit ratty if I'm honest, so it irritates the hell out of me to find Kane's girlfriend loitering in the kitchen with a cup of coffee. No, it's not coffee, it's that disgusting matcha-green stuff she downs by the bucketful. In normal circumstances, it would be good to see my son's girlfriend making herself at home. Now, I resent her lolling around like she owns the place. I'm starting to wonder if her midnight spells on the piano are her way of marking her territory like a cat spraying a house.

There's no sign of Kane.

'He's still in bed, he had a bad night,' Rocky informs me. 'He's really upset about his uncle going missing. It's best to let him rest.'

Who does she think she is to tell me when I can see my son? 'I'm going to make sure he's fine.'

'That's a bad idea.'

She's going to get both barrels at some stage but now is not the time. Twisting on my heels I leave her and rapidly make my way upstairs. I open the door to Kane's room. Rocky's right, he's in a bad way. He's asleep but not at rest. He's mumbling, his limbs twitching and jerking, tossing and turning as if he has a fever. His skin is waxy and pulled tight over his skull. His hair is matted and twisted like old rope. His flesh sweats and is wet as if he's been pulled, drowned, from the sea.

Alarmed I rush over to him and sit on the bed. My hand hesitates above him and then smooths his hair back as if trying to soothe away the pain. His eyes flash open. They catch mine and recoil in horror and sink back into their sockets. They remain fixed on me, staring and glassy with a vacant expression. They never blink. What does he see when he's looking at me?

'Kane?'

I'm so worried. So frightened. What's happening to my son? What is he seeing? His eyelids suddenly flutter and close before his breathing becomes more regular.

Urgently, I wrap his limp, wet hand in mine. And vow, 'I've promised your brother to get the truth. Now I'm promising you too, so you can be at rest.'

I leave him with a tender motherly kiss on his cheek.

My mind turns back to my meeting with Paul. And the secrets hiding in the dark about what really happened on the beach that day. Downstairs in a drawer in a writing desk there's a large brown envelope. It contains some of the things the police asked me to send them at the time of their investigation. Now it's become my investigation.

The police asked for any copies of photographs from the holiday, especially from the day Sam was lost, as well as credit card receipts, in fact anything that might help them build up a picture of what happened.

Mark was furious with them at the time. 'Do my wife and I really need to be doing this when we've just lost our son?'

In his role as liaison officer, Paul had intervened to calm the waters and had helped us to collect any evidence the police needed. I hunt for the envelope that I kept everything in. It's slightly scuffed, its adhesive long gone. I take it to the cosy armchair near the window. Inside are photos and dog-eared pieces of paper. Carefully I take out one of the photos. One immediately captures my attention. I can't stop looking at it. I raise it to the light coming in from the window so I can properly see it. It's a snap of the three children: Kane, Sam and Frances. They are standing in a line with their arms around each other's shoulders with Sam sandwiched in the middle. They look so happy. Such a happy family. Laying the photo in my lap, I stroke a finger lovingly down Sam's face. It still stuns me to think that a few hours after this image was taken he was gone. As I push the photo away there's another that catches my eye. Olivia and Frances are holding hands. The mother looks proud, but her daughter's face looks like thunder. Poor Frances. It obviously hasn't been easy for her having Olivia for a mother.

Olivia dominates another photo, wearing a wide-brimmed glamorous summer hat. I took that picture by chance as she was making her way up a sandy path towards a cliff walk with a bag under her arm. She'd taken to visiting rural churches in the area to do brass rubbings of mediaeval knights and their ladies. This was a very un-Olivia hobby, but I assumed it was probably just an excuse to get away from the rest of us. She'd disappear for hours at a time leaving Frances with Simon and me. She's quite a distance away and Olivia has her back slightly turned to the camera, the wind blowing her hair up as if from an electric shock. I'm not clear why I took it. Perhaps it was my way of saying I was glad to see the back of her.

I put the photos back in the envelope, not needing or wanting to look at the others. After that there's the paperwork from the holiday to go over. Leaflets for summer shows we never saw, exhibitions at the local museum that were interesting enough but that bored the children. Tickets for day trips and credit card receipts for lunches, dinners and ice creams. Scribbled notes from purses and wallets that must have meant something at the time but it's no longer clear what. When some are unfolded, grains of sand trickle out onto the floor like yellow ghosts of a dead holiday.

The receipts for the hotel are there all stapled together with the others. Mark booked the place on his card, probably by way of an apology for the fact he wasn't coming. It was all done on the cheap. Receipts for service stations and petrol, on and on these scraps of paper go.

At the back is yet another receipt. It's not tacked on, it's almost there as an afterthought. It's got nothing to do with our holiday. It's for a hotel further down the coast from the town where we were staying. The hotel is called the Stacks. A room was booked there at about three times the price of the accommodation we had stayed in.

Double deluxe.

Sea view.

Room 206.

When I look it up on the net, the Stacks Hotel seems to be a rather luxurious place where the advertising boasts the place is quiet and discreet with all the facilities and is popular with honeymooners. The promo shots are all of super smiley couples, the most prominent one showing a couple staring into each other's eyes sharing a romantic dinner with roses and champagne scattered around. I pull out my phone and put the address into the map app. It's about four miles down the coast from where we were staying.

The date on the receipt shows the room was booked for the same week as the family holiday.

I'm at a total loss. Why on earth did Mark book this?

I think back, racking my brains trying to remember if Mark showed this receipt to the police at the time. Did he tell them he had booked a hotel down the coast? My head starts hurting as I try to remember. Then again, there's so much from that time I don't recall. But if he had shared it with the police surely they would have said if there was anything suspicious about it?

Still, why did he book a hotel on the coast? Mark should have been in Norwich.

I pick up my phone again to call him and find out but my mobile sticks to my frozen fingers. Instead, I fetch the photos out of the envelope again and find the one of Olivia heading off towards the cliff path to do some 'brass rubbings'. The Stacks Hotel is about an hour's walk away in that direction, faster if she found a bus stop. Without prompting myself, I hear Frances's words echoing around my head.

'She's little better than a whore.'

'Do you know the number of strange men I met around the break-fast table on Saturday and Sunday mornings?'

I check the receipt again. And again. And again. I look at the website for the Stacks Hotel and try to think of an innocent explanation as to why Mark was there. Perhaps he did it as a favour to a friend who didn't want to use his own credit card. Perhaps he was planning to turn up on the holiday after all and surprise us but didn't want to stay in the same place but then something happened that meant he couldn't come. Perhaps his credit card was spoofed and he never mentioned it because it was trivial compared with losing our son. Perhaps a lot of things.

Or perhaps while our son was being swept out to sea, Mark and Olivia were enjoying the 'facilities'. Perhaps my ex-husband is a cheat and my sister is a whore.

Chapter 24

'Was my sister sleeping with my husband?'

That's the blunt question I put to Frances when I manage to catch her on her way to work.

Frances freezes in her tracks, her troubled eyes search my tight features. I'm slightly surprised because I'd have expected her expression to appear stunned not troubled.

'Mum . . . and Mark?'

There's no way to pretty it up. 'Were they having an affair?'

'What? Like now?' Her question scrambles out sounding disjointed.

I stop. Take a breath. I'm feeling hyper and need to slow this down. More calmly I say, 'Ten years ago.'

Her mouth forms into an O of understanding. Then she carries on walking, me having to catch her up. 'My mother and Mark? That's not very likely, is it?'

I let out an internal sigh of relief. This is what I want to hear. I've back-pedalled since discovering the receipt. Mark and my sister? Together? It's absurd. They're such an unlikely pairing. Olivia's ferocity would've gobbled Mark up.

'I'm not interested in whether it was likely, I'm interested in whether it happened.'

Frances's pace becomes brisk, her following words backing me up. 'He's not her type. Mark hasn't got a title for starters, doesn't own an estate and doesn't drive around in a flash sports car. Let's be honest, and no disrespect to you, but he's not exactly a looker either.'

I take her by the arm and bring her to a halt. I show her the receipt that I'm carrying around like a sacred text. She inspects it. 'What's this?'

'Mark booked a hotel room a few miles up the coast while the rest of us were on holiday and never told me. Your mother kept disappearing on so-called trips to churches to do stuff to help her interior design business.'

Frances shrugs. 'That's true.'

'But . . .' I hang on to the word. Then, 'On the day Sam disappeared, the police have verified that she wasn't at the church she said she was going to. She was caught on camera not far from the hotel on this receipt.'

Frances tilts her head back and the expression of pity hits me hard and makes me step back.

In despair at my naivete, I softly say, trying to hide any appearance of hurt, 'They were having an affair, weren't they?'

My niece's pity switches to concern. 'I'm sorry, Aunt Alison. They were seeing each other at the time.'

Seeing each other. The words hang dangerously over me like a plastic bag about to cover my face.

Seeing each other. What a sanitised turn of phrase to describe something so cruel.

Seeing each other. As if they were teenagers stealing glances across a crowded room. As if it were a chance encounter, a fleeting moment of weakness. As if it weren't a calculated, deliberate betrayal that has shattered the very foundation of my world.

'They might still be now for all I know,' Frances adds, slashing my bleeding wounds even deeper. Her darkening gaze bores into mine. 'I told you – she eats men for breakfast. I told you Mum's evil. She'll probably only have gone with Mark to get back at you . . . Aunt Alison!' she shouts after me. 'Where are you going?'

I've marched away. I know exactly where I'm going.

◆ ◆ ◆

The first employees are leaving Mark's workplace when I arrive. He won't be one of them, he's always the loyal employee who wants to show willing. Shame he wasn't the loyal husband. Checking the listing of the companies in the building I find his located on the first floor. The movement of people near the entrance makes it easy for me to bypass reception and use the stairs to reach the first floor.

Through the thick Perspex twin doors, I see Mark in another room tucked in the back of the open-plan office. It's some type of conference room because he's one of dozens around a long table listening to a man giving a PowerPoint presentation.

A perfect scenario for what I'm about to do.

I barge into the room. Startled by my surprising entrance, all confused eyes are on me. The man doing the presentation I recognise as Mark's partner in the firm. It's him, not Mark who says, 'Alison?'

Mark is frozen in his chair.

'I'm terribly sorry to interrupt like this' – my determined stare sweeps the room – 'but I need to make a point of my own.' I don't give anyone a chance to answer, instead take my place at the head of the table.

My ex-husband finally makes a panic-stricken move, jumping up and trying to make an apology at the same time. 'I'm sorry about this.'

'Were you fucking my sister?'

Gasps fill the air. Mark staggers back.

I round the table towards him. 'It's not a very hard question! Were you shagging my sister while our son was dying at sea?'

It's the last question that turns the tide against Mark. The air has grown thick with silent condemnation. One woman crosses her arms, her face a mask of cold disapproval, while another tilts her chin down, looking at Mark over the rims of her glasses with clear disdain. Office gossip doesn't get much better than this. There'll be enough here to keep them going for months.

Blood rushing to his face, Mark turns to his partner, who is looking on with a single raised brow. It's his partner who speaks to me. 'Alison, usually always great to see you. However, on this occasion I think this is a discussion that best takes place in a more private environment.'

I allow Mark to take my arm and frog-march me out of the room and the building. He swings me into the narrow dead-end street near his office.

He hisses in my face, his fury evident in the heat of his breath touching my skin. 'I always told everyone you weren't mad but I see now I was wrong.'

'Is. It. True?'

His neck snaps back, snatching his face out of my space. 'I was involved with Olivia. Briefly.'

This is where I should rant and rave. Maybe deliver a stinging blow of outrage to his lying face. I do neither. I feel strangely numb. The confirmation hangs in the air, crushing and stifling, but I can't seem to react. My hands should be shaking. My voice screaming in accusation. But I'm perfectly still. So still. The anger I expected to explode within me is eerily absent, replaced by a vast emptiness. An emptiness I haven't been able to fill since Sam.

It's confirmation that parts of my old life were a lie. The people closest to me were hiding terrible dark secrets.

'But it was her fault,' Mark continues. 'Flashing her legs at me at family functions and whispering those smutty lines of innuendo that she does so well. And you weren't helping. You're not the easiest person in the world to live with.'

I almost let out a sour laugh at this bastard's audacity. 'That's right, Mark, blame the two women. Your ex-wife and one-time sister-in-law. This has got nothing to do with you not being able to keep it in your pants. Let's not forget you've got form.'

Three years after we were married, when Sam was still a baby, Mark had an affair – an 'encounter' was how he put it – with a co-worker at an office Christmas party. He assured me it was a one-night stand. Once he'd assured me that it would never occur again I didn't make too much of a fuss because I wanted our marriage to work.

The truth is I'm only here for one reason. 'I need you to answer a question for me.'

He looks at me incredulously. 'Is that it, Alison? Aren't you going to ask me why I had an affair?'

'No, Mark. I'm not. And you know why? Because your reasons don't matter.' I take a step closer, my gaze unflinching. 'The days when women are expected to understand, to forgive, to shoulder the emotional burden of some man's mistakes are gone. We're done with that.'

My numbness gives way to a surge of righteous anger. 'I don't owe you the chance to explain yourself. I don't owe you my anger or my tears. What I owe myself is what I came here to do. And it's to find out about this.'

I shove the receipt at him. 'You booked room 206 at the Stacks Hotel the same week as the holiday. Why?'

Squinting, he looks at it. 'I don't know. I can't remember.'

'Was it for you and Olivia to have a little love nest while the rest of us were holidaying?'

He looks again and a moment of recognition comes over his face. 'That was the plan but it didn't work out. In the end we had an emergency at work and I couldn't get away so the room was left empty.'

'So Olivia wasn't visiting churches as she claimed. She was with you at the hotel.'

'Like I said, at the last minute I couldn't make it.' He sounds and looks peeved with me now. The nerve!

'But Olivia was definitely seen not far from that hotel.'

'If she was there it wasn't to see me.'

I think this through. Maybe Olivia went to the hotel and while she was there Mark contacted her about being a no-show.

I put the receipt back. And leave with a stinging parting shot. 'If you're planning on cheating on your current wife, it might be a good idea to pay cash rather than use a card when you're paying for services.'

I think about Olivia, my own sister, choosing – of all the men out there – her sister's husband to have an affair with. Then again, Olivia has always gone out of her way to try to humiliate me.

Chapter 25

The Sisters

Alison sat at the wedding reception, overhearing the whispers of the two women at her table.

'It won't last five years, you mark my words.'

'He's at least twenty-five years older than her.'

'Between me and you, I'd bet my life she's only married him for his money.'

'I hear there's already a delivery on the way. Four months.'

'I thought he was a Jaffa.'

'A Jaffa?'

'Jaffa orange. No pips. His other marriages produced no children.'

The gossiping would have ceased instantly if they knew that the bride's sister was among them. Alison had received her invitation to Olivia's wedding only ten days ago.

The invitation was for one, excluding Mark, although he seemed content to stay at home. Alison had never met Gilbert, Olivia's intended. The sisters' lives had taken different paths with Alison supporting and nursing their father for four years until his death while Olivia found success in interior design among the affluent communities further up the coast. Olivia's disappointment at losing out on a scholarship to

London so she could live in the capital had soon been swept aside by her single-handed pursuit of embedding herself into the more local wealthy community. This marriage to a noted member of it was Olivia's symbol of success.

Finances always tight, Alison had let her bank account become overdrawn to purchase an appropriate outfit plus hat for the church. Only subsequently did she realise she should have read the invitation closer. It was an invite for the reception only.

When she'd tried to return the hat in an attempt to claw back some of her much-needed money the store reminded her of their no refunds policy.

When she'd arrived at the grand hall, Alison had navigated the crowd to find her sister. Olivia was a vision in her frothy white gown and flipped-back veil. The sisters embraced awkwardly.

Smiling, Alison remarked, 'Dad would be proud. Unless you're still keeping it hush-hush that he was a fisherman.'

Olivia's face paled. 'That's a cruel thing to say on my wedding day.'

'Sorry.' Her apology was quick and heartfelt, although noting Olivia didn't deny her accusation.

Olivia's face brightened as she glanced over Alison's shoulder. 'There's Gilly's neighbours. I'll catch up with you later.'

Alison nodded and headed towards the top table, only for Olivia to stop her. 'Where are you going?'

Alison's brow furrowed. 'To the top table. I'm the bride's sister.'

Olivia stepped back. Alison knew that gesture well. Her sister used it to create a distance between herself and her background.

'Gilly's family . . .' Olivia began firmly.

Alison gently cut in, 'No worries. I'll find my place. Enjoy your special day.'

She smiled, not wanting to disrupt her sister's wedding. But inside, she hurt. So bad. Swallowing a lump of sadness, Alison said, 'I hear you're expecting.'

'Yes.' Olivia's face glowed. 'I'm over the moon.'

Having located her assigned seat at the table, Alison continued to listen to the women diss her sister. She could have intervened by revealing her identity. Instead, she sipped her wine and listened to the guests trash Olivia's reputation on her wedding day.

Chapter 26

I'm not going to pretend. I'm drinking. I think I've been drinking for some time, but, you see, I don't always recall what's been going on. And it's not just booze, it's the pills too. Uppers to keep me awake, downers to help me sleep. Or both at the same time when I'm really stressed out, like now. I think this explains the empty whisky bottles and pills scattered sometimes on the floor of my room up in the attic. I can't be sure though because: I. Don't. Remember.

I don't know what to call what happens to me. Blackouts? A brain that's wired all wrong? I can't tell you. What I do know is this all started after Sam went missing. What happened after that is hazy, a blur. When I've asked for an explanation, Mark and Kane both tell me to rest. So not only have I lost a son, I've lost big stretches of my own life as well.

At the moment I'm frantically searching the bathroom cabinet for something to help me get through the night. You see, the booze isn't enough on its own, I need the pills too. Perhaps I'll get the combination of meds and alcohol wrong and OD and die. I don't care, not anymore. In the past when I've been careless with these things, I'd chant my sons' names – Sam, Kane, Sam, Kane – to remind myself there's something to live for. Not this time. Even the reminder I have a living son doesn't seem to help.

Earlier I was brave thinking I was numb to what Mark and Olivia had done, but as the day has worn on the numbness has given way to a throbbing, burning pain.

The world tilts and sways around me as I stumble towards the stairs, my vision blurred by a mist of anger. I won't cry. I reserve my tears for Sam alone. I grip the banister, my knuckles turning pale as I struggle to keep myself upright. Each step is a battle, my legs feeling like I've just run a marathon. The stairs seem to stretch on forever, a daunting challenge in my intoxicated state. I sway dangerously, the world spinning around me, and for a moment I fear I might tumble over the banister. But I cling on, which sums up my life so well. Alison, the woman who learned to cling on.

Step by step, I drag myself onwards, my movements slow and clumsy. The world fades in and out of focus, the edges of my vision foggy as I fight to maintain my grip on reality. Finally, I reach the landing and retreat to the attic, numbed with humiliation and pain. A safe place to lick my wounds. I collapse on the bed. Instinctively, I reach for Dad's tip jar. All I find is thin air. Of course, my precious tip jar of memories has gone. Taken from me like so much else.

My natural instinct after leaving Mark was to go to Olivia and unbottle my fury in her lying hateful face. How could she? Betray me like this? My own sister and the man I once loved and was married to, sneaking around behind my back while . . . It cripples me to even think it! . . . While Sam was out there. Alone. No one to hear him scream. The waves dragging him under. I trusted them. I trusted her. Despite our differences, I never thought Olivia would stoop so low, to steal my husband and destroy our family. And him, Mark – I spit his name with all the force I can muster in my head – seeking comfort in her arms while all the time claiming he couldn't come on holiday with us because of work. Bastard! It's a betrayal so deep, so gut-wrenching, I can hardly breathe. I feel like I'm drowning. That's what lies do, they squeeze and squeeze you so tight that you're not even aware when the squeeze has twisted into a choke, leaving you fighting for your life. How could they be so heartless? So selfish. To put their own desires above the well-being of our family. It's a question that haunts me, a question I may never have an answer to.

Have you ever felt the soul-crushing pain of betrayal by people you most trust in the world?

◆ ◆ ◆

I jerk awake, my heart beating hard against my ribs. When did I fall asleep? I don't remember. My mouth tastes stale and sticky. That will be the whisky. I'm lying on the bed partially twisted on my side, my legs hanging over the edge. My eyes are sticky against their lids. God, my head hurts so much. Then I hear it. It penetrates my throbbing skull. The music. The piano.

Rocky's back playing it downstairs.

Why is she doing this to me now, when I'm emotionally at an all-time low? Curling into a ball I slam my palms over my ears to drown the music out. Drive it away.

Leave me alone. Please leave me alone.

But it's no use. Then again, I'm not surprised, as if my hands could stop the power of this music from getting through. Fittingly, she's performing Chopin's Funeral March.

I've always hated this piano piece with its slow, mournful, dragging rhythm and the way every note drips with despair. It's a piece that speaks of death and loss. And betrayal because betrayal is like a type of death. It's a taunting reminder of how empty my life has become. I want to scream, to yell at Rocky to stop. To silence the music that's wrenching me deeper into a place so dark I'm not sure I'll ever be able to come out of it.

Pull yourself together, an inner voice of strength urges me. *What would Dad think of you now, wallowing in your own self-pity? He taught you that a working woman like you stands backbone-straight, head held high, tall and strong. Don't ever let anyone make you believe that you aren't good enough.*

It's my father's uplifting words that finally get me on my feet. I'm still a bit shaky so I stumble down the stairs heading for the music room. Every step closer the music seems to pound louder and louder as if she's beating her hands with full force against the keys.

I thump my fist against the door. 'Rocky! Let me in.'

The volume of the music increases, vibrating through my body.

There's no answer of course. She knows how to play this game now. Knows I can't go inside the music room. I drop to my knees and awkwardly peer between the space under the door. There's a flickering muted yellow light in there but the main light isn't on. I can't see anyone. There's no movement.

'Rocky!' I bellow. 'Come out!'

Kane is bound to appear at any moment disturbed by my shouting. Strangely, he never appears. He doesn't seem to hear the music either.

The music abruptly stops, replaced by a ringing silence. I get steadily to my feet. If Rocky thinks she's outwitted me she's got another think coming. Olivia and Mark might have made a fool of me but I won't allow her to make one of me too. I'll show her.

Movements still unsteady, I go into the kitchen and stagger towards the kitchen knives. I pull one out and test its point against my finger. Beautifully sharp. Perfect. I lurch into the dining room. Its solid wall of bricks is all that divides me from the piano room on the other side. Except it's not completely solid. There was once a serving hatch here, which Mark had closed off so Sam could have some quiet while he practised. He'd patched the serving hatch with wood and plaster.

The music blasts back as if Rocky senses me. This time the piece she's chosen distresses me. It's mine and Olivia's favourite: 'My Old Man Said Follow the Van'. How did Rocky know about my connection to this song? Who told her? It couldn't have been Kane because I've never talked to him about it. My mind races. How did Rocky know . . . ? Unless it's not Rocky in there. It's someone else playing the piano. Someone who knows all my little secrets. I shake off my mad doubts. Of course it's Kane's girlfriend. Who else could it be?

I raise the knife and, with all my might, savagely plunge it in the wall. In the place where the hatch once was. I rotate the blade and dig. And dig. I won't stop until I have a hole so I can look at Rocky who has the audacity to take Sam's place in the music room.

The knife jumps slightly when it reaches the other side and pieces of dry plaster fall on my hands. There's a hole. It's about an inch wide. I press my watery eye up against it and look inside. A yellow and orange glow dances inside.

However, I'm compelled to turn away. This is the first time that I've looked inside this room for the past ten years. It's almost too much to bear, these forgotten but familiar walls with their pictures and shelves in these haunting shadows. I force my eye back to the hole. Only half of the piano is visible. Its lid is open and sheets of music are scattered over it. With a heady sense of relief and with a deep sense of release, I know I'm not going insane. There's no sign of Rocky.

Next time, I'll be ready for her. I have a plan that will catch her red-handed.

Knowing I will get her next time, I sink down onto my backside, legs shooting in front of me, the back of my head resting on the wall. A wave of tiredness washes over me. My head flops to the side. My eyes begin to close.

Chapter 27

A cold burst of air jolts me awake. That's strange because I don't recall leaving the attic window open. The coldness travels and tickles along my naked arms and legs. Why are my limbs exposed? Why are my feet and arms aching so much? Where's the duvet gone? Then again, I was so upset last night that I no doubt had a restless night, tossing and turning and have kicked the duvet off. Still, the bed feels so hard beneath me. The scent of flowers is in the air.

That's when I know that something isn't right. Heart pounding, my eyes bolt open. I'm out in the open, with the sky above and a man looming over me. I figure out that I'm lying on a bench. Where the hell am I? Disoriented and groggy, I sit up, blinking against the early morning sun that warms my strained skin. The graceful morning song of the birds in the background feels at odds with the panic rising within me.

As my surroundings come into focus, I realise with a growing sense of dread and embarrassment that I've been lying asleep on a bench in the memorial gardens. My eyes land on Sam's brass plaque, glinting in the sunlight a short distance away, and a wave of confusion washes over me.

How did I get here?

The man standing before me is wearing a uniform, which I recognise as those worn by the groundsmen who tend to the park.

He regards me with deep suspicion, his eyes narrowed as he takes in my shabby appearance. I feel the need to explain myself, but shame clogs my throat.

Managing a weak smile, I mumble, 'Good morning. I'm afraid I came down here early and had a bit of a funny turn, so I lay down on the bench to get my bearings right.'

We both glance down at my body, and I see with horror that I'm wearing nothing but a nightdress under my coat, my feet clad in slippers. My legs and hands are scratched, likely from climbing over the stone walls to get into the gardens, which are closed at night.

He shifts uncomfortably, clearly too embarrassed to call me out on my flimsy explanation. 'Do you need a doctor?' he asks, concern lacing his voice.

'No, no, I'm all right now, thank you. Lovely morning,' I reply, trying to sound like this incident is perfectly normal despite the mounting panic in my chest.

He's not convinced. 'Are you sure that I can't call someone?'

The sun may be warm, and the birds may be singing, but I'm far from OK. I'm utterly beaten, my mind reeling as I try to make sense of my situation.

'Who are you going to call? They've all betrayed me,' I mutter, the bitter words tumbling out before I can stop them.

The groundsman sighs, his eyes filled with understanding. 'You're not the first one I've found here, seeking solace in the early morning hours. When the heart yearns to be with a lost loved one no locked gate can stand in the way of that longing.'

Shaking his head slightly, he walks off with his broom. I'm left alone on the bench, my mind spinning as I try to piece together the events that led me here.

With trembling hands, I reach for my phone, only to find a simple devastating message from Frances:

We're still by the sea. The police say that a body was recovered from the sea first thing this morning. Mother is going to identify it, but there's not much doubt who it is.

Simon!
There's another text from her:

Mummy wants you to stay away.

The news hits with the force of a runaway train. I stare at the screen, numb and disconnected.

Simon's dead! I can't believe it. My baby brother is gone.

As grief overwhelms me, my mind drifts back to our childhood days in the fisherman's cottage. I'm ashamed to say that when I look back it's as if Simon was never there. Too many times he was overshadowed by Dad's ferocious determination to teach Olivia and me the piano. Simon was a dead loss at the piano, so he didn't receive the same time with Dad as we did. Simon, bless his beautiful heart, tried his best to keep up. He'd sit at the piano, his brow furrowed in concentration, but the notes never seemed to flow as effortlessly for him. Yet, he never gave up, always eager to be a part of our musical family.

Simon's true passion lay on the rugby field. He was a force to be reckoned with, his determination and skill shining through with every game. But even there, in the shadow of his more gifted sisters, it felt as though his achievements were often overlooked. The cheers from the sidelines were always a little louder for us, leaving Simon to celebrate his victories in quiet solitude.

Amidst the constant activity in our family, there was one person who never failed to recognise Simon's worth – our mother. Mum was the embodiment of love and compassion, her heart so vast that it could encompass us all. She had a special place in her heart for Simon, always making sure he felt seen and appreciated. In her eyes, Simon was never forgotten, never overshadowed. When she was taken from us too soon, it was my brother who felt the blow of her loss most deeply of all. I think that's why he became a teacher. Mum shared her love and care with him, now he wanted to do that to others.

Did I drive Simon to his death?

I shake my head in denial, gut instinct telling me Simon had his demons. What were those demons that haunted him? Whatever drove Simon I sense is connected to what happened on the beach ten years ago.

As I sit on the bench, the sun's warmth doing little to chase away the chill that has settled in my bones, I realise that I'm facing a daunting task the least of which is piecing together how I came to be in the memorial gardens. That will have to wait. My brother's death has speeded up my determination to find out what really happened to Sam.

I force myself to stand, my legs shaky and unsteady beneath me. The scratches on my hands and legs sting as I move, a painful reminder of my mysterious journey to this place. I take a tentative step forward, then another, the cool ground seeping through my slippers to my feet.

As I make my way out of the memorial gardens, I can't help but glance back at Sam's plaque, a wave of grief and confusion washing over me. Sam, my beloved son, gone too soon. And now, another body recovered from the sea.

I head to the one person I can trust to help me find answers that unlock the dark secrets of the past. I just hope that I have the strength to face whatever lies ahead.

Chapter 28

'Good grief! What in hell happened to you? You look like you've spent the night in a builder's skip.'

Even a shower and a change of clothes haven't made me look presentable enough to go and see Ralf. Fortunately, some of the buttons and switches in my head have come back to life.

'Simon's dead,' I inform Ralf, feeling kind of dead inside myself. 'They found him this morning.'

Ralf sighs, his only outward expression of emotion. 'That's bad luck. Where did they find him?'

A chill races through my body as if a violent wave has crashed over me leaving me drenched in icy seawater. 'The sea. He was recovered from the sea.' I stare beseechingly into Ralf's eyes. 'How many more members of my family is the sea going to take?'

Ralf answers, 'I'm sorry that this has brought up such painful memories. But I have to say, in your brother's case it was bound to happen.'

I remember that's what Frances said. 'Why? Why was it bound to happen?'

He avoids my eyes and reaches for a cigar and lights up. 'Unfortunately, in his chosen profession, suicide is on the increase with teachers.' His chin tips back as he lets out a perfect ring of smoke. 'Any other developments to help in our case to stop your ex?'

I push the Stacks Hotel receipt across his desk for him to see.

Studying it intently, a spark of excitement flashes in Ralf's gaze. 'What does this mean?'

'Look at the dates. Mark said he couldn't join us on the holiday so why is he booking a hotel a few miles down the coast on the same week? Now, why would he have done that?'

Ralf examines the receipt more closely. 'Maybe he fancied a break?'

'Oh, he fancied something all right.' I feel a little level of satisfaction with myself for uncovering Mark's deceit after all these years. 'He was planning on entertaining my sister there.'

He hands me the receipt back with disbelief. 'Mark? With Olivia? You're kidding me. That's like Cleopatra dating a cardboard cut-out.' His mouth turns down. 'No, swap Cleopatra for Attila the Hun.'

'That's a bit nasty.' Although secretly I'm chuckling inside. 'Why don't you and Olivia get along?' I ask.

Ralf stretches his neck. 'When I was sorting out your father's estate, she accused me of trying to cheat your family. Claim additional expenses.' His eyes blaze. 'You can call me many things – and many have – but a cheat isn't one of them.' Ralf continues, scoffing, 'I wouldn't think Mark was rich enough for her tastes. You know Olivia, she doesn't do cheapskates. Have you spoken to either of them to confirm this?'

I nod. 'Mark doesn't deny they were having an affair.'

After sucking in a heavy punch of smoke, Ralf says, 'Your ex-husband is a real piece of shit. What the hell did you ever see in him?'

His question takes me by surprise. I still remember the day I met Mark. It's vivid in my mind, even now. I'm walking through

136

the supermarket car park when suddenly – crash! We collide, and my shopping tumbles everywhere. But there he is, immediately on his knees, helping me gather my scattered groceries. And his smile . . . a warmth of sunshine broke through the heavy clouds of looking after Dad.

I look down at my tightly wound hands. 'He was nice. He made me feel good about myself. Seemed to appreciate me for who I was.' My head flicks up. 'Don't get me wrong, I never resented having to look after Dad, not once. But it wore me down and I forgot about myself—'

'And here comes along a boring knight in shiny armour to make you feel all beautiful and lovely again.' He shakes his head. 'So, he and your sister were doing the dirty in a hotel room.'

'That's what he denies,' I utter emphatically. 'He booked the room but claims that he couldn't make it in the end.' My voice hardens. 'The ex-cop I told you about.' Ralf can't help doing an annoyed eye roll, which I ignore. 'He told me that Olivia wasn't in the church where she claimed to be.'

Ralf pulls a face. 'Maybe she went for a walk after she visited God knows what.'

My hands fist in my lap almost as if to stop myself from leaning across and grabbing him to start shaking some sense into him. 'Don't you get it? Mark and Olivia were at that hotel. Together.'

'But you just said that Mark told you he cancelled the booking. More to the point, all that receipt proves is that your ex-husband booked a deluxe double for a shagfest. It doesn't prove he was in it, much less that he was entertaining Olivia there. Unless that is you've got some additional evidence?'

The nasty taste of betrayal fills my mouth again. 'And why would I believe a man who was cheating on me with my own sister?' Silently smoking, my lawyer says nothing, which needles me. 'You're not taking me seriously, are you?'

'It's not that.' With a firm twist of his hand, he stubs out his cigar in the ashtray. 'You need to forget about Mark and Olivia. Forget about churches and hotel rooms. Forget about receipts.'

Something has happened because he looks grim. It puts me on edge. He pulls out a thin black file.

'Your amateur detective work has rather been taken over by events, I'm afraid.'

'What is that?'

He puts the file down, his palms laid over it as if he's worried it will somehow slide over to my side of the desk.

'I've been in touch with an associate from the police. He did me a big favour and accessed the notes from the original inquiry.' He switches back to the usual sarcastic Ralf for a second. 'You know, the one done by real police detectives not a cop from the tea and sympathy brigade who's relying on canteen gossip for his news. As a favour, my guy copied the key parts into a file and sent them on to me.'

'What does it say?'

Ralf studies my face. I know what it looks like, I checked it in a mirror before setting off. I look washed out, a person going through the motions rather than living. He looks down at my legs, which are covered in scratches and bruises from climbing into the memorial gardens last night. Finally, he looks at my hands. I clasp them together so he can't see the marks on those too.

'Have you been to see a doctor yet?'

Of course I haven't. 'Yes, sort of, there's an appointment booked anyway.'

He nods as if he suspected as much. 'Let's make an agreement. I'll share with you what I found out as long as you go and see a doctor.'

'Of course. Now tell me what's in that file.'

He levels a serious and concerned expression on me. 'Alison, I'm worried about you. I don't know where you got those scratches, but I'd bet my life it wasn't somewhere good. I'm going to level with you.' The tips of his nails drum against the cover. 'This file is a tough read and you're going to need to be in a better place than you are now in order to cope with the information.'

'I've got a right to know what's in that file,' I grind out.

He shakes his head. 'Not until you've seen a doctor. Don't try and blag your way out of it either. I'm going to want to know the name of the doctor, what he or she diagnosed and what treatment was prescribed.'

He's boxed me into a corner. 'Then you'll let me read that file?'

'I'll read the important bits to you. Meanwhile, there's another thing. A little dickie bird told me that you had a drink with Frances after your first visit here. I hope you're not trying to involve your niece in your investigation. Or your son, for that matter. Naturally, you'll understand that the pair of them will still be badly traumatised and they don't need you confusing them into your alternative version of what happened.'

He waves the black file at me. 'Especially as we've now got the real one. Leave them alone and let them get on with their lives. I know you think I'm a rather dubious individual who sails a little close to the wind sometimes. Perhaps that's true. But you've been my client for a long time and I'd hate to see you going over the edge because of this matter. You want my personal advice rather than my legal one? Let Mark get on with his case and if you go and see a doctor, I'll tell you what the police think really happened.'

I don't answer. I look down at my hands and legs and touch my puffy face with my fingertips. I think about Kane and the way he looked lying on his bed like a washed-up corpse brought in by the tide. I think about Rocky playing the piano in the night. I think about Frances sitting in the darkness on the breakwater. I think about Simon's empty car on the seafront with police tape wrapped around it.

'I'll go and see a doctor.'

Ralf sighs with relief. 'If I was in your shoes, I would not want to find out what is in this file. Because it may destroy you.'

Chapter 29

'What seems to be the problem?' Doctor . . . I don't remember his name, asks me.

He's an old-school member of his profession with his half-glasses and bulging belly that's in contrast to the stay healthy advice he preaches to patients. But I'm here, just like Ralf asked me to be. Behind his desk the doctor peers down at my medical notes. He shouldn't need notes, he only has to look at the state of me to see what the problem is.

I tell him, 'I'm under a lot of pressure at the moment.'

The door to the consulting room swings open and a nervous-looking woman comes in. The doctor, who seems to be under some pressure himself, snaps, 'What is it?'

'I've explained to my patient what I think my diagnosis is but he doesn't seem to be willing to accept it.'

Annoyed beyond belief, the doctor struggles to his feet. 'Excuse me, Alison, we've got a student doctor who seems to lack some confidence.'

I smile at the student, who is mortified by his words, to show I'm on her side and not that of this arrogant and rude individual. After the door closes behind him, it's just me and a computer screen full of medical notes.

Naturally, I want to read them. After checking with an ear to the door to make sure there's no one outside, I lean over the desk and use the mouse to scan backwards through the notes. Over the past few years, there are just the normal run of medical issues. But if I look back at the months after Sam was lost I can see it's just one visit to the doctor after another.

It summarises what happened to me during that time.

What I read leaves me shaken.

It's in cold professional jargon, sprinkled with Latin words and psychological buzzwords, along with a list of the drugs and treatment they prescribed me at the time. It hardly does justice to the agony that I endured, but then medical notes don't win any prizes for doing justice to agony. What it lists as happening is barely recognisable to me, but then I was barely recognisable to myself at the time. The same words keep coming up again and again in my medical notes like a mantra: 'grief', 'guilt' and 'trauma'.

Oh my goodness! I had a breakdown. Was hospitalised. I don't remember any of it.

'*Why don't you just go back to that lunatic asylum you were in?*' That's what Simon had shouted at me. I didn't understand at the time. Now I do. It leaves my head pounding.

My breakdown produced morbid symptoms, a refusal to accept that my oldest son was dead.

Some of the sentences and phrases in my medical notes are like hot needles being poked into my eyes:

'The patient is convinced that the loss of her son was her fault, in spite of all the evidence to the contrary.'

'As a result of her son's loss, family dynamics have broken down and the patient is no longer in touch with her family.'

'The strain has effectively ended her marriage.'

Those words I can cope with. But this? 'The patient accepts that she has relied on alcohol to manage her condition and consumes various unprescribed medications without supervision . . . The patient suffers from hallucinations and blackouts, panic attacks, erratic behaviour, and various episodes that have required hospitalisation.'

That must be a lie, I don't remember any of this. The quacks in this surgery made this up. Then I read 'memory loss'.

Then the final and utterly brutal lines. 'The patient believes that she can commune with her late son and that he is able to hear what she says. She insists that she holds meaningful conversations with the deceased.'

Tears begin to fall. My stomach rolls over. I look around for something to smash the screen with. I turn away from the computer. I can't read any more. I'm dead inside. This isn't a description of me from ten years ago. It's a description of the person that I'm becoming. My soul is blasted away to nothing.

The door opens but not all the way. The doctor is still outside in the corridor. 'Just tell him if he doesn't want to accept our diagnosis, he's welcome to get a second opinion.'

I stagger back to the chair, my gaze unseeing.

When the doctor returns to his seat he seems oblivious to my condition. Rather than be angry, I'm grateful. The last thing I need is awkward questions. Now he is studying my medical notes. He looks slightly puzzled as the notes on the screen are from ten years ago not the current ones. He takes some time to read it all but then there's a lot to read. He hasn't noticed that I scrolled backwards with his mouse, back through the notes to the time of my crisis. It looks as if he's quite impressed by my tale of woe. 'Sorry for the interruption there, Alison. You have to be firm with patients unfortunately. What seems to be your problem today?'

I'm only here to keep Ralf happy so I can find out what he's got in that file. I certainly don't want to tell this doctor what's been going on in case he hospitalises me.

'I seem to be suffering from headaches a little lately.'

He checks his notes. 'You told the receptionist it was an emergency? This isn't really an emergency.'

I don't feel guilty anymore about lying to him. He's not worth the truth. 'A headache feels like an emergency when you've got one.'

He sighs. 'Yes, I can prescribe you something but to be honest you'd probably be better off going to a pharmacy, they're very helpful these days.'

He prescribes me something which I've no intention of taking, organises some blood tests that I've no intention of attending and suggests some patient groups where advice for headaches is shared which I don't even listen to. I was once a member of one of those and I'll never do it again. He also tells me to get my diet sorted out.

Back out on the street, I'm light-headed with shock. Was that really me they were talking about in those notes? Who was I in those days anyway and who am I now? I feel an urgent need to have a drink or take something to slow down the blood that's pumping its way around my veins at a disturbing speed and the bright lights in my head. I resist it. An urgent need to go to the memorial gardens and speak to Sam. I resist that too.

My poor son. Kane. As if losing his brother wasn't bad enough, he lost his mother for a time too. How frightened he must have been. I force myself to remember Ralf's wise words when he heard about Simon. His warning not to take on the guilt for Simon as well. How I take the blame for everything.

He's probably right but this time, the blame is on me. I should have been strong when Sam was lost. I should have stood up, not collapsed inwards. Now I'm doing it again, crumbling inwards when I need to be strong.

But I've come to a decision. There will be no more drinking. No more pills shoved down my throat. Of course, now I realise why I couldn't recall how the empty bottle of booze and pills ended up on the floor of my bedroom. Memory loss, that's what my records said I had. Well, no more.

But the one thing I can't stop doing is talking to Sam. What harm is it doing anyone if a grieving mother speaks with her son?

I'm going to be clear-headed in my pursuit of the truth. As Dad would say about fishing in the stormy sea, I'm going to use my strong arm to find out what happened to Sam. Feeling renewed, I straighten my back, and as I walk my head begins to clear.

I open my bag and dump the bottle of pills into the first bin I come to.

With a brisk pace I head off to Ralf to see what terrors are inside that file.

Chapter 30

'I thought you'd be back this week. Have you been to see a doctor?' Ralf asks.

I sit across from my lawyer, my troubled gaze on the black folder on his desk. It might as well be radioactive for all the dread it's radiating. God, I'm so nervous. My mouth is dry, and I have to consciously unclench my jaw. Every muscle in my body seems wound tight. I'm aware of every breath, every small shift of my body. It's as if I'm both hyper-aware and completely disconnected at the same time.

Whatever Ralf's about to tell me, I know it'll change everything. Again.

Will I survive?

'The doctor prescribed plenty of rest,' I answer.

'Which we know you're probably not going to do.' He finishes with a knowing expression.

I feel no guilt whatsoever about telling him white lies. That's partly because I need to know what's in that file and partly because I know he would have no compunction in telling lies to me.

'The doctor thinks I'm suffering from severe stress. He wants me to see a counsellor and he's prescribed some things to calm me down and help me sleep. He's also proposed some lifestyle changes, diet, exercise, the usual things.'

Ralf is satisfied. 'That's what I thought.'

We both look at the black file. It's me who speaks first. 'What's in it? What did the investigators say?'

He picks the file up and thumbs through it. 'Are you sure you want to hear this, Alison? It might mean another visit to the doctor.'

My back is straighter and my voice is firmer. 'What's in it?'

He looks down at his file. 'You know Simon used to be a teacher?'

Simon? My dead brother? His was the last name I was expecting to hear.

'He was a good one,' I explain. 'He was always good with children. It was adults he couldn't manage. Six months or so back, from what I understand, he took a break from the classroom and has been volunteering at his local community centre.'

Ralf pulls a face to suggest that's not accurate.

'He didn't choose to take a break; he wasn't left with much choice.'

Oh hell, I don't like where this is going. 'I don't understand. What do you mean?'

'There was a nasty incident at a school he worked in. Simon was accused of striking an eight-year-old.'

'What?' My head's ringing.

'He lost his temper and cuffed the child around the head. He denied it of course and there were no witnesses but the school were pretty confident he was guilty. There was a previous incident where he was supposed to have thrown a book at another kid. Fortunately, it missed.'

My head feels like it's about to explode. 'Don't be so ridiculous. Simon wouldn't hurt a fly. That was his problem, he was too gentle, so people sometimes walked all over him.'

Ralf is undeterred. 'The school didn't want a scandal so he was persuaded to resign. Or "was resigned" to be more accurate.

147

During the investigation, the police found this out when they did their background checks.'

'Ridiculous.' I refuse to believe this.

But why would Ralf lie? The police lie?

Ralf is solemn. 'In the week after Sam was lost, Simon was the subject of four interviews with the police. They were sympathetic at first but less so as the interviews went on, until finally he was spoken to under caution. You know, be careful what you say or it might end up with a prosecution barrister using it against you in court.'

He pauses for effect. 'You see the police suspected there was foul play on the beach and they concluded that whether by accident or design, Simon was responsible for Sam's death. What exactly happened we'll never know, but that's what they thought. Simon couldn't keep his story straight for five minutes, he had what one cop called the "guilty vibe" which police can feel after a long time in the game.'

I feel overwhelmed. My brother did something to Sam?

'What about Kane and Frances? Were they in on this crime with Simon too?' I spit out with grating sarcasm.

'Consider this.' He leans forward. 'Simon was a teacher. He understood children, so maybe he manipulated them.' I swear at that, which doesn't deter Ralf from carrying on. 'He told them to never tell. If they did, they would get into trouble. Kane and Frances just went along with whatever they were told to do by an adult.'

I shift out of the chair and am on my feet. 'What you're accusing Simon of is murder. MURDER. The murder of my son. The murder of his nephew.'

The horror of it brings me almost to breaking point.

'Alison.' Ralf looks at me calmy. 'Sit. Down. Please. You're working yourself up into a terrible state.'

He's right, so I slowly resume my seat. 'I won't believe this.'

He nods his understanding, but his following words convey something very different.

'Think of Kane and Frances. They've been given a story to perform by a trusted adult, so they performed it. Then they're stuck with it. They can't very well turn around later and tell the police the story they told was bollocks and bullshit. That they made it up. Maybe they wanted to help their Uncle Simon.'

Ralf presses on. 'Let's face facts. Simon was running from something. That was probably his past. Maybe his involvement in Sam's death? Suicide is a rather grandiose way to apologise when you've got nothing to apologise for. It all fits, Alison.'

It does all fit. Simon's behaviour when I went to see him was completely out of character. Violent. Was this the real Simon? The one he kept hidden from the family. The one that exploded on the beach.

And what about the letter he said he would send me? It never turned up. Was the letter a lie as well?

I'm silent now.

Ralf picks the file up and puts it in a drawer. 'I'm sorry, Alison. I don't know if Mark was in a love nest up the coast with Olivia and it doesn't matter. You're never going to know the truth about what happened to Sam and the most likely explanation is the one the police came up with putting your brother in the frame. The only reason they let him go was because they couldn't prove anything.'

I'm still silent.

'I know what you're going to do, Alison. You're going to want to interrogate Frances and Kane about what really happened that day. Can I advise you once again and very strongly not to do that. If they're telling the truth, it won't make any difference. If they're not, it won't make any difference either. Sam and Simon are dead and that's all there is to it. Leave Kane and Frances alone to get on with their lives.'

I'm staying strong. 'You have to understand that I've made a promise to Sam to get to the truth.'

'I don't even know what that means,' he mutters.

'You wouldn't.' My tone is acid and riddled with an aching sadness. But above all I am devastated.

◆ ◆ ◆

Simon DID NOT hurt Sam.

MURDER him.

There's no way my brother laid a hand on my son.

No bloody way!

Only when I go outside do I realise that being in Ralf's office has left me feeling suffocated. Choking with the information he was trying to make me swallow. Now walking in the cool air and lukewarm sun provides me with the space I need to think.

I won't believe what the police suspected about my brother. Or that he hit children in his care in school. Simon? My little brother? I remember a night when we were children. The couple in the cottage next door were fighting again, their shouts and threats echoing through the walls. Simon, barely seven, crept into mine and Olivia's room, scared out of his wits. I'd tucked him close, whispering soothing words until he fell asleep. He was so small, so vulnerable. How could that frightened boy grow up to . . . ?

No. I can't even think it.

The only way to find out the truth is to ask Simon. I head for the car to drive to his house. Only when I begin opening my car door do I remember.

Simon's dead.

And the dead can't defend themselves.

Chapter 31

There's no sign of Rocky or Kane when I get home, which gives me the chance to get things done. I find every bottle of alcohol in the house and pour the contents down the sink. It's disturbing how much there is. Half bottles, empty bottles, bottles placed behind packets of cereal or in vases. Bottles that I don't remember even buying, never mind drinking.

Each one emerges like a secret coming to light, proof of a deception I've practised against myself.

It's no wonder the doctor's notes gave me such a fright. I'm beginning to repeat my behaviour of ten years ago and for the same reasons. If I hadn't been so drugged up after Sam's death I would have had my wits about me and been clear-headed enough to follow the police investigation. How can I have missed the fact that they interviewed Simon four times? Four bloody times?

Only a couple of items survive the cull. One is a magnum of champagne for Kane's graduation that I now worry may never come. The other is an unopened bottle of whisky that Mark bought for Sam and Kane to give me as a Mother's Day present. That wasn't appropriate I suppose but they signed their names on the label and it's always been one of my treasures. I can't throw either of those down the drain for sentimental reasons. But I can't drink them either.

Next, it's the pills that have to go. They're everywhere as well. All sorts of pills and tablets. Some of them prescribed by my doctor, some sold over the counter by a pharmacist, some sold under the counter by the same pharmacist. Pills from the net, pills from the dark net. As the tablets swirl down the toilet bowl, I think it's a miracle I'm still alive.

Now for the other task I have to do. I open my bag and find what I bought in the shop. A miniature camera with microphone. 'Discreet surveillance' is the promise made in the information leaflet. I approach the small hole I made in the connecting wall between the dining room and the music room.

A shiver runs through me. That's what happens when I see inside this room. It's daft really, that I can't just go into the hall and open the door to the music room. I know that will happen one day but today is not that day. I decide to fit the camera looking into this room in case I hear piano music again. Not to prove that Rocky is playing, but to prove she isn't. It's very discreet. Wrapped around a light stand, you barely notice it. The camera itself sits flush with the hole. When it's switched on, there's a feed to my phone.

Looking at my phone, there's a clearer view inside the music room. It's almost exactly as it was the last time Sam played there in the week before our holiday. It doesn't even seem that dusty. The piano stands against the opposite wall. On top of it is a candelabra with some half-burned candles in their holders. This is slightly disturbing. I don't remember that being in the music room but after all this time, it's possible I've forgotten. I certainly remember seeing the flickering light of the candles when I looked through the hole. I thought I heard Rocky playing the piano in the middle of the night. But did I? I remember my medical report.

'The patient suffers from hallucinations and blackouts.'

I leave the feed running on my phone and go to bed. I desperately want a stiff drink and something to help me sleep but there's nothing in the house for me.

◆　◆　◆

Sometimes you can be too tired to sleep. Sometimes you can be too sober to sleep or too clear-headed to sleep. When it finally comes, my slumbering is fitful and disturbed. I hear the piano being played of course but now I know it's not really happening, I'm strangely reassured. Tonight, the music in my ears is not the sort of mournful or morbid music that Rocky would play, but happier melodies that lift me up rather than bring me down. I try to block out the music in my head, to fall asleep. But it's no use, I can't.

I decide on a herbal tea, so I head downstairs to the kitchen. In Kane's room there's a conversation going on, urgent and heated but at too low a level for me to hear what's being said. My phone says it's three o'clock in the morning.

When I pass the music room door I see a faint light coming from the slight gap under it. On my knees and looking under, it's clearly coming from a single candle burning steadily within. Someone has been in this room tonight.

It's time to see if my plan has worked.

Excitement is burning within me because I'm going to catch Rocky. At last.

I rewind the footage on my phone until about half an hour ago when the film shows the door to the music room opening. A half-light comes in but the camera doesn't seem to be picking up whoever enters.

That's strange.

The door closes again and the room is in darkness. There is a faint shadow of a figure moving around the room as if looking for something. The figure brushes past the camera, so close that it feels as if they touch me. Goosebumps run over my skin. I turn up the volume on the feed. Feet can be heard moving up and down on the floorboards. Then the room falls silent and the figure stops moving. The sound is of the piano lid being raised. The figure sits. Begins to play.

Why can't I see who it is?

The music stops and a match is lit. The outline of the figure becomes more distinct but their back is to me so I can't see their face. The match gutters and dies. Another one is lit before finally the figure manages to light a solitary candle and begin playing again. The orange wafts backwards and forwards on the walls and on the figure. But the gloom is so deep that it's impossible to make a judgement about their shape or body. The shape matches Rocky. Doesn't it? But I can't tell for sure.

The piano plays on for ten minutes, Chopin I think, until it abruptly stops. The shadowy figure gets up from the piano seat and cups its hands to blow out the candle. The flame blows to and fro but doesn't go out. The figure gives up and moves out of shot to the right. A brief kerfuffle by the door, before it opens again and a shaft of light comes in. The door is closed and the room goes dark except for the lone candle on top of the piano.

I sit and watch this footage again and again. And then again and again, over and over, desperately trying to find evidence that it's Rocky. It has to be.

But there's something about the way the figure moved.

The way its fingers caressed the piano keys.

There's only person who matches the hazy description of the shadow.

Sam.

Has my son come back to me?

Chapter 32

This has to stop. I can't go on like this. It can't be Sam I saw last night, can it? Which means I have to make myself go into the music room. Conquer this fear.

So here I am the following afternoon, standing in front of the door to the music room. Close enough for my hand to reach out and grasp the handle. My anxiety levels are through the roof because I'm going to do it. Walk inside the room. I have to conquer this. It's one of the final hurdles to me understanding the past. I'm not kidding myself that this will be easy but I can't be imprisoned by the past anymore. The tremor rushes through my blood as I reach towards the handle. My trembling palm closes around it. It's made of metal but it feels like warm flesh in my hand. Damp, and soft and alive. Breathing deeply, I turn. The latch clicks, a sound too loud in the still air.

Now push. Go on. Push.

With a half step forward, I open the door. A wave of stagnant, dusty air hits me in the face causing me to cough. I look inside and, of course, the first thing I see is the piano. Sam's piano. Majestic and gleaming, yet so hauntingly still. It sits under the window to be in the light. Dark brown and well used, it's the same one that Dad would play, the one he taught me and Olivia on. Despite its age it seemed like the most natural thing in the world to pass it on to Sam. I picture it now, the first time he ever played it. He was just coming up to two years old. I was sitting on the stool, tinkering with the keys with Sam nestled in my lap. All of sudden his little chubby hands had banged and banged against the keys. He wouldn't stop, playing with hiccupping gurgles of laughter. It's these happy memories that had stopped me from coming in here. All those joyful moments we had in here together. The thought of entering this room without Sam is unbearable. It means having to face the guilt of failing Sam. I still can't bring myself to go inside the music room. However, standing here on the threshold looking in is a huge step forward for me.

Without warning, a force slams into my back, pitching me forward. I cry out as I stumble, lose my footing and crash land to the carpet on my knees. A shock wave of pain tears through me, but it's nothing compared to the icy dread settling over me. I twist around, searching for the person who did this. But the doorway is empty.

The music room begins to take on a nightmarish quality. The walls loom at impossible angles, inching closer like a tomb closing in on me. The ceiling is pressing down while the floor starts to shake.

A musical note strikes the air. My gaze snaps to the piano where the keys have become jagged and dangerous, the black keys monstrous rotten teeth. A terrible sense of grief, sadness and longing for my son grips me.

I need to escape.

But I'm frozen. My legs and arms won't move. The air thickens, clogging my lungs.

I need to get out of here.

Sick churns in my gut. There's a stink in the air now. I know what it is. The stench of my guilt. A sob wrenches from my chest. I begin to move, my nails clawing at the carpet as I drag myself towards the door. The music room spins as inch by torturous inch,

I drag myself forward, the carpet leaving burn marks against my knees.

Suddenly a force from nowhere yanks me forward and I skid out of the room. I look up. See a face peering anxiously down at me.

A pale and shocked Paul.

I'm shaking uncontrollably as Paul guides me to the living room sofa. The terror of being in Sam's music room still grips me, making it hard to breathe. Paul disappears into the kitchen, returning moments later with a glass of water.

'Here,' he says gently, pressing the cool glass into my trembling hands. 'Get this down you.'

I take a sip, the water doing little to wash away the taste of fear. Paul sits beside me, his presence solid and reassuring.

'Tell me what happened,' he urges softly.

My answer tumbles out in a rush. 'I was just standing there, looking into the room. I wanted so much to be able to walk in there. Like any normal person would do. I couldn't . . . I couldn't make myself go in.' My strained face stares at him. 'But then something pushed me. I felt hands on my back, Paul. Real hands!'

He listens intently, his brow furrowed with concern. I can see him slipping back into his old role as a FLO where he'd have been trained to show empathy, listen and make no judgements.

'And then?' he gently prompts.

'It was like being back there, that day.' Swallowing the salty, bitter taste of tears, I utter quietly, 'I could almost hear the piano, Paul. I could smell Sam. I'm on my knees . . . I couldn't breathe. And then . . . then something was pulling me out. It was you.'

Paul nods slowly, his eyes never leaving my face. 'Alison,' he says carefully, 'I need to ask you something, and I want you to be honest with me. Are you still taking your medication?'

The question catches me off guard. 'I was for a time. But I think it was messing up my head. My memory. I've recently been to the doctor where I agreed to stop.'

'That was a good move.'

However, the expression in his eyes tells a different story, so I push out, 'I'm not crazy.'

His tentative reassuring smile is an attempt to calm the sudden tension between us. 'I'm not suggesting you are.'

I look away, unable to meet his gaze. 'I've been doing a bit more booze than usual,' I admit quietly. 'Not much. It helped me take the edge off things. Well, at least I thought it did.'

Sighing, Paul leans back, his features set with a faraway expression. 'I've seen this type of behaviour before. Grieving parents, desperately searching for answers. It can consume you, make you see things that aren't there.'

'This was real,' I insist. *Just like the piano playing is real.*

So I tell him about the piano playing at night. I finish with, 'I placed a secret camera so I could catch Rocky—'

With a bite in his voice he interrupts. 'Using a secret camera to film people without their knowledge is illegal, even in your own home.' Despite his gentle warning, his curiosity gets the better of him. 'Did the film show Rocky playing?'

How do I tell him this? He'll think I've lost the plot for sure. I take a breath. 'I saw a shadowy figure.' I stare down because I can't bear to see his expression when I say, 'I think it's Sam. My son back at his piano.'

I'm only underscoring for him that he thinks I'm crazy. Delusional. A grief-stricken mother finally losing her grip on reality.

I imagine his face shifting from concern to pity. Part of me wants to take it back, to laugh it off as a joke or a misunderstanding. But I know what I saw. And even as I brace for his disbelief, a small, defiant part of me hopes that maybe, just maybe, he'll believe me. Because if he doesn't, if he dismisses this as the ravings of a broken woman, then I truly am alone in this.

'Let me tell you about a case I worked on,' Paul says, his voice filled with a soft patience.

I risk a glance at his face, my tension easing when I find no ridicule or mockery in his expression.

'A little boy went missing,' he continues his story. 'His father saw his son's face everywhere – in crowds, in passing cars. One day, he became convinced he saw the boy inside a neighbour's house. Instead of waiting for the police, he broke in and burst into the neighbour's home, certain his son was inside.'

A chill walks down my spine. 'What happened?'

'His son wasn't there, of course,' Paul says sadly. 'He had imagined it all. That's what the power of grief can do. Make you see and hear things that aren't really there.'

'I'm not like that,' I protest weakly, but the words sound hollow even to my own ears.

Paul leans forward, taking my hands in his. 'Alison, you've been through so much. It's natural to want answers, to look for signs. But at what cost?'

I think about the years I've spent searching, the nights I've lain awake replaying that terrible day. Well, the bits of it I can remember. The relationships strained, the opportunities missed. All in pursuit of a truth that seems to slip further away with each passing year.

'I can't give up,' I murmur, as if to reassure myself. 'I can't let Sam down.'

'You haven't let him down,' Paul says firmly. 'You've honoured his memory every day. But maybe . . . maybe it's time to focus on healing. On living.'

I shake my head, unable to accept the idea of moving on. How can I, when the mystery of Sam's death still haunts me? The truth is still out there.

Then it occurs to me, 'What are you doing here?'

It wouldn't have taken him long to get here, since the drive from the seaside where he lives to here is less than an hour.

'I came to talk with you about something I've found out. I knocked and when no one answered I looked through the window and saw you on the floor. Luckily the window to the room wasn't locked.'

Paul watches me for a long moment, his eyes filled with a mixture of concern and something else – understanding, perhaps. Or resignation. Finally, he speaks, his voice barely above a whisper.

'I'm really reluctant to tell you what I found out—'

'Because you think I'm going bonkers? Losing the plot?'

He shakes his head sternly. 'Never that. I want you to consider what I'm going to say next very carefully.'

I wait.

Finally, he asks, 'Is looking for the truth worth your sanity?'

Chapter 33

I walk with Paul in the dying afternoon sun. We're in the small park near my home, where there's a pretty field of wild bluebells that bloom every year and within a month are gone. There was only one answer to the question Paul had asked. I don't care what it costs me, I have to know the truth. So he told me to get my coat and took me for a walk. Now my racing mind is trying to deal with the information he told me.

'Witness? What witness? I was never told about a witness!' My fingers clench involuntarily, nails digging into my palms.

Paul's voice is low and steady as he continues, 'I'm not trying to be cruel, but I think that for much of the time back then, you weren't taking in what people told you. The investigation team informed your ex-husband.'

After seeing the doctor's records I know that Paul is only telling me the truth.

'This witness,' he carries on, 'claimed he saw a second man on the beach with your family that day. This was after the tragedy happened. But before the police were called.'

My mind is blowing up. I can't believe what I'm hearing. It's almost too much to take in. I stop walking, gripping the back of a nearby bench for support. The rough wood under my fingers grounds me, reminding me that this is real, not some twisted nightmare.

'Do you know who this witness was?' I manage to force out.

Paul nods, his expression grim. A gust of wind dances between us, carrying the scent of newly mown grass. 'He identified himself as Andre de Pierre. Turns out that wasn't his real name and the investigation was never able to find out who he really was. He was definitely an artist, a blow-in from London who was renting a cottage locally because he liked the light on the coast and felt it helped with his art. Mr de Pierre was the only one who responded to the many police boards asking for witnesses to come forward.'

We start walking again, our pace slow and measured. A group of teens runs past us, their youthful laughter a stark contrast to the heaviness of our conversation. I envy their carefree joy, remembering a time when Sam's laughter filled our home.

Paul pulls out his small notebook and flips the pages.

'He claimed he was on the cliff walking at 2.45 p.m. with his dog. He knew this for certain because he went for regular walks along the cliff at 2.30 p.m. on the dot every day. It took him fifteen minutes exactly to reach the spot where he claims he saw what he saw. He said there were two male adults and two children, one boy and one girl, in what looked like a huddle on the beach. He was very firm about that.'

'Hang on,' I butt in, my mind rewinding to the past. The memories are hazy, clouded by grief and time, but something doesn't add up. I rub my temples, trying to focus. 'I might be wrong but didn't Simon call the police to report Sam missing nearer three o'clock?'

Paul says, 'It was actually 2.57. The calls to the emergency centre recorded that exact time. Which was later than De Pierre's sighting.'

My heart's thundering. I don't like where this is going. The path curves around a small pond, its surface rippling gently in the strengthening breeze. Dark clouds are gathering on the horizon, promising rain. I watch a duck glide across the water, envying its serenity.

'What did this other man on the beach look like?'

'De Pierre was up on the cliff walk so he was at some distance unfortunately, but he did mention the other man was oddly dressed, as if he'd thrown his clothes on in a hurry. Andre was sure he saw the guy go down to the beach from the cliff top and speak to Simon and the children before heading off in the other direction up the beach carrying something under his arm. Apparently, Simon was asked by the lead detective about this other man.'

A lump forms in my throat. The question marks about my brother are back. I swallow hard before asking, 'What did he say?'

'He insisted that there wasn't another man on the beach. Also he said that he wasn't aware what time he contacted the emergency services. Obviously he was in shock and he was frantic with worry for Sam but he was adamant there was no one else. But our witness on the cliff says there was.'

I try to imagine the scene on the beach that day, but the details are frustratingly vague. A cool gust of wind makes me pull my jacket tighter around me. 'What about the children?'

Paul closes his notebook and looks at me. His eyes, usually so reassuring, now hold a mix of concern and something else – regret, perhaps?

'If the children were spoken to there's no record of it. Or at least, that's what my friend on the investigations remembers. With only De Pierre's version contradicting Simon's it was decided the artist was probably wrong.'

When I see the sour turn of his mouth, I sense there's more bad news. 'Tell me,' I say, bracing myself for whatever's coming next.

'The supposed witness had, to put it mildly, a somewhat *artistic* personality and had a real problem with the police. Y'know, calling the police fascists and corrupt. There was suspicion that he also had a drinking problem. So in the end, the investigation was glad to see the back of him.'

I close my eyes, feeling the warmth of the fading sun on my face. Perhaps Ralf was right and Simon's guilt stretched further than letting my two boys out of his sight. It feels unforgivable to think this when my brother's dead. But my promise to my son comes first.

'And where is this De Pierre guy now?' I ask, opening my eyes to meet Paul's gaze.

'I've been trying to track him down by tracing some of his paintings to various exhibitions around the country. Leaving messages in places that I know he's stayed. If I find him, I'll let you know.'

We start walking again, our steps slow and thoughtful. The park is busy now, filled with after-school families and dog walkers. Their normalcy feels alien to me, a reminder of the life I once had and lost. The wind is picking up, carrying with it the first few drops of rain.

'Paul. What do you think this means? Could Simon have . . . could he have done something to Sam?'

Paul tries to hide the conflict in his eyes from me, but I see it. 'There's no point jumping to conclusions. There are a lot of unanswered questions here, and we need to be careful.'

My hands tremble slightly, and I shove them into my pockets to hide it. 'Do you think there was a stranger on the beach? Someone speaking to my brother?'

'Let me track down De Pierre and we'll have our answers.'

'Was there another man on the beach that day?'

I'm on the phone to Frances. Once I get back home, my jacket off, I call her straight away.

'A what?' She sounds sleepy. I hope I haven't woken her up from an evening nap.

'My contact with the police mentioned that an eyewitness on a cliff walk saw you, your Uncle Simon and Kane on the beach together. With another man. This was shortly before Simon rang the police to report Sam missing.'

'Oh yeah, after the cops arrived there were lots of people on the beach—'

'No, this was before the cops turned up. A witness claims to have seen another man.'

'Oh, him. I thought the cops decided that so-called witness was a crank?' Frances sounds fully awake now. 'I don't remember another man being there. It was total chaos.'

Another thought comes to me. One I don't want to have. 'You aren't covering for Uncle Simon?'

'What do you mean?'

Simon was accused of striking an eight-year-old. He lost his temper.' Ralf's damning words about my brother being a violent man come back to me.

'Did Uncle Simon do something to Sam?'

'What?' Her outrage makes her voice rise. 'Are you kidding me? Uncle Simon wouldn't hurt a fly. And what's this got to do with a strange man?'

It's clear Frances knows nothing. Maybe the investigation was right and this De Pierre character got it wrong. Probably trying to create trouble for the police considering his fraught history with them.

'Thanks, Frances.'

'I hope a good night's sleep will bring you peace.'

If only. I cut the call and am halfway to the kitchen for a glass of water when the doorbell goes. Who's calling at this time of . . . I check the time on my phone . . . 7 p.m.? It's not late but it's starting to get dark. I peer outside.

There's a stranger standing at my door.

Chapter 34

The stranger at my door looks like a homeless man of some sort carrying all his possessions with him. Under one arm is a large file of documents and under the other a bulging rucksack. He looks a bit weird too, wearing a well-worn straw hat, canvas trousers and an overcoat. Or is it an overall? It's hard to tell in this light. Last year there was a spate of addicts knocking on doors spinning tall tales about urgently needing money to visit their sick mums in hospital to fund their next fix.

Something tells me he isn't a druggie.

'Alison? Alison Taylor.'

How does he know my name? My nerves start kicking in.

'I'm Andre. Andre de Pierre.'

The witness from that day. The man Paul told me about.

I start to pull back the door further, then think: 'How did you know where to find me?'

'Word reached me that a man called Paul Simpson was looking for me. A former cop.' His face droops with disdain when he mentions that, and I remember what Paul told me about the tension between this man and the police.

'You still haven't answered the question: how did you know where I live?'

His voice drops low. 'People talk, Alison. People always talk.'

Something tells me if I don't let him into my home this evening, I might never see him again.

'You can't be too suspicious these days,' he tells me as he comes inside. 'My reluctance to be suspicious has cost me millions of pounds. Art dealers, collectors, gallery owners and jealous rivals, you can't be too suspicious of those types of people.'

Inside, I can get a good look at him. The hardness of his life is carved across his face. But what draws me is the intensity of his light brown eyes. They seem to be observing everything.

He looks at the clock on my wall. 'I can only spare you an hour. I'm off to Paris tomorrow morning, the City of Light.'

After he declines my offer of tea, I take him into the front room. We sit opposite each other. Before I can start questioning him, he opens the file he is carrying. Well, I see now that it isn't a file, but one of those large portfolio folders artists use to keep their work in. It contains his sketches, drawings and paintings.

'Would you like to see some of my work?' He doesn't wait for a reply. 'This one is from what I call my stripes period.'

I'm too desperate for his help to say no. Actually, that isn't quite true. I'm drawn to his work.

He shows me a painting that consists of black and white stripes. It's like looking at the hind quarters of a zebra. 'Stripes focus the eye.'

'It's very good.'

Next, he shares one of his sketches. 'I sometimes like to sketch people while I'm talking to them. It helps me clarify emotionally who I'm dealing with.'

It's the face of a woman unlike anything I've ever seen. It's a mishmash of different shapes and odd angles, some sharp, others rounded. Her eyes are triangles while her nose is a circle. All her features seem to be pushed to one side. She seems so sad to me. It's disturbing and captivating all at once. Shivering, I look away.

Scared that my hour is going to be frittered away I seize my chance. 'Perhaps tell me what you saw on the beach that day?'

For a moment he hesitates before saying, 'Of course. On one condition.'

My spine stiffens. Suddenly it hits me that I'm alone in my home with a strange man. If anything happens, will anyone hear my screams?

'What do you want?' Holding my breath, I wait for his answer.

He smiles, showing me a mouth missing most of its teeth. 'You. I want you.' He pulls out a piece of paper and charcoal. 'I want to sketch you as we speak.'

I sigh with relief, then try to get some answers. 'Paul told me you saw my family on the beach the day my son was lost. Can you tell me what you saw?'

'One moment.' He holds out his charcoal and appears to try and align it with my face as if measuring me up, then he starts drawing. 'I was walking Matisse on the cliffs at the time.'

'Matisse?'

'My dog. What a beauty he was. He still had a spring in his step despite getting on in years. It's important for dogs to have regular exercise, so during my spell in Norfolk I took him out at half past two every afternoon. That was when my painting was in its circles period. Would you like to see an example?'

'I lost my son that day.' He pulls back slightly at the sting in my voice. 'I don't mean to be rude but I really need to know what you saw.'

Andre's hand moves in swift, confident strokes across the paper. He glances up at me, his intense gaze scrutinising my features before returning to his work.

'The beach was nearly deserted,' he said. 'There was a group on the beach. Two adults, one of whom I believe was your brother

Simon. Two children aged I would say about ten. One girl and one boy. That would be Kane and Frances, your son and niece.'

I'm impressed with how he remembers everyone's name and relationships.

He pauses, tilting his head as he studies the emerging sketch. His hand shifts across the paper in a broad arc, capturing some unseen detail.

'I understand that the identity of the second adult is the one which interests you. A man. I suspected at once something was wrong. An artist has an eye for that sort of thing.'

Andre's gaze flicks up to me again, his eyes narrowing as he takes in some nuance of my expression. The charcoal in his hand dances across the paper, leaving bold, dark lines in its wake.

'This second adult was obviously in charge of the situation—'

'What makes you think that?'

His mouth twists in a very sour manner. 'I've had a lot of experience with men like him. Always bossing people around, determined to get their way. He spoke to your brother for some time, as if explaining something to him. He put his arm around your brother – not to comfort him – I think he was trying to calm him down.'

Andre leans back, assessing his work with a critical eye before moving in close to add some fine details.

'He then bent down and spoke to the two children. After that he took off down the beach, half running, half jogging. He was constantly looking around as if someone was chasing him but the beach was actually deserted. He was carrying something under his arm, a blanket or a sheet or suchlike. He disappeared from view after that.'

Abruptly he tells me, his eyes shining bright, 'The weather always sets the stage for darkness to creep in, whispering omens of the horrors to come.'

A shiver runs through me.

Andre's hand stills on the paper, his eyes locking with mine as if to gauge my reaction to both his words and his artwork.

Andre continues drawing. 'I told all this to the police at the time. They seemed interested at first, but then as good as accused me of making it all up. Let me tell you something about the police, they're the real criminals. Do you know the number of times I've presented them with clear and irrefutable evidence of occasions I've been defrauded and robbed by people in the art world? Do you know what they do with the dossiers I've presented them with? Nothing, absolutely nothing.'

I hate doing this, but I want answers. 'Please, Andre, the stranger on the beach. What did he look like?'

'He walked with authority and confidence, despite the slippers—'

'Slippers?'

'Yes, like he'd rushed there from his home. He wore shorts too. One interesting fact: he wore a T-shirt that was put on the wrong way round. And yet another interesting fact, his hair was a mess. He had an expensive haircut but it looked as if he'd slept on it.'

I nod in understanding. 'As if he'd dressed in a hurry, perhaps summoned from somewhere at short notice?'

'Exactly.'

A hotel perhaps?

'Would you recognise him again?'

He's still drawing. 'Probably not, he was too far away. I just felt his vibe, so to speak.'

'Did you catch any of the conversation?'

'I'm afraid not. The wind was blowing off the sea onto the land that day.'

That's disappointing, but thanks to Andre I feel I know a little more about what happened.

I'm already thinking ahead. It's time for my sister and I to have a frank conversation and not just about her committing adultery with my husband. Does Andre's description fit Mark? Then again, Mark is not the kind of man who gives off a 'vibe'. If it wasn't Mark, who was it? I'm convinced the man on the beach was staying at a nearby hotel.

The Stacks Hotel? Room 206?

Andre packs away his things, except for his drawing of me. 'I'd better go or I'll miss my train.'

As I escort him to the door, he turns back to me. 'Perhaps there is one other thing I noticed on the beach that day. This little group of people, they looked like conspirators plotting. You know? Like something out of Shakespeare.'

Plotting? That's what stays with me as I sit alone in the front room after Andre has gone. It's easy to see why the police didn't take him seriously. To the gentlemen of the law, he must have looked like a complete time-waster, especially when he started showing them his paintings. Still, my gut tells me he's telling the truth.

Why would he lie about something like this? What would he have to gain?

I want to delve deeper, but the truth is my head is killing me. It's like someone has taken a chainsaw to it. Well, there's nothing I can do tonight. But there is something I must do. I text Paul about Andre's visit.

He texts back: You invited him in?

Me: Yes.

Paul: I found out he was sectioned.

Me: What did he do?

Paul: Stabbed someone with a paint brush. Could be dangerous.

A chill goes through me as I consider the risk I've taken letting him into my home.

After finishing messaging, I slump back. A damning question occurs to me. If Andre is dangerous, was he somehow involved in what happened to Sam? Is he implicating others to throw the scent off himself?

As I stand, Andre's drawing catches my eye. I pick it up. It turns out he wasn't drawing me after all. Instead, its simple lines show a number of figures in a loose circle. One is crouched down talking to two squiggly lines which suggest they represent two children. Horror creeps over me at what I see in the background.

A small figure being consumed by the sea.

Chapter 35

Olivia's house is not quite grand enough to be called a mansion. The drive is too cramped. The trees in her front garden are in a huddle rather than neatly spaced with room to breathe. The classical pillars that frame her front door are too short to suggest Ancient Athens. It's just a big house with pretensions, a little like its owner really. It still hurts that she made such an effort to distance herself from our father. When you start denying your roots, you lose your way.

She doesn't answer the tinkle of the brass bell at once. She's probably staring at me on her spy cam. The double door swings open and I'm expecting it to be her housekeeper. She wouldn't shut up about having one when she married up. But it's Olivia who greets me. Then I recall hearing that her former husband got stung in the stock market meltdown a few years back. Obviously there's no money left for housekeepers.

My sister looks like she's stepping out for a day at the races, all decked out in a fitted floral-print dress and ridiculously high heels with a string of rose-toned pearls to complete the look. Because heaven forbid my sister would ever be underdressed, even for sitting around her house. She acts like some glamorous lady but the sad truth is she looks old.

She's obviously surprised to see me. She folds her arms. 'The tradesman's entrance is round the back.'

'If I see a tradesman, I'll tell him.'

She looks me up and down. 'What are you doing here? If you've come to beg an invite to Simon's funeral, you're wasting your time. Not my decision of course. I tried to persuade Katie to let you come but she was adamant on the subject.'

'I want to ask you about our holiday ten years ago. Some interesting new information has emerged and I'm hoping you might be able to shed some light on it. Or I could go to the police.'

'What information?'

'If you invite me in, we can discuss it.'

She sighs, pretends to look at the watch she isn't wearing and shrugs. 'There is no new information. Everything was all done and dusted at the time. We all know you've got your problems, Alison, and you have an issue with reality, but I really don't think at this stage . . .' She catches my eye. She can see I'm serious. 'Oh, very well.'

She leads me through the hall and into a drawing room with a fake chandelier and a fake stone fireplace. With an impatient hand she indicates for me to sit on an armchair, while she spreads herself over a very comfy two-seater sofa.

'What is this about?' There's no offer of a drink, not even a glass of water. Why am I not surprised!

'You were screwing my husband.'

Olivia smirks, running a French manicured finger over her pearls. 'You've finally found out about Mark and I having a little tryst? Poor Alison, always late to the party.'

Her attitude leaves me breathless. She could at least say, *'So sorry, Alison, it all happened in a moment of weakness.'* But no, her motives were cruel and calculating.

I carry on. 'The week of the holiday, Mark booked a room in a hotel further down the coast. A little love nest for you both. I remember how you kept slipping away to go and do brass rubbings in local churches.'

Leaning back, Olivia folds her legs. 'For your information he booked the hotel room but then couldn't get away from work so it was left empty. Typical Mark, always letting work get in the way of having a seriously good time.' She settles a penetrating gaze on me. 'And he was having a good time, Alison, believe you me.'

I fight for control. She's not going to rile me. Not this time. *Think of Sam. Think of what Andre told you about the man in the slippers who looked like he got dressed in a hurry who arrived at the beach.*

She's laughing at me but this time there's an uncertain edge to it. 'Who told you about the hotel reservation?'

A faint Norfolk burr is creeping into her voice, something that often happens when she's nervous and stressed out.

'I found a credit card receipt in Mark's name for the booking. He's admitted the room was intended for you and him.'

She rolls her eyes. 'Typical Mark, leaving a trail of evidence behind him like that. Mind you, I don't suppose he had much experience in the affair or indeed the sex department.'

She lets out a little tinkle of laughter as she tries to drag me in the mud. 'He was desperate. I don't blame him for remembering, it was probably the highlight of his life. Personally, I'd forgotten all about it. All it took was for me to flash a bit of leg and he was on it like a starving dog with a bone.'

That gaze of hers digs right through me. 'Not that I could blame him of course. There wasn't much in the way of leg and bone at home, let's face it.'

I consider Olivia carefully. While she's literarily dogging me, she should be enjoying herself, but the blood is heightened on her cheeks. Her gaze keeps skidding away. That's when I figure out what she's doing. She's trying to cause me maximum pain to distract me away from her and Mark. From the hotel room?

'That the room was left empty is one possibility,' I say. 'Another is that you kept the room booking and used it with another one of your men.'

She says nothing.

I plunge on. 'If it wasn't Mark in that room, who was with you?'

Without warning, all the fake laughter drops from her face, replaced with a gleam of pure menace. She unlocks her legs and shifts to the edge of the sofa as if getting in position to jump me.

'We don't really want to go down this road, now do we?' Her Norfolk roots are on full display in her tone. 'How would it ever make things right between us? You want me to admit that I've only ever played the bitch with you because I was jealous of you? All right, I admit it.'

I inhale deeply. Never in a million years did I think Olivia would fess up to that.

'But why? I don't understand why you would be jealous of me. You're the one with all the money. You got what you wanted out of life.'

There's a hardness about her face as she considers me. 'Extra lessons from the piano teacher at school. The way Dad rubbed your back after you played for him. I never got any of that. Any special attention.' The rest of her words are blistering and brittle. 'I had to fight for everything I got. No one paved the way for me.'

She continues. 'Do you want me to admit the Mark thing was one way of me getting back at you?' She shrugs. 'Very well, I admit it. But believe me, Alison, everything I've done since Sam was lost, I've done for the family.'

She sounds sincere for once and her voice is soft. But it doesn't matter. 'Who was it?'

'What difference does it make if it was another one of my lovers?'

'I'll tell you what difference it makes. It's a fact that Simon called your mobile. That's on record with the police. So the only way a man would turn up at the beach—'

'What man?' Olivia looks ruffled for the first time. 'There was no other man.'

I press on. 'You left that day to supposedly go to the church. But you went to the hotel. Mark couldn't make it so you called another lover to meet you there.' There's a loud scoff at that. 'When Simon contacted you, your lover was there too. You sent your lover to the beach to . . .' I hesitate. This is the part I'm still trying to work out.

'What?' Olivia barks. 'I sent my phantom lover down to the beach to do what? Sell bloody ice cream? Parade donkeys to entice the kiddies for rides?'

'You ordered him down to . . . clear something up before the police were called.' I know it sounds weak and not formed. 'What I don't know is who that lover was. Or what needed clearing up. But I'm going to find out, you can be sure of that.'

Her face and voice harden again and her brief spell of sincerity is broken. 'I see. You want to ruin everyone's life in a petty act of spite and revenge. Let me tell you how it was. Mark never went to that hotel and neither did I. Do you really think someone like me would go and have a quickie in a hotel with fake palms in the courtyard and a tatty cocktail bar called The Elite Lounge?'

'How do you know there were fake palms in the courtyard if you've never been there? How do you know what the cocktail bar was called?'

She purses her lips at me catching her out. 'It doesn't matter how you wash yourself, Alison, you'll always smell of our father's disgusting fish.'

'That's an honest smell, Olivia. It's better than the whiff of fakery and self-hatred you give off everywhere you go.'

She's furious I won't buckle. 'You want to pull the building down on top of all of us, including you and your own son? You can try but I won't let you do that. I'll do whatever is necessary to stop you. Now, get out of my house and don't come back. Ever.'

As I get up to leave I take a look at Olivia one more time and am shocked by what I see. It's in her eyes. She doesn't think I see because it's a momentary flash and then it's gone.

Why did my sister look like she was running scared?

Chapter 36

The Sisters

Alison and Sam arrived at the Guildhall School of Music and Drama in London, nerves thrumming with anticipation. Sam was auditioning for a coveted place, a chance to nurture his prodigious musical talent. There were only three places available this year. Alison was instantly reminded of her own scholarship here, the scholarship she turned down to look after her father. Now Alison's heart swelled with pride as they walked down the corridor. Her son, her shining star, was finally going to receive all he deserved. Sam had practised hard and long for this, although he told her that if he didn't get in that was no problem. That was her Sam all over, always upbeat.

But as they entered the audition room, Alison's steps faltered. There, sitting in the front row, was her sister Olivia and her daughter Frances. A flicker of surprise crossed Olivia's face before it settled into a mask of cool composure.

Of course, Frances played the piano as well.

The sisters hadn't realised their children would be competing for the same opportunity. The air crackled with unspoken tension. Sam was dressed very casually, in jeans and one of his quirky piano T-shirts sporting the slogan: 'I don't need Google I've got Debussy.' Frances was turned out in a frilly dress and ribbons that made her look like a throwback to the 1950s. Sam looked so relaxed, his cousin appeared very uncomfortable.

Sam was called first and took his place at the piano, his fingers poised over the keys. As he began to play, the judging panel were entranced by the hauntingly beautiful melody that poured from his fingertips. His performance was flawless.

When Sam finished, the judging panel erupted into applause, their faces brimming with admiration. Alison's heart soared, tears of joy pricking her eyes.

Then it was Frances's turn. The girl approached the piano, her shoulders hunched, her steps hesitant. As she played, the difference was stark. Mistakes peppered her performance, the tempo uneven, her fingers faltering on the keys.

Secretly Alison watched her sister, noticing the tightening of her jaw, the momentary flash of fury in her eyes. When Frances finished, the room was silent, the judges' polite smiles barely masking their disappointment.

Afterward, Olivia approached Alison and Sam, a brittle smile plastered on her face. 'Congratulations, Sam. You were brilliant.'

But Alison knew her sister too well. Beneath the veneer of graciousness, resentment simmered.

As Olivia and Frances left, Alison overheard the hissed words Olivia told her daughter: 'How could you embarrass me like that?'

Alison's heart clenched and hurt for her niece, who looked humiliated and upset.

The cruel twist of fate was that Sam won a place, but his acceptance letter arrived two days after he died.

Chapter 37

I'm staring at the bottle of champagne on the kitchen counter, the one I'd set aside for Kane's graduation. The dark brown glass catches the light like it's giving me the promise of numbness and escape if I indulge. After the blow-up with Olivia, my nerves are raw, frayed. One glass wouldn't hurt, would it? Just to take the edge off.

No! I can't! I need to stay sharp, keep my wits about me if I'm going to unravel this mess. There's too much at stake. Still, the temptation lingers, a constant whisper in the back of my mind.

I force myself to leave the room and go up the stairs.

'No, no, no, I've had enough of this.'

I go totally still. That's Rocky's voice. It sounds as if she's on the phone. She must be standing outside Kane's room on the landing. And it sounds as if she's pacing.

'You don't know what it's like here.'

Who is she speaking to?

'Kane . . . ? Well, I've done my best.'

She's talking to someone about my son? My heart pinches inside my chest. What does she mean, she's done her best?

She falls silent. Then bursts between clenched teeth, 'It's a mad house. I want out . . . Don't give me that . . . I don't care, babes, make an excuse. It's almost seven. I'm leaving now. You better be there by eight. Or you're on your own.'

I shuffle down the stairs as quick as I can and retreat back to the kitchen. Less than a minute later, I hear Rocky's footsteps in the hallway. The front door shuts.

I give it less than a minute before I grab a jacket and follow her. Who has Rocky gone to meet?

◆ ◆ ◆

We've all seen the cops and PIs tailing people in the TV shows and films where it all looks surprisingly easy. But it isn't. I nearly lose Rocky on the first mildly busy street she comes to. Her pink hair saves the day though because it's easy to spot. There's another bad moment when she pauses at a bus stop to inspect the timetable. I don't know how I'm supposed to follow her onto a bus without being noticed. While I pretend to look in a shop window, she looks up and down the road to see if anything is coming.

When she judges there isn't, she presses on. Finally, she passes a cab office and drops in. A few minutes later, she emerges with a middle-aged guy. They get into a cab and drive off.

I've lost her.

In despair, I turn on my heels and get ready to walk home before having an idea. I go into the cab office with a story at hand.

The controller is the type of stony-faced woman you do not muck around.

'Good evening. Look, I'm terribly sorry but my daughter has just caught a cab from here and the silly girl has left her purse at home. Is it possible for me to order a cab to where she's gone so I can give it to her?'

The expression on the woman's face shows she doesn't approve of my parenting style. 'You're that girl's mother? You should have a word with her. She looks a bit mad.'

'Well quite, but what's a mother supposed to do?'

Less than twenty minutes later, a cab drops me off outside a bar. The bar's hoarding has no name on it, only a scrawled painted symbol that looks like graffiti, I suppose in an attempt to make it trendy and groovy. It's pretty obvious that blending in here isn't going to be easy. Getting past the door isn't going to be easy either. Two bouncers are manning it and neither is impressed when I walk up and try to get in.

'Are you sure you're at the right place? I wouldn't have thought this would be your scene.'

'Really? Why?'

The bouncer explains. 'It's a bit of a young, alternative vibe in here. I'm not sure you count as either. No disrespect, I'm doing you a favour by keeping you out.'

I'm running on adrenaline. I think of using the 'my daughter's lost her purse' tale but change tack. I know how these places operate even if I've never shown up at one personally.

'I'm from the licensing authority and we visit bars and clubs regularly to ensure the rules are being kept to. As it happens, my boss has got a mutually beneficial arrangement with the owner here to ensure that I don't see anything I shouldn't. But I have to visit anyway. I'm not sure the owner is going to be very happy if they find out you've refused me entry.'

I worked in a bar many years ago and know all the types of behind-the-scenes shenanigans that go on.

The two bouncers look at each other. They should ask me for ID or suggest I just say I've visited but why would they? They're getting paid anyway and they let me in.

Stepping out of the way, they tell me, 'Enjoy your evening, madam.'

The muscle on the door was right. This isn't my scene at all.

It's a mosaic of dark blue spaces but occasionally a white strobe light crosses the bar and for a moment you can see in more detail before it goes dark again. Secluded booths and tables keep nosy parkers at bay, there's a dance floor with nobody dancing, a long bar with high chairs and there is noise, so much noise. So loud in fact, you can barely hear yourself think. The crowd is very Rocky. Girls with exaggerated make-up and clothes and boys who want to look different and who all end up looking the same. There's plenty of drugs too and I wonder if the owner really is paying off the licensing authority.

It's going to be hopeless finding Rocky in here. If you want to hide in the bar, no one could stop you.

The furniture is distressed chairs and sofas into which the patrons sink. In the booths, you can only see heads of the people inside bobbing over the top. Short of leaning in and inspecting closely, I wouldn't be able to identify my own mother in this place. Even Rocky's pink hair isn't going to help me this time. It's complete chaos in here. I order a drink from the bar. Soft drink. I find a place concealed in the shadows behind the stairs that lead up to reception. This is probably a wasted journey. Rocky might not even be here and if she is, it's unlikely that I'll spot her or her mysterious date. But I'm determined to stick it out. I'll wait until the early hours when the joint closes if necessary.

A young woman comes down the stairs in the dark blue light. For a brief moment the strobe light crosses her face. During that moment, I think she looks like Frances. As she crosses the floor, the light catches her face again and this time, there's no doubt.

It is Frances.

It's a Frances I've never seen before. She's got the look of the people who frequent this bar, not the svelte young professional I'm familiar with. Black is her colour of choice – skin-tight jeans, leather jacket and lipstick. Her face appears solemn and serious and slightly upset. I stand up ready to call her name but she's already swallowed up by the din, so she'd never hear me. She's a shadow now, crossing to one of the booths. Another shadow stands up and the two shadows embrace closely, becoming one shadow. The strobe light crosses the floor again. Lights up their bodies.

Pink hair.

The person hugging Frances is Rocky!

I do a double take as if my eyes are deceiving me. But they're not. What the hell are Rocky and Frances doing together?

I've been made a fool of again.

Are they also making a fool of Kane?

Are Frances and Rocky lovers?

There's an intimacy about them that lovers have.

They sit down. It crosses my mind to go over and confront them. I decide against it. It's difficult to confront people when they can't hear what you're shouting and you can't hear what they're shouting back. But it doesn't matter anyway; after maybe only twenty minutes, one of the shadows gets up and makes her way across the bar. On the stairs, she passes only a feet away from where I'm sitting but of course she doesn't notice me as she goes. The strobe light creeps around, crosses her face and hair and it becomes clear that it's Rocky who's leaving. I stay put with my drink to see if my niece has any more visitors that I might recognise, but she doesn't.

All sorts of things run through my mind.

Who Rocky really is has been on my mind for a while.

But now I begin to wonder who my niece really is too. What do I know about Frances except she's lovely and friendly and has done her best to support me? I try to put out of my mind that she's Olivia's daughter and reject the notion that an apple doesn't fall far from the tree. She did grow up in that house with my sister though and that's not the ideal environment for raising a child. It wouldn't be unrealistic to think that maybe some of my sister's talent for deceit and malice had rubbed off on her only child. It's not fair to blame the child because of the parent but it's not fair to expect me not to think of it. I took at face value her assurances that there was no stranger on the beach and that she was nowhere near the scene when Sam was lost.

Was I naive?

It's time for answers. From both Frances and Rocky.

I decide on which one I'll tackle first.

Chapter 38

Rocky gets to my house before me. I find her in the garden, sitting at the round wrought-iron table. It's dark but a wall light shows she's got a drink while furiously tapping away on her mobile. When she sees me come through the back door, she snaps the phone back into her pocket.

'Mind if I join you, Rocky?'

She stands up. 'I'm off to bed—'

I cut her off. The time for games is over.

'Enjoy yourself this evening? I'm sure you can spare me a few minutes.'

Maybe she picks up a hint in my expression that I mean business because she slowly re-takes her seat.

She tries to look blank. 'I haven't been out.'

'Really?'

She avoids my searching gaze. 'You're the one who's been out, not me.'

I don't want to argue with this girl. I just need to find out what's going on here. 'We've never really had a chance to get to know each other, us two, woman to woman.'

She guffaws. 'You can't blame me for that. Let's face it, you're not exactly Mrs Main Street, are you? You're a bit scary actually. You didn't like me from the moment I walked through the front door.

I know you've had your problems with the tragedy and everything, so I'm not saying anything but if we got off to a bad start, that's on you, not me.' She scoffs, 'Accusing me of playing the piano.'

The jury's still out on that one! I don't tell her that.

I'm annoyed until I realise that she's got a point. 'Perhaps we could have got on better if you'd been slightly franker with me.'

She's baffled. 'Franker? What are you talking about?'

'I overheard you on the phone earlier. I then followed you this evening to that awful bar where you met my niece, Frances.'

Rocky starts convulsively. 'I get where you're going. You saw me with Frances.' I'm slightly wrong-footed by her not denying it. It isn't what I was expecting. I thought she'd be trying to bluff her way out of this.

'So you know my niece? Why didn't you mention this?' Recalling the intimacy between them I add, 'You looked very chummy with her. Are you two-timing my son?'

Rocky shrugs. 'No, I'm not sleeping with her.' I'm relieved at that because the last thing Kane needs is a girlfriend fooling around behind his back. She carries on answering the questions I've put to her. 'Why would I tell you I know Frances? It's not a secret. She was my bestie at school.'

I stare at Rocky, totally floored, my mind struggling to process this new information. The casual way she drops this bombshell leaves me reeling. Her silver rings catch the moonlight as she waves her hand, the gesture so nonchalant it's almost infuriating.

'Your best friend?' I repeat. 'How is that possible? Why didn't Frances ever mention you? Plus her mother sent her to a school that's pretty exclusive.'

A dozen questions race through my mind. How long have they known each other? Why keep it a secret from me? And most importantly, how does this change everything I thought I knew about Rocky's presence in our lives?

She tells me, 'My father's loaded as well. Let's just say the life he had mapped out for me isn't one I'm going to take up.'

'Are you even Kane's girlfriend?'

Abruptly, I see the tension enter her body, the seriousness replacing her casual manner. 'Frances and I had an agreement and I'm through with it. Leaving. Out of here. She's trying to persuade me to stay on and look after Kane—'

The hairs on the back of my neck stand up. 'What do you mean, look after Kane? Is there something wrong with him?' A terrible possibility comes to me that leaves it hard for me to breathe. 'He's not dying?'

'No!' The word slams out of her.

A shattering sigh of relief escapes me. 'I want you to tell me everything from the beginning.'

'The first thing you need to understand is that Frances is more than my bestie. She's my guardian angel. My one true real friend.'

There's such an open, adoring expression on her face I say, 'It sounds like you're in love with her.'

A tiny smile ripples across her lips. 'If only! If and when I find a guy who can measure up to Frances's qualities, I'll be one lucky lady.' She draws in the cool night air. 'I'll tell you the story but let me do it backwards.'

'All right,' I say, settling back. 'I'm all ears.'

'When Frances found out Kane was attending the same college as me, she asked if I'd keep an eye on him for her and report back on how he was. He seemed fine to me until this spring. Then he started to go downhill.'

'How did she know which college he was at? They haven't seen each other in more than ten years. Not since Sam . . .'

Rocky rolls her eyes slightly. 'That's where you're wrong. They chat regularly.' Seeing my astounded expression, she adds softly with kindness, 'That's the problem with parents, they never know what their children are really up to.'

Rocky's words wound me, challenging everything I thought I knew about my relationship with Kane. All the times he must have come home after seeing Frances and he never said a thing. Perhaps he was worried that I wouldn't like it, despite me frequently stating how happy it would make me if he and his cousin were reconciled even if their two mothers were not. Then again, Kane has come back to me almost a stranger.

How much don't I know? What else has Kane been keeping from me?

Kane's Not Girlfriend goes on. 'It all kicked off when he heard that his father was going to have his brother declared dead. I watched Kane struggle to deal with it all.' Her gaze lights up. 'I might not be going out with him, but that doesn't mean I don't care about him. Frances suggested he come home to rest and chill. The three of us agreed I'd come home with him to support him.'

That hurts. 'What makes you think I wasn't capable of supporting my son myself?'

It's the first time she looks unsure of herself. 'Can I say it as it is?' After my terse, brisk nod, she softly says, 'You need looking after yourself. You can't do you and Kane at the same time.'

I want to argue with her. No mother wants to be told she can't take care of her child. Nevertheless, it's the truth.

'I heard you on the phone telling Frances you wanted to get out of this mad house,' I throw at her. 'That's why I followed you. Is that what my home's like to you?'

'You and Kane need professional help. And I'm not a professional.'

This girl may have gone behind my back but she has acted with the best of intentions towards my son. 'It's very generous of you to help Kane. I appreciate it. Haven't you got your own life and studies to be getting on with?'

'Frances means everything to me. I probably wouldn't be alive if it wasn't for her.' Rocky's eyes grow distant, her fingers absently tracing the outline of one of her silver rings. 'If she asks me to do something, I do it.'

She shifts in her seat, her gaze suddenly intense. 'Look at me, Alison, just imagine what it was like for a strange-looking kid like me in the school playground when the mean girl gang clapped eyes on me.' Rocky's shoulders hunch slightly, as if remembering old pain. 'It was non-stop bullying until Frances stepped in. She hates bullies.' She pauses, collecting herself before continuing. 'There was this group of mean girls who were always beating me up at the school gates, that is until one day Frances got them to stop. I don't know how she managed it and I didn't care.'

She looks me directly in the eye, her voice soft but firm. 'That's what she's like. Super loyal to people and I'm super loyal to her. It went without saying I'd look out for Kane if she asked me, including coming home with him for a time.' Rocky finishes with, 'I think she gets it from her mother. I've met her a couple of times. She tried to ban Frances from seeing me but of course Frances ignored her and saw me in secret. The mother's not a woman to be crossed either.'

'My understanding is Frances and Olivia don't get on.'

Rocky's laughing again. 'Get on? She hates her mother!' She sees another question forming in my gaze. 'And before you ask, neither Frances nor Kane have told me what happened on the beach that day. And, to be perfectly honest, I don't want to know.'

I ask, 'Will you do me a favour, Rocky? I think you're good for Kane. Will you stay until I get this business with his father sorted out?'

Rocky eases back, thinking beneath hooded eyes. 'OK. But I'm doing it for Kane.' She gets up. 'Can I give you a word of advice? Maybe it's best all round for Sam to be declared dead, allowing his brother to re-join the living.'

Rocky is gone.

I keep getting things wrong because I don't check what I think I know. When I saw Frances and Rocky together in the bar, I took it for granted that they were up to no good. Now it appears that Frances was doing good by asking her friend to support Kane. It also appears that Rocky was doing good by coming and supporting my son who was supposed to be supporting me.

I'm still having difficulty pinning down why Frances didn't tell me about Rocky. Perhaps she thought it would upset me. All the same, I don't like it. It's not that I don't trust Frances. But I need to stop relying on what I think I know rather than what I actually do.

Chapter 39

'Ralf's not in today,' his receptionist says to me sweetly. She should really have it on tape and just press play.

It's not my lawyer I've come to see though. 'What about Frances?'

'She's not available either, I'm afraid. I can leave a message if you like.'

Declining her offer I walk out, but instead of leaving I move around the side of the building until I locate Frances deep in discussion with someone in an office near the back. When I tap on the window, she doesn't appear surprised to see me. No doubt her very good friend Rocky has let her know that I've been asking about their relationship. No doubt Rocky's passed on other bits of information as well.

With a beaming smile, my niece raises her fingers and thumb to suggest she'll be five minutes. When she comes out of the entrance to find me outside, it's difficult to match up this young professional with the woman I saw in the 'squiggle' bar the night before.

She gives me a quick hug. 'Aunt Alison, you're looking a little cheerier.'

Everyone looks a little cheerier when the facts fall into place. 'You on the other hand seem a little tired. Late night somewhere, maybe?' My arched brow communicates the rest.

She looks more contrite. 'Rocky told me you saw us at the bar.'

'I'm baffled why you didn't mention that she's a close friend of yours? Or that you've been keeping in touch with Kane all these years. It's this last that hurts the most.'

Her face fills with pain and embarrassment. 'I'm sorry, Aunt Alison. Me and Kane often talked about it but the feeling was that if you or Mum found out, one of you was bound to hit the roof. If it helps it didn't happen immediately but we bumped into each other when we were in our early teens, through school it must have been. We had a lot to talk about.'

I can imagine. 'And Rocky?'

'I asked her to look out for Kane. If we were speaking, I'd have told you of course. But you and I only linked up again once we met here. After that I did wonder if you might suspect that Rocky was some kind of plant on my behalf for whatever reason, so I didn't mention it.'

'And is she? A plant?'

She looks so hurt. 'That's not a very nice thing to say to me. All I was doing was trying to get Kane through a bad time in his life.'

It's my turn to be embarrassed. 'I'm sorry if what I said sounded like an accusation, I didn't mean it to.'

She smiles again but her gaze is guarded. 'No problem. I know how much pressure you're under.'

I reach into my handbag and pull out a piece of sketch paper that's folded up and pass it to her after opening it up. 'Perhaps you can help me some more. A friend traced the eyewitness who saw the family on the beach that day.'

'What's this?'

'The eyewitness is an artist. He drew that for me. It's the scene he saw from the cliff.' I point out the figures in the sketch. 'That's Simon, that's you and that's Kane. The question is, who is this person, crouching down and explaining something to you and Kane?'

Frances studies the sketch closely for a while like a valuer assessing a fair price for a work of art. 'It's not exactly photographic evidence, Alison. It's just a sketch with some squiggles done by a crank, ten years after the event.' Handing it back she adds, 'I've told you I don't remember anyone on the beach with us that day. I certainly don't remember anyone kneeling and explaining anything to Kane and me. Who? What? Why?'

All good questions. She might be right about the crank and the sketch. But she's changed her story from 'there was no one' to 'I don't remember anyone'. I've nothing else to ask her about the beach but there is another favour I need to ask her. 'Is Ralf in today?'

'No, he's off. He didn't say why.'

I move closer to her and lower my voice. 'He's got a file in his office. It's black, very thin. He put it in his top right-hand drawer after sharing what was in it with me. I wonder if you could go and retrieve it for me and photocopy it. I need to know exactly what's in it.'

'What is in it?'

'Ralf spoke to a contact in the force who got hold of the original police notes for him and cut and pasted the important parts into a file and sent it on. According to Ralf, the original investigation suspected your Uncle Simon might have had something to do with Sam's death.' I keep talking over her astonished gasp. 'I need to read this evidence myself. Is it as Ralf told me? Or did he edit things out?' I add, 'No doubt for the best possible reasons.'

Frances's features suddenly turn stark. She looks around as if she's afraid someone will hear her. 'I can't do that. You know how suspicious Ralf is. If he catches me rifling through his office it's "Goodnight Vienna" for me and I might not get a chance somewhere else. Be reasonable, Alison, I'm doing my best for you but that's going too far.'

I keep coaxing her. 'What could be more natural than his intern going into his office to retrieve a document? If he asks any questions, I'm sure you can talk your way out of trouble. You seem to be very good at that.'

As she looks anxiously over her shoulder, I plead, 'Please, Frances. Top right-hand drawer of his desk, black file, inside is a copy of the police notes from the original investigation concerning Simon and Sam.'

Suddenly she looks at me. 'You don't think that Uncle Simon really . . .'

'Getting me that file is the first step in finding out.'

'I'll try but I'm not making any promises.'

I shadow Frances back to Ralf's office suite. She punches in her code, then strolls down the corridor towards the boss' room like she owns the place.

Ignoring the receptionist, I slip back outside and creep along the building's edge. Through a gap in the blinds, I spot Frances rifling through Ralf's drawers, starting top right. She skims files, replacing each before moving on. After a final sweep of the office, she heads for the door.

I backtrack quickly, re-entering the building. I key in the code I memorised watching Frances's fingers. She emerges into reception, beckoning me with a casual flick of her wrist. We step outside once more.

She's nervous but firm. 'It's not there.'

'It's got to be. I saw him put it in the drawer after he read it to me.'

She's getting angry now. 'What do you want me to say, Aunt Alison? That it is there when it isn't? If it was off-the-book information supplied to him by the cops, chances are he destroyed it. He's not stupid. Look, this has been fun but I've got to go back to work. Whatever you do, don't tell Ralf that I was nosing around his office.'

She walks off in something of a huff.

A banner hangs from the second floor of the office block, advertising available floor space for rent. A similar message is on a board outside on the street.

Once again I go into the block, slip past the glass door that marks the entrance to Ralf's and go up a staircase to the floor that's for rent. Cardboard boxes litter the dusty floor, scraps of paper are trapped under doors, someone has begun to clean the windows but given up halfway through. A deserted kitchen area has some crusty cups and empty packets. The taps are stiff and the sink is stained.

I collect some of the boxes together, create a makeshift sofa out of them and find some films to watch on my phone at a very low volume. It will be many hours before the last of Ralf's staff leave and any alarm is set. Frances is wrong about one thing. Ralf isn't that careful with his security, taking the view that who would want to burgle a solicitor's office? In the meantime, I've got time to kill but it's not a problem. I've got nowhere else to go.

It's not that I don't trust Ralf or Frances to tell me the truth about the files or anything else. But the journey I'm on has taught me one lesson above all others. If you want the truth, you have to find it out for yourself.

Chapter 40

I'm awoken from an uneasy sleep in the boxes by the sound of a car horn blowing and an angry voice outside on the street. It's nearly six o'clock.

'Get out of my way, that's my space!'

It's Ralf. He's returned from wherever he's spent the day and is trying to park his car in his prime parking spot in front of the block. There's a brief argument with another motorist that I view from the window of the empty floor.

Frances is waiting for him outside on the street but she's dismissed with a curt, 'Not now, babe, I'm busy. Tomorrow.' He calls her back. 'Is everyone else out of the building?'

Frances doesn't look happy about being brushed off and gives him a sullen nod by way of an answer before setting off down the street. Ralf comes into the building downstairs but he isn't there long. When he comes back out of the building and locks up, he's in a hurry.

He has a phone to his ear with a client who clearly isn't happy. 'I haven't got time for this, I'm busy . . . What does that prove . . . ? So, what . . . ? Stop ringing me up every bloody five minutes. Stop worrying. Everything's in hand.'

With purpose he's back in his sports car and, with a screech of wheels, drives off at speed. I give it thirty minutes to make sure he's not coming back, before leaving the second floor and making my way down the staircase to the ground floor. My one worry was there would be a security system that detected intruders when the building shut up shop for the evening.

No alarm goes off. I didn't hear any indication that an alarm was set, but even if there is, I won't be long. All I need to do is make a quick check of Ralf's office because Frances may have missed the black file. If I find it, I'll use my phone to photograph what I need.

After pressing in Frances's code, the lock drops.

I go inside the deserted offices.

It feels rather like being a kid climbing into a neighbour's garden to collect a football despite being repeatedly warned not to do so and being unsure if the neighbour's devil dog is on the loose and hasn't had his dinner.

Slightly more relaxed, I scoot down the corridor to Ralf's office. The door isn't even closed much less locked. I slip inside and ease into Ralf's ultra-comfy executive chair, one of those that leans back so you can sleep in it and spin like a roundabout. Only the best for Ralf.

I get to work and open the top right-hand drawer. On a pile of junk that has been stuffed in there, is the file. It's right there in plain sight. Frances didn't look very hard. She didn't look very hard at all.

I take more deep breaths and my fingers are clamped to the file when it's pulled out. Do I really want to read this? Really? What has Ralf kept from me about the police investigation for reasons of his own? Or because he doesn't want to upset me. What else is there about Simon in this file? Ralf's a rogue but he has a good heart. He's trying to protect my feelings. Across the office is a photocopier. Instead of my phone I opt to use it.

The photocopier purrs into life and I take the first sheet out of the file. Do I want to look at it? I can't but I must. I get the shock of my life.

It's blank.

So is the second sheet. And the third and the fourth. I thumb through the ten odd pages and they're all the same. No writing in sight. Pensive and confused, I stumble back to his chair and put the file back on the table and try to stay calm and think about this.

It's possible that he only pretended to have a file copied from the original police investigation. It sounds much better than having a mere phone call from his contact who told him what was in it. Having an imaginary file to flick through in my presence matches Ralf's taste for theatrical dramatics. He is a lawyer after all.

The other possibility is that there was no police contact. That Ralf has lied about what he was told. That would match Paul telling me that he hadn't heard anything about Simon being a suspect. That would be very Ralf too.

But why throw that kind of vile shade on my brother? Trash Simon's reputation like that? To make me feel better by suggesting no blame could be attached to me? How could he think that would make me feel better?

Maybe Ralf was trying to blame Simon to make me stop looking, to save me any more anguish. Blame the dead man who can no longer defend himself.

Something makes me wonder what else Ralf has tucked away in this drawer.

He's got the lot. Unpaid parking tickets, threats of legal action from dissatisfied clients, complaints from colleagues accusing him of unethical behaviour. Plenty in here to prove in a court that he's a rogue.

Personal things clog the drawer too. A card from an unidentified woman: 'I hope you die of a rare, incurable and very painful disease.' And another: 'Don't ever contact me again, do you hear? EVER!' It's signed by a single initial and bizarrely a kiss is added. I suppose that could be sarcasm.

Membership cards, passes, frequent-users plastic, and paper debris from holidays, lots of it. He appears to be very keen on holidays, particularly of the romantic variety. A boarding pass for an airport near Venice. A plastic key for a hotel room in the heart of Paris. His less fortunate lovers get trips closer to home, booked in fake names.

I take out a receipt for dinner for two. It's from the Elite Bar at the Stacks Hotel in Norfolk from twelve months ago.

The Stacks Hotel?

I'm really desperate to believe this is an awful coincidence. Now I begin ferreting like an agitated animal through the drawer. There are more receipts from the hotel going back over many years but none from the week of our holiday. There's no proof here that Ralf was in the Stacks Hotel that week. Unless he's destroyed it, of course.

I think about Andre the artist's description of the stranger on the beach. Professional, confident, used to making decisions. A man who'd dressed in a hurry and had his T-shirt on the wrong way. How he was kneeling down and explaining something to Kane and Frances. What was he saying to them and what was Olivia doing while he did it? Why doesn't Frances remember the stranger being on the beach that day, never mind what he explained to her?

My heart thumps in my chest like a burglar alarm going off.

I'm sat rooted in Ralf's chair while my head sways as if it's caught in a strong breeze. I don't know what to do or where to go. I've found dynamite in Ralf's drawer and it feels like it might go off in my face. Olivia didn't like the hotel very much but Ralf obviously does. He's been going there ever since for his assignations. He even uses the same name, Jack Collins, when he books it. I take my phone out of my pocket and call the hotel.

'Hello, I'm calling on behalf of my employer, Jack Collins. I know it's late but is it possible to book a room this weekend for Mr Collins?'

The receptionist gives a slightly suggestive giggle. 'Let me see, I can't give him his regular room but I might be able to fit him in another. Would that be OK?'

'His regular room?' I slowly ask.

'Room 206.'

I ring off. And sit there. OK, he obviously has a thing for the same room that Mark had booked, but that could be coincidence. Who am I kidding? There are no coincidences in the awful story of Sam's death.

I force myself to go through every last item in the drawer to see what else Ralf might have squirreled away in this box of secrets. As if what I've already found was not enough. It's typical of Ralf to leave incriminating evidence lying around where prying eyes might find it. He's so arrogant that he thinks he can talk and manoeuvre his way out of anything. There's no denying his talent for lying, though. I cringe when I remember how he insisted that I see a doctor before he would share this file of blank sheets with me. How he asked me if I were sure that I wanted to hear what was in it because it was a 'tough read'. How he put my interests first to hide his. The more I think about it the angrier I become. That's good, it helps me get over the shock of what I've learned.

There are only three people left alive who can tell me if Ralf really was on the beach that day. And if he was, there are only three people who can tell me what he said to the children. Ralf himself, Frances and Kane. One way or another I'm going to find out whether he was really there, what he said and why he said it.

I'm starting to have more suspicions about Ralf. To confirm if my hunch is true I know exactly where to go. I pick up my phone and call Paul Simpson.

Chapter 41

Was Ralf the man in the hotel all those years ago?

Was Olivia with him?

Was he the man in the slippers on the beach?

These questions thud and hurt my brain as I walk towards the hotel with Paul.

There are still fake palms in the courtyard of the Stacks Hotel; however, from a distance they do look like the real deal. Up close is a feel of quaint homeliness that doesn't come through on its website. Lucky me for me, Paul knows the owner of the Stacks, their relationship stretching back to Paul's days with the local police force.

Just before we enter the reception, Paul warns me, 'The manager can be a bit tetchy. It doesn't take much to ruffle his feathers. So leave the talking to me.'

Paul's not exactly short with me but I still feel his bristling disapproval that I invited Andre de Pierre into my house. On the way to the hotel he proceeded to give me a lecture about stranger danger and how so many crimes actually happen within the four walls of your home. I know he's right, but what mother wouldn't have done what I did? Without the artist's witness account I wouldn't be further along the road to unmasking the secrets that hide what happened to my son.

Paul phoned ahead, so the manager is already waiting for us at reception.

'Leonard' – Paul greets him with a professional handshake and wide smile – 'it's been a long time.'

Leonard is what my dad would've called short and stout; he's a small man with a sizable tummy. But there's an erectness, a poise to the way he holds himself. Also a shrewdness to his gaze that he's developed over the years in his role as a manager.

'Paul.' His face falls slightly. 'I was sorry to hear about Nancy.'

Nancy must be Paul's wife who passed away last year. For a flicker of time, Paul's expression is one of grief that I know so well. Poor Paul.

Leonard continues, 'I thought you had retired.'

'I'm doing some private work now.' Paul's gaze indicates me.

'Why don't I order some coffees on the terrace where we can talk.'

I don't have time for drinks, so I cut to the chase. 'We're investigating the disappearance of a child. He was lost ten years ago on the beach.'

Paul sends me a warning look, a reminder that he's to do all the talking. The simple truth is that I can't just stand here with my mouth shut.

The other man gives me a strange look. The type that makes me feel uncomfortable and small. With a slow movement of his head and body he turns to Paul, cutting me completely out.

'I remember. Ten years back. A terrible tragedy.'

It's as if I don't exist to him and that's when I figure it out. Leonard is one of those men who doesn't like talking business with women. Probably thinks our brains can't handle it. 'Tetchy', Paul diplomatically described him as. Chauvinistic pig is more accurate. However, if keeping my mouth closed means I'll uncover the truth then I'll do it.

Paul tells him, 'New information has come to light. We need to confirm the identity of a witness who we believe was staying at the hotel at the time. Room 206. We'd like your assistance with that.'

The manager scowls. 'There are established protocols for requesting and accessing this sort of information. No disrespect, Paul, but I'm afraid just turning up isn't really an official channel.'

Paul gestures to me. 'This is Alison. She's the mother of Sam, the boy who was tragically lost that day. As his mother, I'm sure you'll agree that she deserves to know the full story of what happened to her little boy.'

Leonard nods, showing a momentary flash of sympathy, then he turns his back on me, addressing Paul again. 'If there's one thing a business hates, it's bad publicity. A police inquiry into a premises, however innocent, is bad publicity.'

Paul addresses me. 'Why don't you get a drink on the terrace while I sort things out with Leonard?'

Paul follows the manager to his office while I head for the terrace. Outside there's a view over the sea. Everywhere you go here seems to have a view over the sea. Various guests are scattered around at the tables; they all look comfortable and well off. It's all very sedate and respectable but there's a slight air of the stuffy about some of them, as there is about this hotel in general.

The place was probably once a country house that offered a secluded getaway for bankers or politicians who wanted somewhere away from prying eyes and fronting the fresh air of the North Sea. The ivy that grows up its walls and crowds the windows looks like a deliberate feature to hide what's going on inside.

◆ ◆ ◆

'It's bad news.'

A very agitated Paul is standing next to me. I've been sitting here admiring the sea with a tall glass of lemonade with a slice of lime in it.

Quickly he perches on a wicker chair at the table. 'The hotel didn't have security cameras back then so there's no way of identifying who may have stayed in room 206. That's assuming someone did occupy the room. Add to that there's a very high turnover of staff, seasonal workers and the like, so there is virtually no one left working here from ten years ago. Leonard's going to take me to their records office but I wouldn't get your hopes up.'

Then he's gone again.

A few minutes later a voice asks, 'Are you all right there, dear?'

An elderly woman is sitting at a neighbouring table. Her silver hair is a stiff bob around her tiny head and she's taking an avid interest in me with very knowing eyes.

'Are you unwell?' Her voice is cultured, each word precisely spoken. 'Only you're mumbling to yourself and grinding your teeth. You can have one of my sick bags. I carry them everywhere.' She starts opening her bag.

My raised hand stops her movement. 'I'm fine, thank you, just a little under the weather, that's all.'

She gets up, her back slightly bent and makes herself comfortable at my table, her bag sitting on the table right next to her. 'You've come to the right place to rejuvenate yourself. A wonderful sauna here.' She leans in. 'I'd recommend Jeremy, he knows where all the pressure points are. I don't think I've seen you before. Are you staying here long?'

'Just a flying visit.'

'Do yourself a favour and book yourself in for a few days. No disrespect intended but you look like you could do with a good old dose of TLC. I'm here in the summer for six months every year. Now, the winter months I spend cruising round the world.'

Suddenly her face creases with laughter. 'It's my way of giving the finger to my children. They're hoping I'll die so they can get their hands on my money but my plan is to spend it all before I go. That'll teach the greedy, ungrateful little so-and-sos. Children aren't always a blessing, are they? Do you have any children, dear?'

In front of me is the beach. 'Two boys. Or rather there were two. One of them was lost not far from here in an accident out at sea.' The word 'accident' sticks in my throat now. 'It happened about ten years ago.'

She's horrified. 'Yes, I remember. The little boy and his brother? They were your sons?' Her bony hand reaches over and takes mine. 'It was awful. All the sirens, the helicopters and boats going out and looking for him. The poor gentleman who was staying here, he must have been one of the family.'

It takes a few seconds before I catch up with what she's telling me. My hand stills beneath hers. 'The poor gentleman? What do you mean?'

She takes her hand back and nods as if we're sharing a secret that shouldn't have been mentioned.

She plays the innocent. 'No, you're right, it must be my mistake. Anyway, it's time for my walk.'

She's about to get up, but my following words keep her in her seat. 'I don't know what your name is, but this is rather important. What makes you think a member of my family was staying here?'

It's not Ralf who comes to mind now, but Mark. Mark was family. Was he lying to me?

She whispers, 'I'm not one for gossip, dear, and I don't like to cast aspersions on people.'

'Gossip all you like and cast any aspersions you want.'

Given permission, she settles in. 'Well, dear, there was a gentleman staying at the hotel at the time of your son's accident. All week, this man used to get visits from someone, sometimes in the morning, sometimes in the afternoon, sometimes in the evening. It was pretty obvious to some of us that these were illicit assignations. Nookie on the side. You get my drift.'

She coughs as if she's getting rid of a bad taste after having uttered the word 'nookie'. 'Anyway, on the afternoon of your son's accident, he came racing out of the hotel looking very worried and took off in that car of his at high speed. I was having a late lunch at the time on this very terrace.'

This fits with Andre the artist's description of the mystery man on the beach wearing slippers and who appeared to have dressed in a rush.

'What about the woman he was seeing?'

'The lady friend appeared from the hotel too. She looked upset and took off at high speed. I think she called a cab. This was about the time that helicopters were flying around down the coast and boats were putting to sea. That was the last we saw of either of them. The gentleman and his lady friend were in a terrible state so we assumed later when we heard the news that they must be something to do with the family. Possibly even the mother – you know, a mother's tears.'

I know a mother's tears well. 'Did you hear what their names were?'

'I'm afraid not. I can tell you what they looked like though.'

I know who the lady friend is. It's a pitch-perfect description of Olivia, right down to the fact that she walked around with her nose in the air and clearly thought the hotel was too low rent for her. But it's the man's description that stays with me.

Paul appears with a disappointed face and the old lady returns to her table. 'I'm afraid there was nothing in the office to help. It looks like we've drawn a blank.'

But he's wrong. We haven't.

The old lady's description of the man I will never forget: 'Flashy and cocky with it too. Full of himself. He drove a noisy car, you know, the showbiz type. We all noticed him.'

Chapter 42

'I'm sure Ralf was having sex with my sister while you were being lost at sea.'

I've forgotten that I'm not supposed to be speaking to Sam anymore. I don't like mentioning sex to my eleven-year-old either. But I've come to the memorial gardens because I've got no one else I can trust to tell what's happened. At least the lost can't betray you the way I've been betrayed by my sister and that smarmy shark Ralf. I'll share what I've learned with Paul, but he won't understand the devastating emotional punch of what I've discovered. How could he? He's not family. My son is family and he might understand if he can listen.

I so desperately want to believe he can.

'Simon rang your Aunt Olivia after you were lost and then it's obvious that she sent Ralf down to the beach to sort things out. He turns up on the beach to talk to your brother and Frances. This is before they even call the police. Can you believe that? He must have been saying something important to them but I can't work out what it was. Meanwhile your Uncle Simon is just standing there, letting him get on with it. Typical Simon.' That's unkind so I remember to add, 'May your uncle rest in peace. Then your aunt shows up later blaming me for what happened.'

I hoped coming here would help me control my anger. It doesn't do to lose your temper in front of children and Sam is still a child. I am losing it but this is still better than the alternative of heading to an off-licence and buying a bottle of wine, which is what I really want to do. Sometimes I think that a few hours of oblivion and whatever erratic behaviour might follow have to be better than dealing with what I'm learning. All the things I tell Sam are a jumble and half of them don't make any sense. I want to tell him about Rocky and Frances and how I got that all wrong but he doesn't know who Rocky is either. It's all a muddle.

'I don't trust Frances anymore. She's a nice girl but it looks to me as if Ralf is using and manipulating her the same way he did with me for his own ends. I think he's brainwashed her. She saw that file when she went into his office. I told her what it looked like and where it was. It was so easy to find, it took me about thirty seconds. She must have seen it. She must be scared of Ralf or her mother, or both of them. What have they got on her?'

It crosses my mind that even now Ralf and Olivia might still be in a relationship. That they might be plotting together to hide the truth from me. Neither of them was on the beach though when Sam was lost, so what have they got to hide?

'It doesn't make any sense. Why are they doing this? Why did Ralf make up those things about Simon? No one's blaming anyone, so why all the lying? Because Ralf and my sister were lovers? At the end of the day, who cares?'

I do care actually, it's not clear to me why but I do. I'm convinced it has something to do with Sam's disappearance.

The dog walkers and those who come to lay flowers and tend to the memorials have thinned out now. It's getting dark and they'll be closing the gates soon. Some of those who are still walking their dogs or mourning loved ones are walking by where I sit on the bench across the pathway from Sam's simple brass plate. They look over their shoulders as they pass, looking at the woman talking to her missing son. Let them look.

'That Rocky knows something,' I tell Sam. 'She was Frances's best friend at school. Your cousin saved her from the bullies in the playground. Frances hates bullies apparently. Your cousin must be having a hard time, going from Olivia's home to work for Ralf and then back again to her mother's. That's a shooting gallery of bullies, a twenty-four-hour exposure to them. But I don't think Rocky is going to help me. She's too close to Frances.'

In my very worst moments in the memorial gardens, I sometimes came to believe that Sam was trying to talk to me. Not with words, things never got that bad, but with the natural elements around us. When the breeze blew, it was as if he were whispering to me. When a storm came up, it was as if he were angry with me for not being there for him or not taking him to that wretched recital at the pub. When the leaves rustled in the trees, it was as if he was speaking words of comfort to me and telling me not to be upset, that he was all right. On one occasion a double rainbow appeared over the horizon, and I felt it was Sam's way of saying that we were still together, he and I. When the raindrops fell, it was as if they were my son's tears. Perhaps the passers-by are right, I am a mad woman sitting on a bench talking to the dead, but it all made sense to me.

The sky is clouding over now and the gradually fading light turns to gloom in a few minutes. The clouds are rushing over the sky as if they're drawing curtains and putting out lights. Watching those clouds hurrying along, a thought occurs to me. Where was Ralf running to after speaking to Simon, Kane and Frances? According to Andre he went down to the beach from the cliff top where he must have parked his car. Instead of going back to it though, he headed up the beach in the opposite direction carrying something under his arm, a blanket or a sheet. Where was he going, what was he doing and why? What did he do after that?

It seems pretty clear to me that Ralf must have left the scene as soon as he could, leaving Olivia to turn up on the beach shortly afterwards to start blaming me. She must know what happened if she was lying in bed with Ralf when Simon called her. Simon will have told them what happened – he wasn't crafty enough to invent a story himself. They'll have sat in that hotel room deciding what to do next. It will have been Olivia who sent Ralf down to the scene to sort things out and Ralf who would have known what to do. He would have known what to do afterwards to make sure the story was sound and added up. After that he had no questions to answer because it was as if he had never been there. Classic Ralf. To never have been there in the first place. As long as the others all kept silent. Simon, Olivia and Ralf knew how to do that even if it cost poor Simon his life in the end and Frances and Kane went along with it. Meanwhile, I can't prove anything.

There is one other person who knows and who isn't saying and that's my Sam. I listen to the wind and the leaves. I search the darkened skies to see if he's trying to say something to me and only get silence in return. For a moment, I become angry with Sam. He knows but he won't tell me. 'We're all going to be lost, Sam, if you don't find a way to say something.'

A gentle cough behind me is a sign that I have company. 'The gardens are closing in five minutes. Could you make your way to the gates, please?'

It's another one of these guys whose job it is to police the place. He's another one of these shadowy figures trying to stop me getting to the truth. I'm not in the mood to be told what to do. 'It's bad manners to interrupt somebody else's conversation. Can't you see I'm talking to someone? Go away.'

He draws breath. 'Five minutes.'

He doesn't even give me those minutes. He takes a jangle of keys out of his pocket and heads off towards the gates. With a colleague, he begins to pull the wrought-iron gates closed. They're heavy and it gives me time to say goodbye to Sam and hurry the fifty yards to the gates if I don't want to be locked in again. 'I'll come back, Sam. I'm sorry if I was a bit short with you. You understand how it is at the moment.'

I hurry over to the entrance where one of the two guys holds one gate slightly open so I can squeeze through. But I can't. I just can't. I squeeze the other way back into the gardens and run over to where Sam's plate stands. I run my fingers over it, the engraving of his name, look up at the clouds, raise an arm and open my hand towards the sky and scream.

'Sam! Help me!'

Chapter 43

I'm sitting on the bonnet of Ralf's car. The reason being I've already been into his office where I was given the usual 'He isn't available' runaround. So I left and located his car parked a few streets away. Then left him a message telling him where to find me. It's only fifteen minutes before he appears, bristling and glowering.

'What do you think you're playing at?'

I respond a lot cooler than I am inside. 'Like I explained in my message, we need to talk.'

His jaw clenches, a visible sign of the anger he's fighting to control. 'My receptionist informed me you'd turned up in the office. I thought I'd better check my car to see if you'd trashed or keyed it.'

I wriggle my behind as if I'm settling in for the evening. 'Now why would I do that?'

'What do you want, Alison?'

'I want to talk about holidays, affairs, hotel rooms, vicious lies about dead family members, brothers, nieces, sons and lots of other secrets that must never be told.'

Ralf's complacent and self-satisfied grin suggests two things.

One: he's expecting my questions.

Two: he's got answers to them.

'I don't know what you're talking about.' His smile dies away. 'Are you going to get off my motor? Why don't you get into the passenger seat and we can talk?' When I hesitate, he adds, 'Or are you worried I'll drive you off to the woods and do you in? Is that how far down the rabbit hole you are now with your wild accusations and unlikely theories?'

I get into the car and go on the attack when he joins me. I mean to stay calm and wring answers out of him but it's a struggle. 'You lied about my brother! You told me Simon was a suspect! That the police thought he'd done something to my son!'

'Of course I did,' Ralf says, his fingers tapping an irritated rhythm on the steering wheel. 'I was trying to help you out. You don't seem to understand that's what I've been trying to do since the start.'

He turns in his seat to face me, his eyes hard. 'I told you from the moment the letter from Mark's solicitor arrived to let him get on with it. But no, you had to resist, you had to chase wild geese.'

Ralf's gaze bores into me. 'You had to cling on to the idea that Sam might be out there somewhere and now that's turned into a bizarre quest to prove something wasn't right about the accepted version of what happened.'

He leans back against his seat, running a hand through his hair in frustration. 'I was hoping if I threw a little shade on Simon, you might pack it in but no, you had to press on. And now look at you and now look at Kane.'

I'm moments away from hitting him. 'You thought telling me that my brother was a violent abuser who may have harmed my son was helping me out?'

He shrugs. 'Yes, I do. If you'd dropped this business and got on with your life. Be honest, it must have crossed your mind anyway that Simon was to blame in some way. He was supposed to be keeping an eye on the children and he failed. He really was to blame as far as I'm concerned, he might as well have done Sam over.'

What a wicked thing to say!

A curious expression flushes Ralf's face. 'How do you know I made it up anyway?'

Only the hope of getting some answers out of Ralf is keeping me in this car. 'I went through your office and found the file you waved at me. You know, the one with the blank pages you described as a tough read.'

Ralf is impressed. 'Good for you. Nice to see you showing some initiative for a change. Anything else you want to interrogate me about?'

He's back drumming that stupid beat on the steering wheel. I think he's actually enjoying this. I turn my face to him in a futile attempt to show him how I angry I am. 'I know you were in that hotel with my sister that afternoon. Room 206. Your favourite room?' He remains expressionless. 'I know she sent you down to the beach. I know you tried to fix everything down there with Simon and the children. What were you trying to fix?'

Ralf sighs. 'You don't know any of those things and you certainly can't prove them because they're not true. You're wrong, I've never been to any hotel in Norfolk.' He catches my eye. 'All right, that's not quite true, there have been a few visits to that place over the years. I suppose you dug that up in my office as well? Found receipts for the Stacks Hotel. But I certainly wasn't there that day with Olivia so the rest of your story goes down like a badly cooked souffle. Have you got any proof I was in the vicinity? No, you haven't.'

Of course, he's a lawyer, so he's going to try to wrong-foot me with the 'where's your evidence' card.

'Kane and Frances know you were there. Olivia knows too. One day, soon, they'll all tell the truth.'

His smugness grows because he senses he's safe. 'You might be able to persuade Kane, Frances and Olivia to change their story to humour their mad family member, but I suspect the authorities will be a little sceptical about people who stuck to one story for ten years and then came up with another one after all this time.'

I had to be brave to confront Ralf but my bravery has been for nothing. There is one question I want an answer to and he might have the decency to be honest about it. 'When you were shacked up in bed with my sister after that day, did it not occur to you to suggest to her that it was cruel and sadistic to blame me for the loss of my own son?'

Ralf rolls his head back, laughs and drawls, 'Ah . . . ! Now we're getting to the real issue here! Now we're getting to why you've decided to loop Olivia and me into your fairy story of the big bad wolf on the beach. That's why you've turned on me, your only real friend in this whole miserable business.'

Abruptly another piece of the jigsaw slips into place. 'All that talk of you and Olivia hating each other, it was obviously never true. You made it up to keep me and everyone else off the scent of your affair.'

He sneers. 'You're jealous! Jealous of your sister and the fact I was having a thing with her instead of you. And no, I'm not denying it. We weren't in that hotel that day but we were in plenty of other places.' A malicious gleam fires up his eyes. 'We fucked in that seat you're sitting in many times.'

Disgust floods me, but there's no way on this earth I am going to let him see the effect his filthy words are having on me.

'That's what this is really all about,' he says. 'I always thought she was jealous of you. It's supposed to have been the piano thing, wasn't it? You were better than her on the ivories and won the place at the music college which you then blew to look after your father? And marry that loser, Mark? Whereas in fact you were jealous of her. She's better looking, married up, made something of herself and hooked up with a virile lover like me. While you'll always be a fisherman's daughter.'

I punch him squarely on the nose. That will show him how much of a fisherman's daughter I am. I'm not into violence in any shape or form. Well, not usually. This disgusting excuse for a man who pretended to be my friend needed smacking down to size.

Howling in pain and disbelief, he holds his palm to where the blow has landed. 'You can't do that. That's assault! I'm calling the police.'

'Call them. I'll be wanting to talk to them myself when I find out what really happened. What your role really was.'

I slam out of his fancy car. With my fist I smash one wing mirror and before he can stop me, rush around the other side and smash the other one too. There's blood on my fingers and it's smeared on the driver's side door when I pull it open.

My phone rings. With contempt I make a vow to Ralf. 'I'm not done with you.'

I slam the car door and as I rapidly walk away I pull out my phone.

It's Paul. He sounds edgy. 'I'm on your doorstep. Get here right now. I've got some information you'll want to hear.'

Chapter 44

I walk Paul into my kitchen. He looks like he ran here, his clothes slightly in disarray and his hair ruffled. He was the definition of a cat on a hot tin roof when I arrived back home. Jittery, shifting from one foot to the other.

I head for the sink where I turn on the tap and run the water over my knuckles to wash the blood away from where I damaged Ralf's car. The water is soothing and refreshing against my skin.

Paul moves over to inspect the damage. 'What happened? Did someone hurt you?' He looks about ready to take the world on for me.

I shake my head. 'It was the other way around.' As I gently rinse my hand I tell him, 'It turns out the man in the hotel with my sister was my lawyer.'

I make a cup of tea and fill him in. He's incredulous by the end. 'So you think Ralf was the man on the beach? That Andre de Pierre was telling the truth?'

'It all makes sense. Ralf, Olivia, Simon . . .' I inhale deeply. 'I'm hoping what you've found out will help.'

Paul takes strong sips of his tea before answering. 'I've been digging into some old files, calling in a few more favours. I'm kicking myself because I should have remembered this.'

'I can't imagine you of all people forgetting something important.'

'It turns out that both Kane and Frances were interviewed by a police child psychologist straight after what happened on the beach.'

I freeze, the mug halfway to my lips. 'What? Why wasn't I told about this?'

'It was standard procedure,' Paul explains gently. 'But what's interesting is who conducted the interviews. Dr Amma Young.'

The name doesn't ring any bells. 'Should I know her?'

'She's quite renowned in the field of working with children. She's retired now, but she's agreed to meet with us at her home in London.'

I lean back in my chair, processing this new information. A whirlwind of questions race through my mind. What could Kane and Frances have said to this psychologist? Why wasn't I informed about these interviews at the time? And most importantly, could their words hold the key to understanding what really happened that day?

'Tell me more about Dr Young,' I press, leaning forward. 'What exactly is her expertise? And why weren't we given access to these interviews before?'

Paul sighs, running a hand through his hair. 'She is considered one of the foremost practitioners when it comes to childhood trauma. She's developed techniques to help children open up about difficult experiences without leading them on or contaminating their memories.'

I nod, absorbing this. 'But why keep it from us? From me? I'm Sam's mother, for God's sake.'

'It's complicated, Alison,' Paul calmly explains. 'In cases like these, sometimes information is compartmentalised to protect the integrity of the investigation. And to be honest, given your state at the time . . .'

He trails off, but I know what he means. In those early days after Sam's death, I was barely functioning. The thought of my grief being used as a reason to keep information from me stings, but I can't deny the logic.

'What do you think we might learn from her?' I ask, trying to keep my voice steady.

Paul considers me with a steady stare. 'It's hard to say. Children often see things adults miss or interpret events differently. And in a traumatic situation like that day on the beach, there might be details that Kane or Frances noticed but didn't think to mention to anyone else.'

My mind conjures up possibilities. Could Kane have seen something he didn't understand at the time? Or Frances? Sweet Frances who as an adult has gone out of her way to help Kane. Could she have witnessed something crucial?

'When can we go?' I ask, already mentally rearranging my schedule.

'Tomorrow, if you're free. I thought we could drive down together.'

I nod, grateful for his support. We sit in companionable silence for a moment, sipping our tea. There's something I've been wanting to ask him, and now seems as good a time as any.

'Paul,' I begin hesitantly, 'I hope you don't mind me saying this, but I've always felt there was something personal driving you to help me. Something beyond professional duty.'

He sets down his mug, his eyes growing distant. 'You're right. There is a reason Sam's case has always stayed with me.'

I wait, giving him space to continue.

223

'When I was a boy, about Sam's age, I had a best friend named Tommy. We were inseparable, always getting into mischief together.' A sad smile flits across his face.

I can see where this is going, my heart already aching for the young Paul.

As I watch Paul struggle with his emotions, he opens up. 'It was a day just like any other summer day. Bright, hot, the kind of day where the beach calls to you. Tommy and I had been planning our adventure all week.' He pauses, lost in the memory. 'We packed sandwiches, told our mums we'd be back for tea. The beach was busy, but we found a spot to ourselves, away from the main crowd. We were always looking for a bit of mischief, you see.'

I nod, thinking of Sam and how he was always seeking out his own adventures.

'We swam for a while, then decided to see who could swim out the furthest.' Paul's voice catches. 'I was ahead, and when I turned back, I couldn't see Tommy. I thought he was playing a trick on me at first, diving under the water. But then I saw his hand, just for a moment, before it disappeared again.'

I feel a chill run down my spine, despite the warmth of the kitchen.

'I was a strong swimmer, but Tommy . . . I tried to reach him, I really did. But the current was so strong, and I was tired from swimming out so far. By the time I managed to drag him back to shore . . .' Paul trails off, shaking his head.

'Oh, Paul,' I breathe, reaching out to touch his hand. 'I'm so sorry. You were just a child. It wasn't your fault.'

Paul meets my eyes, and I see a reflection of the lifetime of guilt I carry. 'I know that, logically. But knowing doesn't always make the feeling go away.'

'Is that why you became a police officer?'

'Partly,' he admits. 'I wanted to help people, to prevent tragedies like that if I could. But I think it's also why I've never been able to let go of Sam's case. Something about it has never sat right with me, just as it hasn't with you.'

I squeeze his hand again, feeling a surge of affection for this man who has become such an ally in my search for the truth.

'Thank you for telling me, Paul. And thank you for not giving up.'

As Paul prepares to leave, I find myself lost in thought. The prospect of learning what Kane and Frances might have told Dr Young fills me with both anticipation and dread. What if their words confirm my worst fears? Or what if they reveal something I'm not prepared to hear?

I think of Kane, how withdrawn he became after Sam's death. At the time, I attributed it to grief, to the trauma of losing a brother. But now, I wonder – was there more to it? And Frances, always so quiet, so watchful. Did she see something that day that her young mind couldn't process?

Chapter 45

The door swings open, revealing Dr Amma Young. She stands tall and straight, her posture speaking of a lifetime of purpose and discipline. Despite her age, there's a zest about her that many younger people would envy. Her movements are precise and deliberate, no energy wasted. Her gaze is sharp and assessing, as if she's still in the habit of diagnosing at a glance. It's clear that retirement hasn't dulled her edge one bit.

Because she worked with children I was expecting a motherly-type character. Someone soft around the edges, with gentle laugh lines fanning from the corners of her eyes.

Although Dr Young greets us with a warm smile there's a steely authority beneath it. 'Please, come in.'

We step into a small but charming mews house in London's fashionable and terribly expensive Notting Hill. The walls are all pastel with a sense of calm that I suspect is no accident, given Dr Young's profession.

'Thank you for agreeing to meet with us, Dr Young,' Paul says as we follow her into a living room that's filled with knick-knacks that she must have collected from around the world.

'Please, call me Amma,' she insists, gesturing for us to take a seat on a sofa draped with a blanket. Its vibrant colours take me back to a holiday I had with the boys and Mark in Mexico.

She settles into an armchair opposite us, her back as straight as a dancer's.

'I must admit, I was initially reluctant to discuss this. But given your involvement in the original investigation, Mr Simpson, I felt it was important to share what I know.'

My heart races. After all these years, could we finally be close to some answers?

'Is this about your interview with Kane?' I blurt out, unable to contain my anxiety. The thought of my surviving son carrying some terrible secret all these years makes my stomach churn.

Amma shakes her head gently. 'No, Ms Taylor. This concerns my interview with Frances.'

I blink in surprise. Frances? I honestly thought our visit would be concerning Kane.

'What about Frances?' I ask, leaning forward.

Amma takes a deep breath. 'When I first met with Frances, she was incredibly emotional. Crying constantly, barely able to speak through her tears.'

I nod, remembering how distraught Frances had been on the day itself and in the days following Sam's death.

'But,' Amma continues, her brow furrowing slightly, 'something about it felt . . . off. Forced, even. As our session progressed, I began to suspect that her display of emotion wasn't entirely genuine.'

'What do you mean?' Paul cuts in, his cop instincts clearly aroused.

'It's difficult to explain,' Amma says. 'But after years of working with traumatised children, you develop a sense for these things. Frances's grief seemed performative, somehow. As if she was playing a role she thought was expected of her.'

A chill runs down my spine. I remember Frances at the gathering Mark had organised at the house, her face buried in her mother's side, her small shoulders shaking with sobs. Had that all been an act?

'Unfortunately,' Amma continues, 'I wasn't able to explore this further. Frances's mother arrived and abruptly ended the session, refusing to allow any further interviews.'

'That sounds like Olivia,' I mutter, thinking of my strong-willed sister.

'Get out of my house.' Her remembered scream suddenly echoes in my head.

Amma nods. 'I was concerned, but without the family's cooperation, there was little I could do. However, sometime later, I received some disturbing information from Frances's school.' She pauses, her eyes searching my face. 'Are you aware that Frances was involved in an incident where she helped another student who was being bullied?'

'Yes,' I respond quickly. 'I know the girl who was bullied. Her name is Rocky. She sees Frances as her saviour.'

'But there's more to the story,' Amma confirms. 'Shortly after this incident, the alleged bully became very ill. She was hospitalised with severe gastrointestinal issues – stomach pain, nausea, vomiting.'

Paul's expression becomes very grave. 'Are you suggesting that Frances had something to do with this?'

Amma gives us a maybe she did, maybe she didn't shrug. 'The school's headteacher suspected that Frances might have poisoned the girl, possibly with some kind of household substance that contained anti-freeze. But they couldn't prove anything.'

My mind reels. Sweet, quiet Frances? The girl who helped Kane.

'I don't believe this. Frances is a lovely girl. Caring and considerate. Poison a child?' I shake my head in forceful denial.

Amma's voice quietens. 'I'm telling you what the school told me. However, I'm fitting this to my own observations of Frances and the rounded conclusion I came to was that she was a very complex child.'

'Olivia must have been furious at the accusation,' I say, thinking of my sister's fierce protectiveness.

'Indeed.' Amma compresses her lips. 'She threatened to sue the school if they spread what she considered to be malicious lies about her daughter. The matter was quickly dropped.'

A heavy silence falls over the room as Paul and I absorb this information. My thoughts are in turmoil.

If – *if* – Frances was capable of such an act, what else might she be capable of? And how does this relate to Sam's death?

'Dr Young . . . Amma,' I begin, my voice shaking slightly. 'Why are you telling us this now? Do you think it has something to do with what happened to my son?'

For the first time Amma displays some emotion. Her features are strained with concern. 'I can't say for certain, but given the circumstances of your son's death, and the inconsistencies I noticed in Frances's behaviour during our brief session, I felt it was information you should have.'

Paul clears his throat. 'Did you share these concerns with anyone at the time?'

Amma shakes her head. 'By the time I learned about the incident at school, the investigation into Sam's death was already closed. And without concrete evidence, it was just speculation. But it's haunted me over the years, especially knowing the pain your family must have endured.'

I feel as though the ground is shifting beneath me. All these years, I've been searching for answers, never imagining they might lead back to my own family. To Frances, of all people. Then again, all the other people I suspect are in my family too.

'What do you think we should do with this information?' I ask, looking between Amma and Paul.

Paul rubs his chin thoughtfully. 'It's certainly concerning, but as Amma said, there's no concrete evidence. We'll need to tread carefully.'

Amma nods in agreement. 'I wish I could offer you more. But I hope that sharing this might help in some way, even if it's just to provide you with peace of mind.'

Peace? There will be no peace now.

As we prepare to leave, Amma takes my hand, in a surprisingly strong grip. 'Have you spoken to Kane about what happened?'

She won't let go of my hand.

The question leaves me winded. It's the one place I haven't been able to go. I'm terrified about what might happen. My strained expression is all the answer she needs.

She looks me directly in the eye. 'Kane isn't a child anymore. You must ask him what he saw that day.'

I'm silent on the way back and am grateful that Paul gives me the space to think. Now I'm no longer pill-popping or drowning in a bottle I'm much more clear-minded. Which means I can recall more about the past. And the incident I can now remember gives what Amma told us another twist of the knife.

Chapter 46

THE SISTERS

Alison shifted uncomfortably on the sleek leather sofa, feeling out of place in her sister's opulent coastal home. Olivia strode across the room, her designer stilettos clicking on the hardwood floor, the hem of her Chanel cocktail dress swaying with each step as she poured two glasses of wine.

'So, about Dad's cottage,' Alison began, her voice hesitant.

Olivia waved a manicured hand dismissively. 'Oh, that old place? Sell it, keep it, whatever you think is best, darling. I'm sure you could use the money more than I could.'

The patronising tone wasn't lost on Alison. She gripped her glass tighter, remembering the cramped two-bedroom flat she'd left behind in the city.

'It's not about the money, Oli. It's our childhood home.'

Olivia's smile tightened. 'You know I hate being called that.' She carried on over Alison's mumbled apology. 'A quaint little fisherman's cottage, yes. How . . . charming.' She took a deliberate sip of wine, her gaze drifting to the expansive ocean view beyond the floor-to-ceiling windows.

From another room, the disjointed notes of a piano drifted through the house. Olivia's face lit up. 'Ah, that's Frances practising. She's quite the prodigy, you know.'

Alison bit her tongue, resisting the urge to point out that the melody was barely recognisable. Instead, she tried to steer the conversation back to their father's property. 'Look, I know you're not interested in keeping the cottage, but—'

'Did I mention that Frances won first place in her school's talent show last month?' Olivia interrupted, her voice brimming with pride. 'The judges were absolutely blown away by her performance.'

Alison forced a smile, all too aware of the growing divide between them. While she struggled to make ends meet, Olivia seemed determined to forget their humble beginnings entirely.

Suddenly, an acrid smell filled the air. Alison sat up straight, alarm bells ringing in her head. 'Do you smell smoke?'

Olivia frowned, sniffing delicately. Her eyes widened in panic. 'Oh God, it's coming from the music room!'

They rushed out of the lounge, following the thickening smoke to its source. When they burst into the ornate music room, they were met with a shocking sight. The grand piano was engulfed in flames, and Frances stood nearby, her expression oddly blank.

'Frances! What happened?' Olivia cried, rushing to her daughter's side.

The housekeeper appeared, armed with a fire extinguisher. She quickly doused the flames, leaving behind a charred and ruined instrument.

'I didn't do anything,' Frances said, her voice eerily calm. 'It just caught fire while I was playing.'

Olivia wrapped her arms protectively around her daughter. 'Of course you didn't, sweetheart. It must have been an electrical fault or something.'

Alison watched the scene unfold, a chill running down her spine. She observed Frances's unblinking stare, the lack of surprise or fear in the girl's manner and attitude. A nagging suspicion took root in her mind, one she couldn't shake despite Olivia's unwavering belief in her daughter's innocence.

As the acrid smoke cleared, Alison found herself asking a question she never thought she'd have to consider: why would Frances set fire to the piano?

Chapter 47

I've got to ask Kane what happened that day.

But I'm afraid to. The last time I did, when he was a child, things went badly. Got out of control. Nevertheless, I've reached a point when I can almost touch the truth with my fingertips. I was so hoping that I could wade through the lies to discover the truth without involving my son. He's suffered enough. But I'm stuck between a rock and a hard place.

As a mother, do I think of the needs of my living son? Or those of the one that tragically died?

No mother should have to make such a terrible choice.

I'm in the kitchen, so I turn the tap on and fill up my glass with water. The chemical taste is tangy and slightly off. I hear the front door open and close. Rocky and Kane are laughing. I listen to the sound for a while, soaking it up. It feels good to have laughter back in this house.

That brings an idea to me. Maybe I should ask Rocky to ask Kane? I think it over. Is that really fair? The truth is that she doesn't really know him so well. She came to keep an eye on him, to make sure that he is OK. It wouldn't be fair to drag her into the middle of our murky family history. No, I don't have any choice. This is something I'm going to have to be brave enough to do myself.

So, with a heavy heart I make my way up the stairs. Inside his room, Rocky and Kane have their heads together at his computer table playing a game on screen. I don't have to see their faces to know that they're laughing. Suddenly I wish that Rocky was his girlfriend. For real. He needs someone special to lean on.

Maybe I make a noise because Kane turns to the door. 'Mum?'

My tongue nervously flicks out and wets my bottom lip. 'Can I have a word? Downstairs in the living room.'

Immediately he tenses. Rocky lays a comforting and calming palm on his leg.

I turn and leave, to indicate that I mean business. That he should follow. I want this to go as easily as possible so I compose myself on the sofa. Kane hesitates in the doorway as if crossing it will make or break him. And maybe it will. I hope that it doesn't. That this doesn't push him over the edge.

His gaze never leaving me, he comes inside and perches on the arm of the sofa facing me. 'Mum, what's up?'

I take a deep breath. 'What happened that day? The day Sam disappeared.'

The colour drains from his face, and he seems to shrink back into his skin. 'Mum! Don't! Please!'

'I need to know, Kane,' I plead with him. 'I've been too afraid to ask, but I can't keep running from the truth.'

His hands ball into fists at his sides. 'You want the truth? Fine. The truth is, you've never been able to look at me without seeing Sam. Your perfect, golden boy.'

His words hit me like a savage blow. 'What?' I can't believe what he's telling me. What he's accusing me of. 'That's not true,' I say. 'I love you both the same. You're my children. My sons.'

'Am I?' His eyes flash. 'Because sometimes it feels like I'm just a poor substitute for the child you lost. That Sam is your only son.'

An emotional lump forms in my throat, but I swallow it down. 'Kane, no. I know I haven't been the best mother, but I love you. I've always loved you.'

'But not as much as you love him, right?' His voice cracks, raw with pain. 'I'm competing with a ghost, Mum. And I'll never measure up. You even call me by his name sometimes.'

Do I? I'm so shocked I can't move. I don't remember mixing up the names of my sons. Especially the name of one that's dead. If that's what I've been doing, that's a terrible thing. I never had any idea that Kane felt like this.

I reach for him, desperate to bridge this terrible chasm between us. 'Kane, please. I'm sorry. I just need to understand what happened that day.'

A shudder runs through him, and he wraps his arms around himself. 'I can't talk about it.'

'You have to!' The words burst out, harsher than I intend. 'There are parts of the story of what happened on the beach that don't add up . . .'

I never finish because suddenly Kane's eyes widen, a look of sheer panic overtaking his features. He staggers up and back, fighting to get air into his lungs.

No! No! No! Not this. Not again.

Rocky rushes in. 'Kane? What's wrong?'

But he doesn't seem to hear her. His eyes roll back, and he collapses to the floor, his body jerking and spasming.

'Kane!' I cry out, dropping to my knees beside him. It's happening again.

Rocky hovers nearby, her face a mask of concern. 'Should I call an ambulance?'

I shake my head, my voice tight as I try to hold Kane's thrashing form. 'No. It'll pass. It always does.'

I know because this is what always happened when he was asked about that day when he was a boy. Knowing the physical and emotional toll it took on him, I stopped asking.

Until today.

◆ ◆ ◆

'You're a good mum,' Rocky whispers as she sits back down by Kane's bedside.

I'm holding Kane's hand on the opposite side to her. It's been a couple of hours since Kane had his turn. Just like when it occurred when he was a child, but it's taken longer for him to become conscious again and open his eyes.

Rocky's words almost bring tears to my eyes. When was the last time anyone called me a good mother?

She explains, 'At first I thought you didn't care about Kane. It was like he didn't exist to you. The only one that mattered was Sam.' My head dips with shame because she's right. I don't interrupt her. 'But just now, the way you took care of Kane when he collapsed. The way you tended him was so tender. I wish I'd had a mum like that.'

'Didn't you get on with her?'

Rocky shrugs. 'She didn't give me much choice because she did a bunk when I was two. All I remember was she smelt nice. Years later my dad told me that was the fine wines she knocked back.'

We laugh gently at that.

Almost as if I can hear the question in her head, I tell Rocky, 'The first time it ever happened was a week after Sam disappeared. I was making Kane breakfast before he went to school and I just asked him what happened on the beach.' The memory makes me draw in a long breath. 'He stared up at me, his eyes sort of twisted and then he fell. Bang onto the floor. I thought I'd lost another son.'

'Alison,' Rocky tells me softly. 'You don't have to—'

I fix her with an intense gaze. 'But don't you see? That's been the problem in this family. Always hiding behind "You don't have to". Shoving all our secrets inside a box and taping it shut.' My voice is strained. 'I'm tired of it. Tired of all the shit.'

Finally, I dare to say aloud something terrible that's been inside me. 'Someone close to me isn't telling the truth about what happened to Sam. Someone close to me is lying.'

'Mum?' That's Kane's voice.

Thank goodness. A weight lifts off me. His bleary gaze checks me over. 'Did I . . . ?' His tongue sounds heavy.

I'm not going to lie to him. 'Yes. But you're fine. Don't worry, I won't ask you any more questions.'

The air he draws in makes his chest rise. 'I want to. Not now. Soon.'

His words hang in the air with a strange mix of promise and dread. I nod, not trusting myself to speak. The truth is coming, whether we're ready for it or not. And I'm not sure any of us are prepared for what it might reveal.

Chapter 48

The jarring notes of 'My Old Man Said Follow the Van' crash through my restless sleep, dragging me awake. It feels like I've just managed to get to sleep because I was tossing and turning so much worrying about Kane's reaction earlier. The music is not the gentle, teasing version Olivia and I would play. This version is furious. A pounding, electrifying rendition that seems to shake the very foundations of the house. The music reverberates through the walls, each note a horrific shout in the quiet night. The piano sounds so angry.

My heart furiously beats in time with the frenzied tempo. The music swells, filling every corner of my attic bedroom with its urgent, almost desperate energy. There's something about the music tonight that terrifies me. Makes me want to stay here in this room at the top of the house and never leave.

I'd thought – hoped – the music in the night had stopped. Had left me alone. For the last few days, it hasn't been here. In fact it's vanished since I saw the doctor and stopped drowning my sorrows in booze and meds. So why has it come back. Why now?

But this can't be Rocky. Which means . . .

Kane? But he doesn't play. Does he? Or is it Sam? The shadowy presence in the footage I captured in the music room. Or is it me, going mad?

I have to stop it, once and for all.

Stomach churning, I throw back the duvet. Swing my legs over the side of the bed. They're trembling so badly, I'm not sure if I'll be able to stand. Holding on to the bedpost, I stand up. The floor is shockingly cold against my bare feet. The music continues, relentless and demanding.

I make my way to the door, each step careful and measured. The narrow staircase is shrouded in darkness, but the music guides me. It's pulling me, almost against my will, towards the first floor.

As I descend, the melody grows louder, more insistent. I reach the bottom of the stairs, my hand trailing along the banister for support. I keep moving through the jet-black dark until I'm on the ground floor and outside the music room. Suddenly the panic starts rising, because I haven't been able to bear being in this room since I was shoved inside.

The music room door is partially open. A sliver of yellow lights spills out into the hallway. I reach out my hand. Then freeze. Who will I find when I push it open? Rocky? Kane? Or Sam?

I touch the door. Start to push. I'm about to reach for the handle when without warning a pair of hands grip my shoulders from behind. I try to cry out, but no sound escapes my mouth. The world spins, goes dark—

◆ ◆ ◆

I'm sitting at the piano, my fingers flying over the keys. The music – that same fanatical version of 'My Old Man' – is pouring from my own hands. I stare down in disbelief, watching my fingers move of their own accord, creating this storm of sound.

What's happening? How did I get here?

Confusion and fear battle within me. The music flowing from my fingers feels both alien and intimately familiar, as if I'm reconnecting with a part of myself I'd forgotten existed.

The hands are still pressing on my shoulders. The heat of whoever is behind sinks into my flesh. Slowly, I turn my head to look up and discover who it is.

Kane.

What's he doing in the music room?

'What am I doing here?' I ask, my voice barely audible over the music that my hands don't seem to be able to stop playing.

He looks at me for a long moment before answering, 'Don't you know, Mum?'

I shake my head, unable to form words. The music slows, becomes softer, as if responding to my confusion.

What he tells me shatters my world:

'It's been you playing the piano all this time.'

The revelation hits me like a wave, leaving me gasping for control of my very life. It's been me all along, playing the piano in the dead of night.

But what about the camera? The film. Quickly I explain to my son what I did to catch the player. 'It was a shadow.' The air hitches in my throat. I whisper as if still afraid to say it aloud. 'I thought it was Sam. Come back to me.'

Instead of mocking me, my son calmly gets me to tell him where my phone is and when he has it we watch the footage together. I can barely watch. But I'm in for another shock. There's no shadowy figure on the film. No Sam.

It's me.

Me playing on the piano, my fingers gliding and caressing, body swaying while my eyes remain closed.

The pieces start falling into place. No wonder my arms and feet have been hurting me for over a week. My foot pressed against the piano's pedal, my hands exhausted from playing. The booze, the uppers and downers, my desperate attempts to numb the pain and fuel my search for the truth.

'But I've stopped drinking and ditched the tabs,' I murmur, my brain still a mass of confusion. 'So why am I at the piano now?'

'It's probably the stress factor too.' Kane's expression is a mix of concern and relief. 'My illness earlier no doubt pressed some of your major league buttons. Your reaction to stress is to retreat to the place you always felt safest. Granddad and Sam's piano.'

He's right. Looking back, I see it now, how the music from downstairs started when Mark announced that he was going to have our son declared dead.

Shame suddenly washes over me. 'All this time, I thought . . . I accused Rocky.'

Kane softly reassures me, 'It's not your fault. You didn't know.'

'What else didn't I know, Kane? What else have I missed?'

He stiffens, steeling himself. 'After Sam . . . After what happened, you'd do things you couldn't remember. Little things at first, like making his favourite breakfast or buying his usual treats.' I nod, encouraging him to continue. 'But then.' He pauses, swallowing hard. 'One day, I came home from school, and I couldn't find you. Nor could Dad.' He's shaking, the fear of it still with him. 'The police called us. You were found floating face down in the sports hall swimming pool. Apparently, you thought the water would help you rescue Sam from the sea.'

This awful memory hits me hard. I had forgotten. Or it was like a bad dream. But the pain in Kane's face tells me loud and clear that it was real.

'Oh, Kane,' I whisper. 'I'm so sorry.'

He shakes his head. 'It's OK, Mum. I understand now. But back then . . . I felt so crushed and lonely. My big brother was gone, and it felt like I was losing you too.'

I reach out, taking his hand in mine. He lets me, and the simple gesture nearly undoes me. We haven't been this close for such a long time.

'I lost my confidence,' he continues. 'I felt so helpless. I couldn't bring Sam back, and I couldn't help you. When I went to university, I thought things might get better. But then . . .'

'Your father went to court,' I finish for him.

'When I heard he was trying to have Sam declared dead, all I could think was, "Not this shit again." I started missing meals, feeling terrible. That's why I came home.' He falls silent. 'Mum, I need you to understand something,' he continues. 'I don't blame you. Not for any of it. You were hurting, and you were doing the best you could.'

His forgiveness, his understanding, is almost too much to bear. 'But I should have been there for you,' I insist. 'I should have seen what you were going through.'

The truth is, I've failed as a mother to him. It doesn't matter how many times he tells me it's fine, I should have been there for him. After we lost Sam I wasn't the only one in pain.

'Maybe,' he concedes. 'But we can't change the past. What matters is what we do now.'

I nod, feeling a strange mix of sorrow and hope. 'You're right. And I promise you, Kane, things will be different from now on. I'm going to be here for you. Always.'

'I know, Mum. And I'm here for you too. Which is why . . .'

He trails off, and I can see him gathering his courage. The air in the room seems to thicken with anticipation.

'What is it, Kane?' I prompt gently.

His eyes meet mine with a determination I've never seen before.

'Mum, I'm ready to tell you what really happened that day on the beach.'

Chapter 49

10 YEARS AGO: THE BEACH – KANE

Kane jumped out of the camper van, the bracing sea air bouncing against his face. Sam and Frances were right behind him, their whoops of excitement matching his own. With a difference. While they focused on getting to the beach he kept a secret eye on his mother and Aunt Olivia. He wished they wouldn't hate on each other so much. He couldn't understand why they didn't like each other. OK, so the weather was a bit rubbish on the beach but they were away on holiday so why couldn't they just enjoy it?

It was just like his mum and dad. Why did they hate each other so much? Sometimes he never wanted to be an adult.

He glanced at Sam. Kane adored his older brother, always trying to keep up with his longer strides and quick wit. Sam caught his eye and poked his tongue out, making Kane grin.

The sound of raised voices drew his attention back to the adults. His mum and Aunt Olivia were at it again, arguing about who was going to look after the kids. Poor Uncle Simon stood there with an expression that said he'd rather be anywhere but here. Kane felt a surge of annoyance. He was fed up with this constant bickering. Weren't adults meant to be the grown-ups? The sensible ones?

'Race you to the sea!' he shouted suddenly, looking at Sam and Frances. Without waiting for a response, he took off across the sand, his feet kicking up little clouds with each step. He ran right into the sea. The water was freezing. Kane didn't care. He was loving it, feeling free and happy. Frances joined him, their laughter mixing with the sound of the rippling waves while Sam started making strange-looking things with the sand. Kane's eyes drifted back to the beach. His mum sat alone, cross-legged, looking hunched and small. Uncle Simon stood a little way off, smoking. Auntie Olivia had already stomped off for her walk. His mum looked so lonely. Kane felt a pang in his chest, wishing he could make her happy.

After a while, Uncle Simon finished his cigarette and walked over to Kane's mum. He sat down beside her, and they started talking. Kane strained to hear what they were saying, but the sound of the waves and the distance made it impossible.

Suddenly, his mum stood up. Smiling, she turned.

Sam yelled out, 'Mum, can I come too?'

'Next time.'

Then he watched his mum leave the beach.

'Where's Mum going?' he called out to Uncle Simon. *Was she OK?*

Grinning, his uncle shouted back, 'She's gone off to enjoy herself. And that's what she wants you to do too.'

So it was Uncle Simon who watched over them on the beach.

The next thing Kane remembered was he was lurking behind the van. He wasn't sure what he was doing there. The air was cold and biting, the damp seeping into his clothes.

But why was he behind the van?

The next thing he recalled was standing by the bag and Frances came charging down the beach, her face pale and terrified. She was shouting something about Sam, that something had happened to him.

'An accident. There's been an accident.'

Kane's heart leapt into his throat. He started to run, but Uncle Simon held him back.

And ordered, 'Wait here.'

Feeling sick, he watched as his uncle and cousin disappeared around the bend in the beach below the cliffs. He stood there shaking. Something bad had happened, he knew that.

Where was Sam?

Then Frances came back. By the time she reached him she was sobbing, although he noticed there were no tears on her face.

Putting his arm around her, he asked, 'What's happened to Sam?'

Her sobs abruptly stopped. She looked up at him with a sharp expression. 'It was an accident.'

The next thing he remembered were the legs. Sam's legs. His legs in the sand. Not moving. Poking out from behind Uncle Simon.

'What's happened to Sam?'

He didn't remember what his uncle said. A rushing whelmed up inside him while his uncle took him back to where Frances was.

Everything was moving so fast; he couldn't keep up. He wanted to go back to the legs. Sam's legs? Still in the sand.

Then the man came. Ralf. Told him his mum was going to prison and Frances too. He told him a story. That Sam went for a swim and then the sea rose up and carried Sam away. He made him say it over and over again:

'The sea came and took Sam away.'

'The sea came and took Sam away.'

'The sea came and took Sam away.'

Chapter 50

I sit in a paralysing silence after Kane has finally told me what happened. However, when I see the awful wreck his face has become I almost wish I hadn't made him tell me. He looks as if the very life has drained out of him. Exhausted. What hurts me the most is the sadness that has pulled down the corners of his mouth and dimmed the life in his eyes.

He tells me, his voice hoarse and heavy, 'That's the problem, Mum, I only remember things in snatches. I don't know why I was behind the van. But it's Sam's legs. They've haunted me for years. That's what I see when I think about what happened. They look blue and lifeless.'

I go over and put my arms around him. Real tight. I want to feel the beat of his heart next to mine. I want to feel the warmth of his skin. I want to feel the rise and fall of his chest as he breathes in life.

'That's what makes me collapse, Mum.' He can barely get the words out. 'Blue legs, dead. That's all I can see. They well up and I can't breathe.'

I squeeze him tight. He doesn't need to tell me anymore. That day has fractured his mind so much he can only recall some of what happened. Poor Kane, having to live with this has been a nightmare for him.

Above all, I want him to feel that we're a family again.

'Kane—'

He interrupts, strongly with a renewed confidence. 'It's all right, Mum, I can talk about it. I need to talk about it. We need to talk about it.'

'Are you sure?' After he nods I ease back from him and say, 'I knew it was Ralf on the beach. What a liar!'

Gently pulling back from my embrace, Kane shakes his head. 'He was the one in charge. For years I dreamed of him looming over me.'

'But what happened to Sam? Was it an accident?'

Kane looks down. 'I don't know for sure. Sometimes I think Frances was lying and other times not. But if it was an accident why did Ralf coach me and Frances to tell an alternative version of what happened?'

He pulls in a heavy punch of air. 'I know I was scared when he told me that you and Frances would be locked up if I didn't stick to the story.' He rubs his forehead. 'I remember bits and pieces of what he said. But above all he told me one thing.' A terrifying bleak light enters my son's eyes. 'He said if the police came to get you and Frances it would be all my fault.'

What a wicked thing to tell a child. Ralf has scarred my boy for life. If Ralf were here now I don't think I could stop myself from attacking him.

'Maybe it was. All I know is what I was told to say. Maybe I've forgotten some of the details. All the important things I remember though. I remember that. Mum,' Kane draws me away from my murderous thoughts. 'There's so much of that day I've worked years to block out.'

Suddenly another piece of the puzzle slides into place. 'When Frances told me what had happened, what she remembered of that day, she said it was you who had gone off with Sam—'

'That's a lie!'

'That you were the one who came running and screaming along the beach.'

Kane's features twist in confusion. 'I don't understand why Frances would say that. She knows that I was on the beach near Uncle Simon. Unless Sam's death was no accident.'

A chill enters the room.

Fixing my features I smile up at him. Bright and light. 'Go to bed, darling, and rest. We'll sort it all out in the morning.'

It's been a night of revelations. Including not only have I been the pianist I've been searching for, it's me who has been haunting my own house not my dead son.

The door to the music room is half open the next morning, and sunlight is flooding through the window as if a curse has been lifted. Silence reigns inside. I make to close the door but hesitate. Why shouldn't I go into this room now it has become a real part of my home again? Peeping round the door, I can see Sam's piano as it was when he played it. The lid is open and sheet music is scattered around on the floor. That was me of course who did that when I was in here before Kane rescued me.

I get a good look at the room, seeing things I had forgotten. On the walls are cheap but sentimental paintings that we collected during our trips abroad, along with snaps of Sam and Kane as children. Everything is covered in dust except the piano seat where I sat during those nights. The room smells of air that's lain undisturbed for ten years.

Without hesitation I go inside. There! I've done it! That was easier than I thought. Actually, it felt normal, as if I've been doing it every day. I close the door behind me. From the piano seat, I can see everything now. On the floor under the sheet music is a child's sock. I pick it up and hold it against my cheek before gently placing it on a wicker chair where I used to sit while Sam played. These memories are hard but bearable now. On the mantelpiece is a tacky statuette of a fisherman with a rod. It came from my childhood cottage but Mark always hated it, so we compromised by bringing it in here where he rarely came. To be honest, it is a bit naff but it always meant something to me.

And that's when I see it.

Dad's tip jar.

Throwing my head back I laugh aloud with triumph and fist-bump the air. There it is, sitting in its rightful place on the piano. I now understand how it got there.

Me.

During what I'm calling one of my 'lapses', I must have put it there when I came to play the piano. Poor Rocky, I have so much to apologise to her for. I pick it up and nurse it in my arms like a religious relic because that's what it is really. So many memories.

After putting it down, I turn and rest my trembling fingers on the black and ivory keys of the piano and hear a random solemn chord when they press down. Deliberately this time I choose another, a lighter chord, and play a rippling succession of them. Wriggling and massaging my fingers I think of something to play. It can't be haunting or melancholy. This house has heard enough sadness. My hands make the choice for me by playing 'My Old Man's a Dustman'. There's a pause for a moment. What did the dustman wear? That's right, it was 'cor blimey' trousers and he lived in a council flat. My fingers resume playing. I play some old Irish tunes. What gives me most pleasure is not just the music but the fact that my fingers are good to go.

The tunes 'Why Don't Women Like Me?' and 'Hold Your Hands Out Naughty Boy!' are my encore. This room is filled with my own laughter now for the first time in so many years.

I close the lid over the keys to allow the piano to rest.

I pick up my tip jar with the intention of going up to the attic to leave it where it has lived for many years, on my bedside cabinet. One day I'll bring it back to sit on the piano. But not yet. In the hallway I notice a vase with dead flowers in it, so I tuck the tip jar under my arm and reach for the vase to throw the flowers out. I sort of lose my footing and bang into the wall. The tip jar falls from my arms.

It's as if I'm watching it dive to the floor in slow-motion. Lunging forward, I try to reach it. Too late.

It crashes and smashes against the floor.

Distraught, my fingers flatten against my lips. All the memories, all the history of Dad, Sam and me. Gone. I scoop down to pick up the pieces of glass, my fragmented past life. Only the things I kept in it are scattered on the floor. And that's when I notice the envelope folded in two to fit in the jar. I don't remember putting it in there. Then again, as I found out last night there's so much I don't remember.

The envelope is fresh and new and I've never seen it before.

What is it?

Who put it in there?

I turn it over.

'FAO Alison.' That's what's handwritten in a top corner along with 'PRIVATE AND CONFIDENTIAL'.

'Kane!' I call from the bottom of the stairs.

Both he and Rocky appear. I wave the envelope at him. 'What's this? I found it in my tip jar.'

'Oh, that. It came last week. I think it was hand delivered because it was shoved through the letter box at an odd time. It was late in the evening. I put it in your tip jar because that's where I used to put your mail when you weren't here.' He's concerned. 'Is there a problem?'

'Did you see who brought it?'

He shakes his head. 'There was no knock or anything. It was about the time Uncle Simon went missing, I think you'd gone to Norfolk or maybe it was the day before, I can't remember.'

'Thanks.'

He smiles at me, while Rocky says, 'I heard you playing those happy tunes on the piano. I'm glad you're feeling a little more cheerful now. You're an amazing pianist.'

I try and smile back. I don't let on that cheerful is the last emotion I'm feeling at the moment. Tightly gripping the envelope in my hands as if someone might steal it from me, I go up to the attic. Sitting in the peacock chair I examine the handwriting, which I don't recognise.

Then again, I don't have to recognise it because I know who it's from.

Simon.

He did send me a letter after all. That's what he told me after that appalling incident between us before he went missing. I imagine him coming here and hand delivering it himself. I wished he'd knocked on the door so we had a chance to talk about it all. It hurts to think that he wrote this when he already had his own death on his mind.

It chills me to the bone to think it might be a suicide note.

Readying myself for what's about to be revealed to me, I tuck my finger under the seal and open it. It's a letter.

Dear Alison,

I can't read on. The tears are already running down my face. I put the letter back, take some deep breaths and try to calm myself with happy thoughts and visualisations. After one more final deep drink of air, my fingers, which were playing joyful music an hour ago, pull the letter back out again. I force myself to read on.

Dear Alison,

Firstly apologies. Apologies for behaving so badly when you came round to my house. I'd been told by Ralf and Olivia that you were nosing around Sam's death and that I was to stick to our story about what happened, no matter what. I guessed that's what you came to discuss. But I'm tired of our story. I'm so tired of it. Tired of everything. So, I've decided to give you a full account of what happened that day and then I'll see what there is to be done next. This isn't everything. I don't know what the others did when I wasn't there. But this is my part in it. It goes without saying that I should never have agreed to support the story in the first place and it's something I've had to live with ever since.

But in the same way I'm tired of the story. Tired of living with what happened. You will never know how deeply sorry I am for my role.

This is what happened that day on the beach when Sam went missing.

This is my confession . . .

Chapter 51

10 Years Ago: The Beach – Simon

Simon stood and watched his sister Alison happily strolling across the sand towards town to catch the piano performance. He was glad she was going; she deserved some me-time on her own. He was glad Olivia was gone too. He found the tension between his sisters overwhelming. Olivia had gone off to make brass rubbings in churches, her new hobby. He suspected this was just an excuse to get away from the others on the beach and he sympathised. He didn't want to be there. The kids seemed happy enough though with Kane and Frances playing in the sea at the shoreline while Sam went back to making his sculpture after watching his mother walk away. The poor boy looked so sad because he wanted to go with his mum to the piano performance.

The weather wasn't helping. It was cloudy and chilly. A wind was blowing, throwing handfuls of sand over the family as if they were on a building site. All the other holidaymakers that year were away doing something else and the scene was deserted apart from them. It was the most miserable day of the most miserable holiday. But Simon decided if he were in charge, he had to do his best. He picked up a ball and got into teacher mode.

'OK, kids, who's for a game of kickabout?'

He threw the ball in the air but it was caught by the wind and blown across the sand and he had to chase after it. When he returned, the two boys looked on in sympathy but Frances was laughing at him. Simon had noticed the girl had a nasty streak.

He tried again. 'No? What about a game of hide and seek?'

Frances was enjoying baiting him and sneered, 'We're on a beach, Uncle Simon. There's nowhere to hide. Anyway, Sam doesn't want to play hide and seek, he wants to go listen to the piano with his mummy.' She whispered something else under breath that may have been: 'Teacher's pet! Mummy's boy!'

Sam ignored her but Simon couldn't. The adults on this holiday had already fallen out; if the children did too, it might become impossible.

'All right, probably not the right day for this,' he said. 'Why don't we go into town and play the amusement arcades? Would that work?'

The two brothers' eyes lit up, readily agreeing; however, their cousin had changed her mind. 'Nah, let's play hide and seek.'

'You said there's nowhere to hide,' Sam pointed out.

'There's that bit near the cliffs.' Abruptly, she grabbed Sam's hand. 'Come on, Beethoven, let's find somewhere to hide.' Frances was in complete control now. 'Kane, you go and hide. Uncle Simon, count to fifty.'

'All right but don't go too far, Frances. Stay close, please,' Simon begged.

'Whatever!'

Frances led Sam away along the seashore until they went behind the bend in the cliffs.

They disappeared from view.

Simon instantly frowned, not entirely comfortable with that. He was supposed to keep them in sight while minding them. Then again, Sam and Frances were both eleven. They were old enough to be responsible. All the same, a niggling worry churned inside his gut. He got into the mood of the game, covered his eyes and counted to fifty as fast he could. Then he set off to search for the children.

Kane was found easily enough, crouched down and sheltering at the back of the van. Simon left Kane with the ball and bags and headed off to find Sam and Frances.

But there was no sign of them.

Simon began to feel a surge of panic as time passed. Where could they have got to? He felt in his pocket for his phone. Should he ring Alison? She wasn't far away. Or Olivia? He shook with fear when he thought about Olivia's reaction: 'You did what? You've lost my daughter!'

Simon hurried back to where Kane was sitting. 'Any sign of them?'

Please, please, please, let there be a sign of them.

'No.' Then Kane added because he was a good kid, 'Don't worry, Uncle Simon, they're probably playing a trick on you. They'll be back.'

But even then, Simon noticed a glaze in his nephew's eyes as if he knew something was wrong. 'I'll try going the other way.'

But he had only gone a few paces before Kane called, 'Look, Uncle Simon! It's Frances!'

In the distance, a solitary figure was running towards them. Simon's heart dropped.

'Kane, wait here until I come back. Don't move.'

Simon rushed down the beach and met Frances halfway.

'What's happened? Where's Sam?'

His niece looked terrible. 'There was an accident.'

Oh my God! 'Where is he?'

He ran with her as she guided him back beyond the cliffs along the path that led to a bend in the coast.

Francis pointed. 'There he is.'

Simon sucked in a horrified breath.

Sam was lying on the sand, not moving. His eyes were open. Lifeless. One side of his head was bashed in. Simon felt for a pulse. In despair he dropped to his haunches. Dear God. His nephew was dead.

A bloodied rock lay discarded nearby. Simon's immediate thought was that Sam must have fallen and hit his head on the rock. But the rock lay in a strange position for that to happen. When he looked closer Simon saw that Sam's fingers were bent, crushed and bloodied too as if they had been stamped on.

Choking at the sight and driven back in on himself, trying to understand what had happened, Simon rounded on his niece, screaming, 'What have you done? What have you done?'

She in turn shouted, 'It was an accident! It was an accident!'

But when Simon looked into Frances's eyes, he could see no soul behind them at all, only darkness.

'What am I going to do? What am I going to do?' he chanted over and over. He sank to his knees besides Sam's body. And looked up at Frances. 'Go and wait with Kane.'

She didn't need telling twice.

Simon took out his phone and called Olivia.

'Sam is dead! Sam is dead! I think Frances killed him!'

A chaotic, erratic, irrational to and fro lasting for more than a minute between brother and sister before her voice finally became solid and determined. 'You listen to me. My daughter hasn't killed *anyone* and even if the boy is dead *it's not her fault*, do you understand? I'm with someone who is coming to the beach to sort things out. He'll take care of everything. Don't call the cops. Wait for my friend to arrive.'

The phone line went dead.

Simon looked at his nephew, dead and cold on the sand. He wanted to take him in his arms and warm him back into life.

'What's happened to Sam?'

He twisted around to find a distressed Kane walking towards him. Simon blocked Sam's body from his view.

'Let's go back to where Frances is.'

Kane tried to get around him but he grabbed him and held tight. 'Everything is going to be all right. Everything is going to be fine.'

Kane let himself be led away. For fifteen minutes Simon waited further down the beach with the children. They were the worst minutes of his life.

The 'someone' his sister had said was coming turned out to be Ralf, who showed up on the scene in his flash sports car. Any other time Simon would have laughed at him in his shorts, hotel slippers and wrong-sided T-shirt. Under his arm he was carrying a blanket with 'Stacks Hotel' embroidered on it.

As soon as he reached Simon, he pulled him to one side, out of earshot of the children, and demanded to know exactly what had happened.

When he had all the facts from a still shellshocked Simon, Ralf swung into action, firing off questions while scanning the cliffs and beach:

'Where's the body?'

'Are there any witnesses?'

'Have you called anyone else?'

'What did she use to kill him with?'

When he had the answers, he explained things to Simon. 'Here's how it's going to go down. You were with Frances. Kane and Sam went down the beach. Kane came back and said Sam went into the sea for a swim and was swept away. There was nothing anyone could do. That's how it played out. Got it?'

Simon was horror-struck. 'We can't say that. Frances and Kane will never go along with it. And what about Alison?'

'Don't worry about dopey Alison. Olivia will take care of Frances. I'll speak to Kane.'

'We'll never get away with it.'

Ralf seized Simon by the shoulders. 'You'd better hope we do, because otherwise your niece is going to be locked up. A child killer. Then they'll be coming for you. The deadbeat uncle who let his niece murder her cousin right under his nose. Next it will be both sisters who'll probably turn their backs on you for the rest of your miserable days on this earth.' Ralf waited for the words to sink in. 'Don't worry about Alison. It's far better she thinks her son was lost at sea than that he had his head bashed in by her psycho niece. You're already in it up to your neck anyway because you should have called the police at once but you didn't.'

Satisfied he'd sorted out Simon, Ralf went to work on Frances and Kane. Kane was overwhelmed. He knew by now something terrible had happened but he didn't know what. Ralf explained to him, crouching down, smiling and laying a hand on the boy's shoulder.

'Kane, there's been a terrible accident and it's not good for your brother. He's sort of lost and won't be coming back. The thing is that when the police come, they're going to try and blame your mum for what happened—'

'What?' The boy rocked back.

'Yes. And they'll put her in prison. Is that fair? It's not her fault. They'll put you in a children's home where you'll be beaten and kicked. At school the other kids will call you horrible names. Is that fair? It's not your fault either.' Ralf made his voice smooth and calm. 'But if you tell them what I'm going to tell you to say, you and your mum will be able to stay at home. Together. Do you understand?'

Ralf went on. 'And as for Frances, well, she'll probably end up locked up too. For many years. They will accuse her of killing him—'

Kane gasped. 'She said it was an accident.' His small chest heaved. 'Did she do something bad to Sam?'

Ralf let out an ugly word, realising what he'd said. 'She did nothing bad. But that's not how the police might see it. Do you understand?'

He didn't. But Ralf made him rehearse that the sea came and took Sam away over and over until he could repeat it robotically:

'The sea came and took Sam away.'

With help from Ralf, he came to accept that he had to save his mum, Frances and himself. That was the best Ralf felt he could do for Olivia and he'd done it.

'All right, Simon, I'm going to collect the body and find somewhere to put it,' he said. 'Call the police in five minutes. And don't mess up or we'll all end up going to jail.'

With that Ralf ran along the beach in his hotel slippers with a blanket under his arm ready to wrap up a body. When he reached Sam's body the first thing he did was throw the bloody rock into the sea.

Chapter 52

As I career around the road, shooting traffic lights and shunting other cars, in a blaze of vehicles' horns and flashing lights, I realise I've made a terrible mistake. Instead of calling the police first I called Olivia and told her all about Simon's confession. I knew what he'd written was true because why would a dead man lie? Now I know that her daughter killed Sam and Ralf covered it up. I just wanted to confront her before the cops got to her, which would mean the next time we met would be across a crowded court room.

But in my desire to confront her I now realise I've given her forewarning. She'll have time to alert Ralf and Frances. They might even escape the law and that would be too much to bear.

I'm possessed as I drive to my sister's house, shouting out of the window at other motorists, actually climbing out of my car at one stage to tell a bus driver to get out of my way and using the language of a salty sea-dog at hapless pedestrians on crossings. My father never used that language at home but I learned it in the school playground. It's liberating ignoring the rules of the road and telling other drivers what you really think of them in a loud voice, instead of bottling it up inside.

I suppose I'll be in trouble when the police review the camera footage of my journey but if I have to make my case to a jury, they'll understand. I've just found out my son was killed that day on the beach.

Murdered.

It's Frances, Ralf and Olivia who should be afraid of juries.

It's a relief on arriving to find Olivia's car still parked in her driveway. She hasn't done a runner. I calm down and park my car across the drive to block her escape route. Once that is done, I call Paul and tell him what's happened.

He listens carefully before saying to me, 'You're going to be very upset now. I just want you to stay at home with Simon's letter. I'll make some phone calls and get everything sorted out.' He pauses for a moment. 'You are still at home, I take it?' When he doesn't get an answer, his voice becomes urgent. 'You are still at home? If you're not, you need to go home directly and sit tight. I'm calling the police.'

I ring off. No one is taking this moment away from me. I owe it to Sam.

It's only when I walk up to Olivia's front door and raise the knocker that I notice that Ralf's sports car is parked here as well. So much the better, that's two of the four people who took my son from me gathered together in one place. I raise the knocker again but before it falls, I can hear a terrible argument going on inside the house. It's Olivia and Ralf. So two of the conspirators have fallen out.

I push open the letter box and listen.

'Look, Olivia, you just need to calm down! Simon writes a letter to your sister, confessing all. So what? The poor guy drowned himself the next day, the balance of his mind was disturbed. He just covered up his own involvement by blaming you, me and Frances.'

Olivia is screaming, 'And Kane? What about Kane?'

'He's stuck to our story for ten years. He's going to have a problem changing it now and staying credible. Besides, his head is so totally messed up after all this time, I doubt if even he remembers what really happened. Stop worrying! As long as you, Frances and I stay calm and keep our story straight, they can't touch us. But if you go to pieces now, then we're all going to prison.'

I've had enough and hammer on the door knocker, but Ralf and Olivia are so deep in conversation they don't seem to notice. Outside on the lawn is a garden gnome. I pick it up and throw it at the stained glass that forms part of the front door. It takes several goes but when it finally goes through, I reach through the shattered glass, find the latch and let myself in. Ralf and Olivia are in her drawing room where our last bust-up took place. But it's serious this time. Olivia looks shocked to see me but Ralf merely sighs. 'Yes, I thought you were going to show up here for the party.'

I'm not sure which of these two deserves my attention first or what to say. My heart does the talking and to the right person. I go face to face with Ralf. My mouth goes dry because, after all these years, instead of asking the question that's haunted me for so long, the words stick in my throat. I'm not sure I can bear to ask the question.

Where is Sam? What did you do with his body?

Part of me doesn't want to know, doesn't want to face the horrible reality. But I need to. For closure. For justice. For my son.

I feel sick, but I force myself to look into this monster's eyes. I have to know. I have to bring my boy home, whatever's left of him. Taking a deep breath, I prepare to ask the question that might shatter me completely.

'Where is he?'

Ralf plays up his mock confusion. 'Where is who?'

'My son. What did you do with him?'

Olivia is watching Ralf closely. Ralf slips into his well-rehearsed and familiar, soft, empathic voice. 'There seem to be some crossed wires here. What's happened is that Simon – and I'm not blaming

264

him because your brother lost it at the end – has tried to get his revenge on people by throwing metaphorical hand grenades into the metaphorical sea water.' Ralf loves his big words. 'Now, why don't the three of us sit down and talk to each other like civilised adults? We can find a way forward here that can meet all our concerns.'

It's so easy to see how he made fools out of so many people over so many years, me included. I draw closer, so our eyes are only inches apart. 'Where's Sam? I want him back.'

Ralf leans in and whispers to me as if we're sharing a moment together. 'I've got a suggestion for you that I think you're going to like.'

Ralf slips away from me, walks behind Olivia and violently seizes her by the neck and drags her across the room and out into the hallway. I follow and watch as Ralf pushes her into a broom cupboard and uses his hips and hands to shove a sideboard in front of the door so she can't escape. He comes back down the hallway and takes me by the arm and leads me back into the drawing room. Olivia's muffled screams and banging form the backdrop to Ralf's words.

'Right, I'm guessing that your sister has called Frances and she'll be here soon – and when psycho girl turns up, we won't be able to talk anymore. I'm willing to do a straight swap with you here, Alison. I'll tell you where Sam's body is if you agree to destroy Simon's letter and persuade Kane to stick to our story. That way everyone's a winner.'

I actually laugh. 'How am I supposed to explain to the authorities that I found Sam's body if you're kept out of the picture?'

Ralf seems to think this is an irritating detail. 'I dunno, tell them a medium tracked him down or something. Does it matter?'

Olivia is still shouting and banging but we ignore her. I'm firm. 'I want my son. Tell me where he is.'

Ralf shrugs. 'All right, what about this idea? You keep the letter but it's me who goes to the police first to confess, blame Olivia for blackmailing me and then turn King's evidence on them. You find the letter after that and Kane remembers everything. I reckon a good performance in the dock and there's no custodial for me, you get the two real culprits. Come on, Alison, I'm trying to help us both out here.'

'You're going to sell out Frances and Olivia? I want my son back, tell me where you put him.'

Ralf doesn't answer.

Suddenly, a prickle of awareness travels from my neck down my spine. Someone's watching us. Ralf and I turn at the same time.

It's Frances.

She's standing in the doorway with her arms folded. How long has she been there? Listening to us? Spying on us?

Ralf doesn't care what she's heard, he launches himself at her and they struggle together, tumbling across the floor. He's kicked and punched but finally manages to get the upper hand, staggering to his feet, pulling Frances down the hallway, the same way he took her mother. I don't want to stop asking him where Sam is, but this has gone on long enough and I fear where it might end up. Someone is going to be hurt.

Ralf appears back in the doorway again before I can make a decision. He looks exhausted by his struggle with my niece and rests his head against a wall, coughing and spluttering. He takes a deep breath and tries to walk into the room but stutters and stumbles while gripping something in his hand close to his stomach.

What's wrong with him?

He coughs again, finally wretches and spews bright red blood across Olivia's floor, before collapsing in front of me. Only then do I see that clasped in his hand is the handle of a knife that's been rammed deep into his belly to the hilt with extreme force. In shock at this act of violence playing out in front of me, I drop to my knees to turn Ralf over and perform CPR even though I've no idea how to do it.

A flat voice above me says, 'Don't bother, Aunt Alison. He's finished. Don't tell me you're sorry.'

Chapter 53

The Sisters

Eleven-year-old Frances's fingers rested hesitantly on the ivory keys of the polished black Steinway piano. The music room in her large home was located on the ground floor with French doors that opened out onto the garden. The sheet music was open to Beethoven's 'Moonlight Sonata'. She hated playing it because it was far beyond her current abilities.

Fingers heavy with resentment and despair, she began to play. And as usual, every note sounded shit. They came out stuttered and uneven, the timing off. Frances winced at each mistake, her confidence crumbling with every wrong key. A wave of frustration and self-doubt washed over her. Why couldn't she be like her cousin Sam? He made playing look so effortless. So easy-peasy. It wasn't fair.

'Stop! Stop! That's all wrong!' A sharp voice cut through Frances's painful playing.

It was the voice she feared the most. Her mother's. Quickly, Frances snatched her hands away from the piano and pressed them into her lap. Her trembling fingers twisted together until they pinched and hurt. She tried to stop shaking as her mother's high heels clicked with the dreaded beat of a death march across the hardwood floor. Frances felt the bristling heat of her mother standing over her. She never looked up. She couldn't bear to see the disappointment in Mummy's eyes.

'How do you expect any prestigious music school to take you playing like that? Why am I wasting my time lining up auditions for you? Especially after the complete mess you made of the one at the Guildhall.'

Hot tears pricked the corners of Frances's eyes. She hated this. Hated the piano. Hated auditions. Hated her mother's constant pressure. Hated that she couldn't fucking do it.

Hated. Hated. Hated.

But most of all, she hated HIM.

Sam.

Perfect, fucking Sam. If it wasn't for him, her mother wouldn't be doing this to her. She wouldn't be constantly comparing her to Aunt Alison's genius son.

'I'm trying, Mum, I really am. It's just so hard.' In a small, defeated voice she dared to add, 'Maybe I'm not cut out for this.'

'Nonsense,' her mother rebutted brusquely. 'You just need to practise more. Both me and Aunt Alison were effortless pianists. That talent runs in our family, which means you have it too. You just need to work harder.'

Glancing down at the keys, a tear escaped down Frances's cheek. She felt trapped, suffocated by expectations she could never meet. All she wanted to do was paint and draw. Like her mother did for clients decorating their homes. Frances knew she'd never be like Sam, no matter how hard she practised. She didn't have his gift, his love for music. But her mother refused to see it.

'Let's run through it again. From the top,' her mother commanded, tapping the sheet music with a perfectly manicured nail. 'And this time, get it right.'

Her mother's next words were spoken with biting, bitter anger. 'I won't have Alison thinking her son is better than my daughter! I won't allow it!'

The words confirmed what Frances had always known. Her mother was motivated by jealousy of Aunt Alison. It was like her mother had to prove something.

Well, Frances was going to put a stop to it this weekend. She'd nearly put an end to it six weeks ago when she stood over her cousin sleeping in bed with a knife in her hand but she hadn't been able to go through with it. However, this weekend would be different. There would be no hesitation.

Obediently, Frances began the piece again; this time her confidence and self-belief grew. As she played she thought about the coming week-long trip to the seaside. A week would give her plenty of time to make her move. Get rid of her problem once and for all.

Chapter 54

When I look up, Frances is standing over me with another knife in her hand. She leans down towards me and I flinch, expecting to be stabbed too, but she's only offering me her hand to help me get up. She lifts me onto a chair because now I have to hold my hands over my eyes to stop myself seeing Ralf's dead body in front of me, a pool of blood already spreading on the floor.

'For goodness' sake, Aunt Alison, take your hands away from your face. You've seen a dead body before surely?'

It sounds more like a command than a request and I don't want to upset this strange girl who has already killed two people. She is still beautiful, even when I open my eyes and see her sat on a sofa with her knife resting on her lap. Even though she's using Ralf's dead body as a foot rest. I'm shaking with disbelief. I only came here to find out where Ralf and Olivia had hidden my son's body and now this.

'Frances, could you put the knife down, please? It's making me really scared.'

She looks down as if she's only just noticed the blade in her lap. 'I don't want to scare you. I'm here to help you, seriously.' She takes the knife in her hand. 'But I think I'll hold on to it for now, just in case. If you're worried, you can leave, but you'll wish you hadn't.'

I can't leave, not with this girl and her knife and my sister shut up in a broom cupboard. From wanting to kill my sister myself I'm now desperate to save her. I know what Frances thinks about Olivia. The genuine loathing in her voice when she told me, hidden in the shadows while we sat on the breakwater in Norfolk, that she hated her mother. When she sneered at her mother 'sleeping the sleep of the unjust'. I can't leave Olivia here alone.

I'm frightened even to think of how to deal with a situation like this. I don't know whether to tell Frances that I've called the police or not. Will she flee if she finds out, take her revenge on me or take it out on Olivia? I decide to take the risk that she'll flee and leave us alone because I can't think of anything else. 'It might be time for you to go. I've called the police. If you run now, you might escape before they arrive.'

She's not listening. She suddenly seems to have noticed the muffled whimpering and occasional knocking coming from the broom cupboard down the hallway. She gestures in its general direction with her knife.

'Is that her? My mother?' When I don't answer in the forlorn hope that I might avoid giving her away, Frances laughs. 'I thought you didn't like her either?' She kicks Ralf's lifeless body. 'I suppose he did that, did he? Locked her up in the broom cupboard while he prepared to sell us out to you, in return for you getting him off. I heard every word he said. Fair play to you for not agreeing. I would have if I wanted something badly enough.' She rises from the sofa, the knife clasped tightly in her hand. 'Let's go and get her, shall we?'

I follow Frances into the hallway and watch helpless, while my niece pulls the sideboard away from the broom cupboard and opens the door. She reaches inside and drags my sister out into the hall.

Poor Olivia struggles to her feet, apparently under the horrific impression that her daughter is her rescuer. 'Where's he gone?'

Frances tells her innocently, 'He's in the drawing room.'

272

Olivia marches towards the front room seeking revenge on her sometime lover. 'Right, I'll show him what happens when he messes with me like that.'

Frances stands beside me and bursts out laughing when a high-pitched shriek comes from my sister in the front room. This animal-like crying only tails off when Olivia runs out of breath. She takes another gasp of air and begins shrieking again. She eventually stops and begins whimpering incoherently.

In triumph, Frances gives me a playful punch in the ribs before following her mother into the drawing room. Suddenly, I'm alone in the hall, only a few feet from the front door which is half open. I could be gone and halfway down the drive before Frances noticed and I don't think she'd follow me anyway. She's already offered to let me go. I take a few steps and peer out into the outside world, a world of trees and grass and birds singing. A world with no blood.

'Are you coming back?'

Frances's voice is behind me; she sounds disappointed as if my hopes of escape were letting her down. When I turn, she's poking her head around the drawing room door. I come back. I don't know why but I do. Where are the police? Shaking, Olivia sits on one end of the sofa. Frances sits at the other end, toying with her knife. I sit down on an armchair.

We sit in silence for a few seconds before Frances snaps at her mother, 'Go on, tell her! Tell her where Sam is buried. That's what she wants to know, that's all she's ever wanted. She doesn't care who did what to who, she just wants her son back. Tell her!'

Olivia looks at me and then at her daughter. 'I don't know what you're talking about.'

Frances turns to me. 'She knows. We all knew. Ralf insisted we all knew all the details, so that later we couldn't turn around and say we didn't. All of us knew. I bet Uncle Simon didn't tell you that in his letter. Mum says he sent you a sort of confession. But I'm guessing he didn't tell you that.'

No, he didn't.

Frances is fidgeting with the knife now, getting angrier. 'Go on,' she says to Olivia, 'tell Aunt Alison where her son is buried!'

Olivia is looking to make a break for it like a trapped animal with one final hope. When Frances's head is turned, I plead with my eyes for her not to do it. Frances is near the edge. There's no point provoking her.

'All right,' says Frances, 'tell her why you made me do it.'

This is too much for Olivia. 'I made you do it? You've gone insane.'

'Every night with your piano, every night with your "all cows eat grass" so I could learn the notes. Practice! Practice! Practice! Tutors, more tutors, extra lessons. Practice! Practice! Until I was vomiting practice and tutors down the toilet bowl.' She turns to me and her voice softens. 'That's what it was like, Aunt Alison. Torture, sheer torture, sadistic torture.'

She turns back to her mother. 'Just so I'd be better at piano than Sam. That was the only reason, the last round in the two sisters fighting over the piano, only it was me and Sam who had to pay for it. Small wonder when Sam asked me on the beach how my piano lessons were going and whether I wanted to get together and do some duets, I finally flipped. Small wonder I hit him with a rock. My only regret is that it wasn't you.'

She turns to me again, her face visibly twitching. 'There's an abandoned church on the coast road about two miles west of where we were on the beach. It's called St Margaret's. In the disused churchyard is one of those raised oblong graves about four foot high, with a stone covering like a table top. It's the grave of Thomas Holt Esq., who died in 1836. If you look in there, that's where Ralf put Sam.'

I don't know what force makes me get up from my chair and go over to embrace Frances but something does. She took my son away from me and now she's given him back. Frances lets me hug her.

Olivia seizes her chance.

She pounces on her daughter, trying to wrest the knife out of her hands. The screaming pair inflict blows on each other, some of which land on me. We crash onto the floor in a three-way and deadly embrace, rolling together, the knife flashing at angles until I see it no more. Amid the banging and crashing are groans and sighs, before the rolling and tumbling stop and we are all smeared in someone else's blood. Frances's face looks peaceful while Olivia's is contorted with pain. Only when we disentangle and the arms that embraced me flop onto the floor do I realise that my sister has stabbed her daughter in the heart.

In the distance, sirens finally start to wail.

Olivia struggles to her feet and points down at Frances. She seems more like her old self now that she's safe.

'Don't forget, when the police arrive, I stabbed her in self-defence.'

In disgust, I rear back from her. 'Don't you understand? This is all your fault. Even though you married well, socialised with people with money to burn, you still hated me.'

Olivia yells, 'Why did they like you more than me?'

I straighten my shoulders. 'Because I was always proud of being a fisherman's daughter.'

Chapter 55

Even with four of us, the dig at the memorial gardens isn't going well. I can't work with a spade and Paul is too old. Kane has put some weight on and is now back at college but he's still too physically fragile. No doubt Rocky is good with her hands but turning earth over is beyond her. The four of us sit together on a bench opposite Sam's remembrance plinth and plate, linked together by arms around shoulders and held hands. We look more like one than four, which is as it should be.

The managers of the gardens refused at first to allow me to dig up Sam's memorial myself. It's against the rules and they insisted their workers had to do it. When I put my foot down and threatened them with bad publicity they reluctantly agreed.

Paul offered to come and help and it seemed right that he did. I told Kane to stay at college but he came down anyway. Rocky, who initially thought I must have played a role in the death of Frances, cold-shouldered me for a while. After two searching interviews with the police in the wake of what happened at Olivia's, she's begun to accept that perhaps her guardian angel Frances wasn't quite what she seemed. She's begun visiting me and offering her support and I'm grateful for it.

I don't need Sam's memorial now. The police recovered my son's remains, still wrapped in the hotel blanket, from St Margaret's graveyard, just as Frances had told me. Next week we bury him and I'll have an appropriate place to mourn him properly. I don't suppose I'll come here again after today.

I just wanted Sam back and now I've got him. He'll soon be at peace and at rest.

That's all I've ever wanted.

Two of the gardens' workers in their overalls are lurking in the background. One of them walks up to me.

'Are you the lady who lost her son on the beach?'

'Yes.'

He nods. 'The thing is these types of plinths are very well fixed into the ground and you're going to have a problem digging it up. Do you want us to do it?'

The four of us sit and watch the plinth wobbling, then tumbling to the ground. They use a screwdriver to take the brass plate off it. I feel no emotion because my boy isn't here anymore, he's somewhere else.

'It doesn't seem right though that everyone is blaming Frances. It was her mum who messed her head up in the first place.'

Poor Rocky still wants to put in a good word for Frances. I let her because I understand what grief is. 'Olivia's in jail. It will all come out at the trial.'

I don't believe that, actually. The newspaper headline, 'BEAUTIFUL YOUNG WOMAN IS A PSYCHO KILLER' will be too good to resist. Although 'WEALTHY MOTHER SLAUGHTERS DAUGHTER IN KNIFE HORROR' will probably run too. The details won't matter. I don't care because I won't be reading them. Nor do I care how long Olivia stays in prison. It might not be as long as people think. The police are accepting she killed Frances in self-defence and while she's certainly guilty of her part in covering up Sam's murder, she's got good lawyers. She won't serve much time, a few years at most.

The workers load the plinth onto a wheelbarrow and take it away. One of them offers me the brass plate. I take it and put it in my bag. There's just empty earth where I used to come and stand and talk to Sam. It's just a muddy space where I used to listen to the leaves and the breeze and search the sky for some sign he was speaking back to me. Now there's nothing there.

It's time to go, but Paul wonders if I want to go and spend a few moments by the empty earth and have a moment of contemplation. I don't, but the others look at me as if I should. I get off the bench and wander over to the spot where the plinth stood. I feel a bit silly standing here with my head bowed but nothing to say. After I've pretended to contemplate for a decent interval, I turn back. But as I do so, the sun breaks from behind a cloud and we're all bathed in warm golden sunshine.

Perhaps I was right all along.

Sam was always trying to speak to me through the natural world around us.

Epilogue

The auditorium buzzes with the excitement of proud families and giddy graduates. I'm perched on the edge of my seat, my heart full to bursting. My son, my Kane, is graduating today. Finally, we can drink to his success with the champagne I've put aside for this special occasion.

As I watch the ceremony unfold, my mind drifts over the past year. Kane and I have come so far, working hard to mend the tears in our relationship. Those weekend visits home from uni, the long talks, the shared silences – each moment a stitch holding us together.

I think about how close we were to losing each other completely. After Sam disappeared, I was so lost in my grief that I could barely see Kane standing right in front of me. How many times did I look at him and see only the son who was missing? The guilt of that still gnaws at me, but I'm learning to forgive myself.

We both are.

Although in my eyes Kane has nothing to forgive, he still feels that he should have told me what had happened on the beach. Despite me telling him how he was manipulated as a child he still carries the guilt. It will go in time. With love everything comes good.

Sam is still with us, in a way. We talk about him naturally now, sharing memories without that suffocating type of grief. Just because he isn't here doesn't mean he's not part of our family. It's bittersweet, but it feels right.

I remember the first time Kane brought up Sam without that look of fear in his eyes, like he was waiting for me to fall apart. We were in the kitchen, making dinner, and he just casually mentioned how Sam used to always burn the garlic bread. We both laughed, and it felt like a miracle.

Now, we can reminisce about Sam's terrible jokes, his obsession with Debussy and those eccentric piano T-shirts of his. It's like we've found a way to keep him alive in our hearts without letting his absence define us. Kane and I, we're learning to be a family of two while still honouring the memory of three.

The sound of Kane's name snaps me back to the present. He strides across the stage, strong and confident in his mortarboard. My hands ache from clapping so hard, but I can't stop. That's my boy up there! Achieving something I once feared he might never reach.

I think about all the obstacles we've overcome to get here. The nightmares, the therapy sessions, the days when getting out of bed seemed impossible. Kane struggled with so much – survivor's guilt, the weight of being the only child left, the pressure to somehow make up for Sam's absence. And the worst guilt of all, the pressure Olivia and Ralf put on him to stop him speaking the truth. Kane has spoken to me of how this tormented him the most.

But he's done it. We've done it.

As Kane accepts his degree, our eyes meet across the crowded room. His smile could light up the world, and I feel an answering grin spread across my face. This moment, this triumph – it belongs to both of us. And in a way, to Sam too. I can almost imagine him here, cheering louder than anyone.

Rocky's name is called next, and my heart swells with pride for her too. She's become such a part of our little family. I think about how shocked she was when the truth about Frances, her best friend, came out. How she's still coming to terms with it all. But she's resilient, our Rocky. She knows she always has a place with us.

As Rocky leaves the stage, degree in hand, I remember the day she showed up at our door, lost and hurting trying to come to terms with how Frances had treated her. Kane and I didn't hesitate to take her in. Now, watching her graduate alongside my son, I know we made the right choice. She's helped heal us as much as we've helped her.

The ceremony winds down, and I stand, searching the crowd for Kane. I spot him weaving through the sea of black gowns, his eyes locked on mine. When he reaches me, I pull him into a tight embrace.

'My son,' I whisper, my voice thick with emotion.

Kane's arms tighten around me, and we stay like that for a moment, holding on to each other. As I hold my son, I know that whatever the future holds, we'll face it together. We've come so far, and there's still a long road ahead. But right now, in this perfect moment, none of that matters.

All that matters is this: my son's future is bright and full of promise. And those two words that say everything.

'My son.'

ACKNOWLEDGEMENTS

From the spark of an idea to the final page, numerous hands have shaped this book. Eternal thanks to our wonderful editors, Sammia Hamer and Ian Pindar. As always cheers for helping us dig deep. Massive thanks to Jill and all the amazing Amazon Publishing Team. To everyone who played a part, whether named or unnamed, your impact is woven into every page. Thank you all for being part of the *Gone* journey.

A LETTER FROM THE AUTHORS

Guilt is a crippling emotion. To know you're responsible for an event that impacts in terrible ways on the lives of others, especially loved ones, can be a burden that some carry through their whole lives. But when you feel guilty for something that actually isn't your responsibility but you think is, the effects can be even more devastating. That is especially true when others are trying to suggest that it is your fault when it isn't. It was with this in mind that we created Alison. She isn't to blame for the loss of her son but she feels that she is. She feels she should have been there for Sam and his loss is on her. It's partly because of this that she can't accept he's gone. If he isn't gone then she's not to blame for his loss.

We've all seen guilt in people's lives which leads to the 'if only' syndrome. 'If only I hadn't done that' or 'if only something had been different that day'. For Alison it also leads on to 'if only I had asked more questions at the time'.

We wanted to end the novel on a positive note for Alison's sake as much as ours or the readers'. Yes, Sam is gone but she now knows why and has somewhere to grieve for him and she has her other son who's now relieved of his own guilt which wasn't really his either.

Happy reading!

Dreda and Ryan

ABOUT THE AUTHORS

Her Majesty Queen Elizabeth II appointed Dreda an MBE in her New Year Honours List 2020.

She scooped the CWA's John Creasey Dagger (New Blood) Award for best first-time crime novel in 2005, the first time a Black British author has received this honour.

Ryan and Dreda write across the crime and mystery genre—psychological thrillers, gritty gangland crime and fast-paced action books.

Spare Room, their first psychological thriller, was a #1 UK and US Amazon bestseller.

Dreda is a passionate campaigner and speaker on social issues and the arts. She has appeared on television, including *Celebrity Pointless, Celebrity Eggheads, Alan Carr's Adventures with Agatha Christie, BBC Breakfast, Sunday Morning Live, Newsnight, The Review Show and Front Row Late* on BBC2.

Ryan and Dreda performed a specially commissioned monologue for the ground-breaking Sky Arts' *Art 50* on Sky TV.

Dreda is one of twelve international bestselling women writers who have written a reimagined Miss Marple short story for the thrilling bestselling anthology *Marple*. She talked about this on The Queen Consort's Royal Reading Room.

Dreda has been a guest on many radio shows and presented BBC Radio 4's flagship books programme, *Open Book*. She has written in a number of leading newspapers including the *Guardian* and was thrilled to be named one of Britain's 50 Remarkable Women by Lady Geek in association with Nokia. She is a trustee of the Royal Literary Fund and an ambassador for The Reading Agency.

Some of Dreda and Ryan's books are currently in development as TV and film adaptations.

Dreda's parents are from the beautiful Caribbean island of Grenada. Her name, Dreda, is Irish and pronounced with a long vowel ee sound in the middle.

Follow the Authors on Amazon

If you enjoyed this book, follow Dreda Say Mitchell and Ryan Carter on Amazon to be notified when the authors release a new book!

To do this, please follow these instructions:

Desktop:

1) Search for the authors' names on Amazon or in the Amazon App.
2) Click on the authors' names to arrive on their Amazon page.
3) Click the 'Follow' button.

Mobile and Tablet:

1) Search for the authors' names on Amazon or in the Amazon App.
2) Click on one of their books.
3) Click on the authors' names to arrive on their Amazon page.
4) Click the 'Follow' button.

Kindle eReader and Kindle App:

If you enjoyed this book on a Kindle eReader or in the Kindle App, you will find the authors' 'Follow' button after the last page.